SERPENT GATE

"What Kerney understands, and the reader comes to appreciate, is how it all comes down to the land: to the love of it and the need of it and the pure lust of those people who are determined to have a piece of it."

—*The New York Times Book Review*

"A must read. . . . A compelling blend of old-fashioned street-smart detection, tenacity, and modern motivation. . . . Authentic, detailed, and gritty."

—*The Dallas Morning News*

"Michael McGarrity's novels are a perfect blend of riveting action and richly evoked characters, making Santa Fe more irresistible than ever. *Serpent Gate* is his best—a real winner."

—Linda Fairstein, bestselling author of *Cold Hit*

"A masterpiece of plot, setting, and character . . . [to] be savored."

—*Booklist* (starred review)

"McGarrity imbues his fiction with a good deal of authentic police work and local lore but doesn't stop there. Kerney and the other characters . . . have size and dimension, and his plots are suspenseful and action-packed. . . . We can't ask for any more than that."

—*Los Angeles Times*

"Outstanding. . . . McGarrity delivers another complex and powerful suspense novel. . . . Subtle yet full of action, with a chilling closing scene."

—*Publishers Weekly* (starred review)

MEXICAN HAT

"*Mexican Hat* has it all—cattle ranchers, the U.S. Forest Service, militia groups, poachers, land-grabbing murderers, Game and Fish Department investigators and locals who just want to be left alone."

—*Albuquerque Journal* (NM)

"Exciting. . . . McGarrity blew critical and commercial socks off last year with *Tularosa* . . . and now he goes for the boots."

—*Chicago Tribune*

"McGarrity . . . creates tough, believable westerners and allows them to be who they are—warts, AK-47s and all. Unlike many of his colleagues . . . he doesn't mythologize this part of the country. Rather, he offers up the beauty, terror, passions and misplaced (and sometimes murderous) zeal."

—*The Denver Post*

TULAROSA

"Mystery fans shouldn't miss *Tularosa*. . . . [It] moves like lightning."

—Tony Hillerman

"One of the best novels of 1996. . . . Few mysteries are as fresh and powerful as this rich Southwestern tale. . . . McGarrity delivers atmosphere, action, romance, and prime satisfaction."

—*Publishers Weekly*

"A lean, stylish debut, with a hero who's equally at home sniffing out evidence and duking it out with heavies."

—*Kirkus Reviews*

ALSO BY MICHAEL McGARRITY

Serpent Gate
Tularosa
Mexican Hat

Michael McGarrity

Hermit's Peak

A KEVIN KERNEY NOVEL

POCKET BOOKS

New York   London   Toronto   Sydney   Singapore

This book is a work of fiction. Names, characters, places, and incidents are products of the author's imagination or are used fictitiously. Any resemblance to actual events or locales or persons, living or dead, is entirely coincidental.

 POCKET BOOKS, a division of Simon & Schuster Inc.
1230 Avenue of the Americas, New York, NY 10020

Copyright © 1999 by Michael McGarrity

Originally published in hardcover in 1999 by Scribner

ISBN: 0-671-02147-8

First Pocket Books printing August 2000

10 9 8 7 6 5 4 3 2 1

POCKET and colophon are registered trademarks of Simon & Schuster Inc.

Cover art by Gerber Studio

Printed in the U.S.A.

Dedicated to the memory of

MAJ. TIMOTHY B. INGWERSEN,

United States Army Air Force,

Eighth Army,

World War II

RIP

ACKNOWLEDGMENTS

Thanks go to Angela Gill of Kent, England; Terry Sullivan, director of Land Protection, the Nature Conservancy of New Mexico; Darrel G. Hart, director, Recruitment and Training Division, New Mexico Department of Public Safety; and Patricia A. Baca, partner, Daymon & Associates, CPA's, all of whom helped me get my facts straight.

Any screwups are mine alone.

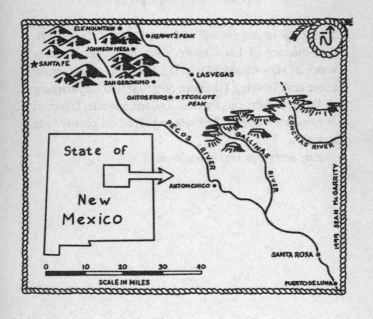

Hermit's Peak

1

Maj. Sara Brannon arrived at her office fifteen minutes before she was due to report to Gen. Henry Powhatan Clarke. She sorted through her mail, looking for a letter from Kevin Kerney. There was no envelope with either a New Mexico postmark or his familiar scrawl. Disappointed, Sara set the mail aside, took off her fatigue jacket, and glanced at her wristwatch. It was evening in Santa Fe, New Mexico, and she wondered if Kerney was home from work. With the demands of his job as deputy chief of the New Mexico State Police and his gloomy description of the small guest house he was renting, she doubted he spent much time at home. Both Kerney and she were working long, hard hours in pressure-cooker jobs, and camping out in less than inviting quarters.

Late March in South Korea had brought a series of cloudy, dreary days that made spring seem a long way off. Sara yearned for sunshine and home. But with several months remaining on her tour of duty, it was too soon to start daydreaming.

Her office desk faced a full wall of situation maps documenting all recent North Korean DMZ incursions, infiltrations, and violations. As commander of allied G-2 ground reconnaissance and intelligence units, she was directly responsible for monitoring North Korean troop activity along and inside the DMZ. Her squads had to catch whatever the electronic eyes in the sky missed. Sara routinely accompanied the patrols to assess their effectiveness and efficiency.

For the last forty-six years, battle-ready armies had faced each other across a swath of rugged mountains two-and-a-half miles wide and a hundred-and-fifty miles long that cut across the Korean peninsula, keeping the zone free of any human activity except intermittent skirmishes. Once blasted by artillery, bombed and strafed by aircraft, burned and left barren by infantry, the DMZ now flourished as a nature preserve. The reforested mountains, abundant grasses, and wildflowers, the deer, brown bears, and wildcats that grazed and fed peacefully in the valleys and the high country, reminded Sara of her family's Montana sheep ranch and Kerney's still unrealized hope to return to his ranching roots in New Mexico.

When G-2 had received advance notice of the itinerary for the secretary of state's South Korean visit, Sara concentrated her attention on Panmunjom, the neutral village within the DMZ fifty miles due north from Seoul. The secretary had scheduled a quick visit to the site, to be accompanied by high-ranking military and civilian dignitaries.

During a series of late-night sweeps at Panmunjom,

Sara had spotted the tracks and scat of a Korean wildcat. On a subsequent patrol, under a full moon, she caught sight of the animal, an adult male about the size of an American cougar. Through night-vision binoculars, she watched it lope quickly across the cleared area around the village and move on.

Two nights before the secretary of state's arrival, she saw the animal again on the same traverse. Halfway across the clearing the big cat froze, turned to catch a downwind breeze coming from the village, reversed direction, and quickly retreated.

Whatever startled the wildcat needed looking into. Sara got permission to go into the DMZ for a closer look. Her team jumped off late at night from a staging area in a canyon south of Panmunjom, and belly-crawled to the open perimeter surrounding the village, where they waited for the full moon to set.

Under cover of darkness, Sara spread her people out and put the area under close surveillance. For hours nothing moved, but Sara sensed that the North Koreans were up to something. She ordered a ground sweep into the village. As Sara and her team crawled across the clearing, automatic weapon fire opened up from three hidden positions, taking out her point man.

Sara popped flares into the night sky, called for cover fire from the infantry platoon stationed behind the wire, and kept the team moving forward as rounds whined overhead. The green dots from the AK-47 tracers, the red dots from the M-60 machine-gun tracers, and the searing white of the flares cast carnival colors across the night sky.

Using rocket grenade launchers, the team took out two of the positions and stormed the third, capturing a wounded North Korean soldier.

As Sara pulled back with the wounded North Korean and two shot-up team members, the enemy answered with return fire from behind the village. Another soldier took a round in the exchange, but Sara got everyone out. They hit the safety of the fence and a bank of ten-thousand-watt spotlights lit up the village. All shooting stopped.

Sara stayed with her wounded until the medics got them stabilized and ready to airlift. Then she reported to the command bunker. A South Korean infantry officer was on the telephone in a terse exchange with his opposite number on the other side of the DMZ. The officer hung up and reported to the American colonel at his side an immediate stand-down by the North Koreans.

At dawn, Sara took a platoon of infantry back into the DMZ to inspect the area. They found three tunnels with shielded ceilings to block any traces of body heat that could be detected by satellites. Dug from the North Korean boundary, the tunnels ran to within five hundred feet of the viewing platform that looked over the DMZ, and were positioned to rake the viewing platform in a cross fire. Commando sniper rifles with silencers and telescopic sights were retrieved from the tunnels. Then each tunnel was sealed and destroyed with explosives.

As a result of the thwarted assassination plans, the secretary of state's DMZ visit was cancelled.

Weeks later, Sara was still waiting to hear what the CIA and Defense Intelligence Agency had to say about the incident. The Beltway spy shops had taken full control of the investigation and dropped a heavy security blanket over the episode. Since the firefight, most of Sara's time had been spent either undergoing intense questioning by teams of Intelligence analysts or debriefing Pentagon and National Security Council officials.

She had put her people in for commendations and medals, but hadn't heard a word back through the chain of command. Perhaps the incident would be buried so deep that there'd be no recognition of her team's outstanding performance. Such a morale-buster wouldn't make the rest of her tour any easier. She would have to think of ways to keep the unit's performance at a peak.

Sara looked at her wristwatch again. She had five minutes before her meeting with General Clarke. She put on her fatigue jacket and walked across the street to the headquarters building.

Upon assuming command of Combined Forces in Korea, Gen. Henry Powhatan Clarke had taken one look at his senior staff dressed in their Class-B headquarters uniforms and issued his first order, making fatigues the duty dress of the day for all personnel regardless of rank or assignment. As commander in chief of a combat-ready army, Clarke wanted the staff that would run the war and the line soldiers who would fight it dressed, equipped, and prepared to respond at a moment's notice.

It was the first of many changes Clarke made to hone his army to a high state of readiness.

In a rare exception to his own policy, General Clarke had worn his Class-A uniform to work. His schedule for the day included a meeting with the United States ambassador and senior members of the embassy staff. Of all the ribbons he wore above his left jacket pocket, his most prized was the Good Conduct Ribbon, awarded only to enlisted personnel. Serving in Vietnam at the age of twenty, Henry Powhatan Clarke had won a competitive service appointment to West Point, and had graduated in time to return as platoon leader during the 1968 Tet Offensive.

At his desk, Clarke thumbed through the Defense Intelligence Agency report that had been delivered to his quarters late last night by a special Pentagon courier. The contents of the report, along with a letter and attached orders from the secretary of defense, had prompted his request to have Maj. Sara Brannon report to him.

A knock at the open door made General Clarke look up. He smiled and moved to the front of his desk. "Come in, Major," he said, gesturing toward the two army-issue, metal straight-back office chairs that, by design, made long sit-down sessions almost unbearable. Clarke liked short meetings that got his people up and moving as quickly as possible.

"Thank you, sir," Sara answered as she sat in the butt-numbing chair with more grace and ease than Clarke would have imagined possible.

She watched as the general gathered papers from the desk and sat across from her. He had pale blue eyes, a round face that belied his toughness, and close-cut, thick brown hair that curled slightly at the ends.

Sara met his gaze directly.

Clarke knew that Maj. Brannon was an exceptional officer. Any man who only saw her good looks—her sparkling green eyes, strawberry blond hair, and the mischievous line of freckles across her nose—would be seriously underestimating her.

"We finally received a conclusive Intelligence report on the sniper operation," General Clarke said. "A North Korean diplomat defected and confirmed the assassination plot was mounted by a fanatical element within the North Korean officer corps. They wanted to force Kim Jung II into a war with South Korea."

Sara nodded and waited.

"The three snipers had orders to kill the South Korean president, the secretary of state, and me." Henry Powhatan Clarke smiled. "Personally, I like to think that shooting an American four-star general would have pushed us into a war."

"I'm glad that didn't happen, sir," Sara said, smiling back.

"So am I, Major. I understand you've been asking my chief of staff about the status of your request for promotions and commendations for your team."

"I have, sir."

"I like an officer who goes to bat for her people."

"They've earned the recognition, General," Sara said.

"Agreed, Major," General Clarke said, as he put some papers in Sara's hands. "Each enlisted rank gets a meritorious promotion and the Army Commendation Medal. Additionally, the wounded men receive Purple Hearts."

"That's good news, sir," Sara said breaking into a smile as she scanned the orders and citation documents.

"There's more," General Clarke said, handing Sara another sheet of paper. "At the request of the secretary of state, and upon the recommendation of the secretary of defense, you are to receive the Distinguished Service Medal."

Stunned into silence, Sara read the citation. Finally, she raised her glance. "I don't know what to say."

"Congratulations, Colonel Brannon."

"Excuse me?" Sara said incredulously, forgetting protocol.

General Clarke laughed. "We couldn't promote everyone else on the team and leave you out, now could we? I can't think of anybody in your academy class who is walking around as a light colonel."

"A few are on the short list, General."

"Well, you'll have seniority over all of them. You'll get orders for your next duty assignment within the week. You're going home early."

"Where to, sir?"

"After you report from leave, you'll be attending the Command and General Staff College at Fort Leavenworth."

"I wasn't scheduled to attend C and GS until next year," Sara said.

"We can't have a highly decorated, new light colonel running around without her C and GS College ticket punched," General Clarke replied with a warm smile. "You'll need it in your personnel jacket for your next promotion to full colonel. Considering that you kept the North Koreans from sending me home in a bodybag, it was the least I could do."

"Thank you, sir."

"No sweat, Colonel. Meet me at the Officers' Club tonight at twenty hundred hours. I'll pin on those silver oak leaves and douse them with beer, as tradition demands."

"I'll be there, General."

General Clarke stood and walked to his office door. "Any time you want to return to my command, Colonel Brannon, just give me a holler. I want nothing but stud officers serving with me, and I don't give a damn what gender they are."

Sara stood outside the headquarters building in the drizzle paying no attention to the enlisted personnel who walked past snapping off salutes. She recovered her composure and started moving in the direction of G-2, across the street. A convoy of troop carriers held her up.

Sara remained on the sidewalk after the convoy rumbled by, trying to calculate the miles from Fort Leavenworth, Kansas, to Santa Fe. She guessed it to be seven hundred miles. It certainly put Kerney within striking distance.

She smiled as a thought crossed her mind. They had been writing to each other more frequently as the time for her to rotate stateside grew closer, making plans for a visit. Maybe she'd just show up in Santa Fe unannounced and early.

Sara's smile turned into a slightly wicked grin. She had hammered her sexuality into submission by working eighteen-hour days and avoiding even those men who were not off-limits under the current sexual relations policies. Avoiding the whole sex issue had been the most realistic way to survive with her career intact in a combat-ready command, and she was damn tired of abstinence.

A young soldier gave Sara a salute and a sidelong glance as he passed by, and Sara wiped the grin off her face. The cloudy day had turned cold. Sara zipped up her fatigue jacket, yearning for the dry desert heat that she'd bitched so much about during her tour of duty at White Sands Missile Range.

She stepped off the sidewalk and hurried to find her Field Intelligence and Reconnaissance Unit squad leaders. She wanted to be the first to tell her people about the promotions and citations before word leaked out from other sources. Then she'd finish her workday and celebrate after General Clarke pinned on the silver oak leaves that evening.

It was, Lt. Col. Sara Brannon thought, one of the best days in her ten years as an officer in the United States Army.

Kevin Kerney sat in the passenger seat of Dale Jennings's truck with the window rolled down, while his old friend from the Tularosa Basin drove down a San Miguel County dirt road in Northern New Mexico, about fifty miles due east of Santa Fe.

It was an unusually warm and pretty early April morning, but Kerney wasn't paying any attention to the weather or the vistas. His thoughts were on Erma Ferguson.

Erma was his mother's college roommate and life-long friend. When his parents died in an auto accident over twenty-five years ago, Erma became one of the few people left in Kerney's life with a link to his boyhood on his family's Tularosa ranch.

Erma taught art at the state university in Las Cruces for almost forty years. After her retirement, she became one of the most renowned landscape artists of the Southwest. She'd never married, never had children.

Kerney had last seen Erma in November on a visit to Las Cruces. In her seventies, she remained a head-turner. She was vibrant, vital, elegant, and classy. They went out to dinner, reminisced about Kerney's parents, and talked about his college years when Erma served as his surrogate mother.

A massive stroke had killed Erma in early February, and now Kerney was about to take his second look at the ten sections of high country ranch land she had left to him. He'd known that Erma owned property she once used as a summer retreat. But the size of it—6,400 acres—came as a complete surprise, as did her bequest of the land and the old cabin that stood on it.

Kerney glanced quickly at Dale, now the last living person connected to Kerney's childhood years on the ranch. Dale's arm rested on the open window and he steered the truck with one hand. His fingers were blunt and calloused, and his long forehead, covered by the bill of a cap pulled low, hid his thinning hair. His closely cropped sideburns showed a hint of gray and his face was weathered from years working in the scorching sun of southern New Mexico.

Dale ranched near the Tularosa, on land handed

down through three generations. He'd been Kerney's closest neighbor and best boyhood friend.

They passed through the village of Ojitos Frios. An adobe church and a cluster of homes—some of stone and others coated with cement or plastered with stucco—sat among irrigated fields that rimmed the base of flat-topped Tecolote Peak. The small valley seemed frozen in the late nineteenth century.

"What is this place?" Dale asked as he drove through the settlement.

"What?" Kerney asked.

"What's the name of this place?"

"Ojitos Frios."

Dale glanced at Kerney with amused brown eyes.

"What's so funny?" Kerney asked.

"Cold Springs, huh? If we find one, maybe I'll give you a good dunking to wake you up."

"I'm here," Kerney replied.

"Not hardly," Dale said. "You've been off in dreamland since I rolled up to your door early this morning."

Kerney laughed. "I guess I have. I still can't believe Erma put me in her will."

"That lady loved you like a son," Dale said. Up ahead a fast moving stream ran across a dip in the road. He dropped the transmission into low gear and rattled the truck through the water, keeping an eye on the trailer hitched to the truck.

The trailer held two horses Dale had brought up from his ranch in the San Andres Mountains. One of the animals, Soldier, was a mustang Kerney had trained and later named in honor of his dead godson, Sammy Yazzi.

Sammy had been murdered while serving in the army at White Sands Missile Range, on land that once belonged to Kerney's family. Working with Sara Brannon, an army officer at the base, Kerney solved the crime, and the men responsible for Sammy's murder were dead.

Even though Kerney had given Soldier to him, Dale always planned to return the horse. Now, maybe soon he could.

Across the stream, the road curved and climbed the crest of a small hill that opened up on overgrazed grassland. Along the streambed Dale could see deep erosion furrows, a sure sign of poor range management.

"Where exactly is this mesa you now own?" Dale inquired.

"A little farther down the road," Kerney answered, starting to feel a bit antsy.

Only three weeks had passed since he'd been informed of Erma's bequest of the land and the cabin, and due to the demands of his job as deputy state police chief, he'd been able to manage just one quick trip up from Santa Fe to look over his unexpected windfall.

What Kerney had seen looked promising. The foot of the low mesa held rich grassland, and a live stream wandered near a ramshackle cabin. But most of the land was on the mesa, and Kerney didn't have a clue what to expect in the high country.

With Dale supplying the horses and coming along for the ride, Kerney planned to see it all before the weekend ended.

The road turned east then north as the valley

widened, and a long ridge line popped up, dense with trees that climbed steep slopes. Beyond, the Sangre de Cristo Mountains rolled back into the horizon, peaks still capped in deep snow.

"That's my mesa," Kerney said, when the cabin came into view.

"That's a pretty dinky mesa," Dale replied, tongue in cheek.

"Don't be a spoilsport," Kerney said. He directed Dale through the open gate and got out of the truck as soon as it came to a stop.

Dale eyed the cabin from the cab of his truck. Old stone walls sagged under a rusted, pitched tin roof. The front door and small windows were boarded up with scrap lumber. It looked completely useless.

He heard the sound of hoofs on metal and left the truck to find Kerney leading the horses out of the trailer and down the ramp.

"In a hurry?" Dale asked as he reached for Pancho's halter. Pancho was his best trail horse, sure-footed and with endurance suited for long rides. Soldier stood nearby, pawing the ground and shaking off his confinement in the trailer.

"You bet I am," Kerney said, reaching for the riding tack in the trailer storage compartment.

Dale stretched his back to ease the tightness from the long drive and looked around. Off in the distance, he could see the outline of Hermit's Peak, two massive summits that stood like the hindquarters of a prehistoric animal. His gaze traveled to some smaller button-nose peaks that dipped off at the front end, and suddenly Hermit's Peak looked like an upturned face with a gaping mouth staring into the sky.

He switched his gaze to Kerney and found him saddled and mounted.

"Let's get going," Kerney said.

"Slow down, cowboy."

"Slow down, shit," Kerney said with a grin. "I want to cover it all before sundown. Saddle up."

Dale grinned back. It had been a long time since he'd seen Kerney look so damn happy.

An old ranch road petered out at the base of the mesa where a stock trail began, winding through a dense thicket of juniper and piñon pine trees. Halfway up the trail got rocky, and the horses picked their way carefully through loose stones and small boulders. They hit the top and encountered a stand of young ponderosas that gradually thickened into a dense climax forest. Kerney turned to look at the rolling valley below. His eyes followed the cuts defining the deep running streams that converged in the village of San Geronimo. Nestled in a shallow depression, the village was mostly in ruins, kept barely alive by the few ranching families who still lived there. The church stood, as did a vacant school and a few homes. But the remaining buildings were weathered empty shells surrounded by piles of hand-cut stone rubble.

The hills beyond the village cut off from view all but the uppermost third of Hermit's Peak, and the mountain looked like two giant loaves of homemade bread set out to cool on a windowsill.

"Every time I look at that mountain, it seems different," Kerney said.

"You're not wrong about that," Dale said, buttoning his jacket. A broad stream of clouds blocked the sun and chilled down the air. "It will be the last nice view we have if these woodlands don't give way to some open country pretty soon."

"You don't like fighting your way through the brush?"

"Nope. Reminds me too much of work."

"Pray for open country," Kerney said.

They came out of the trees a thousand yards from the ridge line, where the ponderosas dwindled away and grassland took over. A barbed-wire fence barred their passage and they followed it, looking for an opening.

As he rode, Kerney eyed the wide mesa. There were small stands of piñon and juniper trees sprinkled over the land and folded rock outcroppings along the edges of shallow depressions. The land sloped westward, and several wandering arroyos had cut through the thin layer of soil down to the rock plate before draining into intermittent catchment basins.

From the map Erma's lawyer and executor, a man named Milton Lynch, had supplied, Kerney knew there was no live water on the mesa. But two windmills tapped groundwater, and Kerney was eager to find them. If they were in working order, it would ease the expense of putting cattle on the land.

They entered the grassland through an old cedar pole gate, and moved down an arroyo into a dry basin. The open range, Kerney guessed, took up four thousand acres of the ten section tract, and showed no sign of recent use. He figured the neighboring rancher who leased the grazing rights had decided to rest the land for a season or two.

As they came out of the basin, Kerney caught sight of a windmill and stock tank. A black dog with brown stockings limped away from a grove of trees, carrying something in its mouth. Even from a good distance away, the dog looked skinny under its thickly matted fur.

It heard the horses, stopped, turned, and retreated in the direction of the trees. Kerney couldn't quite make out the object in the dog's mouth. As he closed in for a closer look the dog froze, dropped the object, skirted around Soldier, and scampered for cover, yelping in pain as it ran.

"That pooch isn't doing too well," Dale said.

"It doesn't seem so," Kerney said as he broke Soldier into a trot toward the object on the ground. He looked down, fully expecting to see a dead rabbit. It was a chewed-up athletic shoe.

He dismounted and retrieved it. It carried a name brand and seemed to be sized to fit a woman. The faded label inside the tongue, barely readable, confirmed it.

Dale caught up, looked at the shoe in Kerney's hand, and shook his head. "That dog sure isn't much of a hunter. A retriever, maybe. Do you want to leave it here and move on?"

"No, it's hurt. Maybe it got dumped or left behind by campers. We'll round it up."

As Kerney started to remount the dog broke cover, carrying another shoe, moving as quickly as the lame hind leg allowed.

Kerney took his boot out of the stirrup, looked up at Dale, made a face, and shook his head.

"Now what?" Dale asked.

"A dog carrying one shoe I'd call mildly curious. But a dog with two shoes piques my interest."

Dale laughed. "Maybe it just likes to collect shoes."

"Maybe." Kerney looked around the empty mesa. "But from where?"

"Good point."

"Think you can fetch that dog for me?" Kerney asked.

"Sure thing," Dale said, reaching for his rope.

"Bring the shoe back with you."

"What are you going to do?"

"Check out that stand of trees."

"Don't you ever stop thinking like a cop?" Dale asked as he broke Pancho into a trot.

"Probably not."

Kerney walked Soldier to a lone juniper at the edge of the grove, tied him off, looked into the shadows, and saw nothing. He pushed his way through some low branches, and knelt down on a thick mound of needles, letting his eyes adjust to the dim light. The dog had dug out a small hollow at the base of a piñon tree. Kerney's eye caught a touch of color in the loose dirt. Using a twig, he brushed away the dirt and uncovered a comb. He backed away and scanned the ground of the surrounding trees. He saw a scrap of fabric that looked like denim. Next to it was a half-buried bone, with a human foot still attached.

Kerney had seen enough. Whatever else there was to be found, he would leave to a crime scene unit and the

District State Police Office in Las Vegas. He came out of the grove as Dale rode up, carrying the dog over his saddle.

"Find anything?" Dale asked, as he handed Kerney the shoe. It matched the first one.

"The shoes were left here," Kerney replied, "with some human bones."

"No joke?"

"No joke."

"What are you going to do?"

"I left my cell phone in your truck. We'll head back and call the district office."

"What about the dog? It's a neutered male. I make him to be about five or six years old. He needs a meal bad and he has a gimpy hip."

Kerney looked at the mutt. Mostly black, with brown markings around the eyes that matched his stockings, he had flecks of gray on his chest and a salt-and-pepper tail. He was hairy, filthy, skinny, and scared.

"I'll keep him," Kerney said impulsively.

"You need to give him water, food, and a name," Dale said.

"I'll call him Shoe, for now," Kerney said, as he opened his saddlebags and reached for one of the sandwiches he had packed for lunch.

He handed it to Dale and the dog wolfed it down. Dale cupped his hands and Kerney poured water from his canteen into them. Shoe lapped it up and Kerney gave him more.

He untied Soldier's reins and mounted up.

Dale held Shoe out to him. "He's your dog. You might as well get used to his smell."

Kerney sided Soldier over to Dale, took the dog, put him across the saddle, sniffed, and wrinkled his nose. "We'll head to that stock tank and clean him up a bit before we turn back."

"Good idea," Dale said.

"We should still have part of the day to explore after things settle down."

"What happens next?"

"Officers and a crime scene unit will come out and search the area."

"Damn, I'd like to see that."

"I'm sure you will."

"You sound grumpy."

"This is not the way I wanted to spend my weekend."

"Do you think you've got a murder on your hands?"

"I always think the worst when people turn up dead."

"Maybe you should call this place Skeleton Mesa."

"That's cute, Dale."

Dale shrugged his shoulders. "Just a suggestion. I think that dog likes you."

Shivers ran through the dog as it laid across the saddle. Kerney could feel it breathing heavily. He ran his hand over the dog's back to calm him and scratched his ears. The dog looked at him with serious eyes. "Not yet. But I think he will."

2

Kerney spent more time than he liked briefing the two officers who showed up at the old cabin. Russell Thorpe, the rookie patrolman who responded to Kerney's phone call, had brought along his field training supervisor. Thorpe was a new academy graduate in his last week of on-the-job training before being released for independent patrol.

Six feet tall, with a weight lifter's build and a boyish face, Thorpe nervously questioned Kerney under the watchful eye of Sgt. Gabriel Gonzales. Kerney figured that Gonzales had warned him not to screw up in front of the deputy chief.

After double-checking Kerney's statement for accuracy, Thorpe bagged the two sneakers as evidence and went to the patrol unit to call for a response team. Sergeant Gonzales tagged along to oversee, and stood by the open door of the patrol car while Thorpe transmitted radio messages.

Kerney found Dale stretched out on the seat of his

truck, snoozing. In the back of the extended cab, Shoe was curled up in a ball. He fashioned a collar and leash out of some rope, put the collar around Shoe's neck, got the dog out of the truck, and shook Dale awake.

"Got any flea powder?" he asked when Dale sat up.

"In the tool box," Dale said. "There's a bottle of equine spray."

"That will do."

Kerney found the bottle, tied Shoe to the front bumper, and began spraying. Fleas started jumping off the dog.

"Chief."

Kerney turned to face Sgt. Gabe Gonzales. Twenty years on the force had set deep creases on either side of the sergeant's face. His eyebrows turned up at the corners of his eyes, and a stubby chin gave him a squared-off, serious cast.

"We'll have a helicopter here in thirty minutes with a crime scene unit," Gonzales said.

"Good enough."

Kerney rolled Shoe on his back and squirted flea spray on his stomach. The dog started scratching busily.

Gabe eyed the dog's performance. "You might want to spray the inside of the truck, while you're at it," he suggested.

"Good idea," Kerney said. "Did your rookie do his job right?"

Gonzales smiled. "By the numbers. He'll be a good one."

"Pass on my compliments," Kerney said.

Gonzales smiled and nodded. "I'll do that, Chief. Do you want a copy of the field report sent directly to you?"

"You bet," Kerney said.

Gonzales went back to watch over his rookie, and Kerney finished up with the dog. He fed him some lunch meat from the cooler, put him in the horse trailer, and then sprayed the inside of the truck. He put a basin of fresh water in with the dog and added a sock. Shoe took the sock in his mouth, shook it, wagged his tail, and sat, looking pleased with his new possession.

"Are you ready?" Kerney asked. He turned to find Dale holding out Soldier's reins and grinning. "What are you smiling about?"

"Hell, I'm having a good time. Cops, skeletons, homicide. This sure beats watching a police show on television."

"We'll stop by the crime scene so you can have some more fun," Kerney said as he took the reins and swung himself into the saddle.

"That's what I wanted to hear."

They cleared the tree line on the mesa as the sound of a chopper broke the silence. They entered the open grassland and the state police helicopter passed overhead, veering in the direction of the first stock tank.

It took half an hour by horseback to reach the grove where Kerney had found the bones. He slowed Soldier to a stop and watched. Gonzales and Thorpe were doing a field search around the perimeter of the trees, while two crime scene techs worked in the shadows under low branches.

Dale sidled up to Kerney. "Aren't you going to see if they found anything else?"

Kerney didn't want to interrupt the search. "We'll wait and watch for a few minutes."

Finally, a figure emerged from the grove and Kerney recognized Melody Jordan, a senior crime scene technician who specialized in forensic pathology. Jordan did all the preliminary assessments of human remains for the department.

Aside from being highly competent, Melody was an attractive woman. No more than thirty, she had lively brown eyes, a mouth with a sexy little pout, and wheat blond hair. Born and raised on a ranch in the Hondo Valley, she had a frank and casual style that Kerney found charming.

Melody walked in his direction, pausing briefly to brush some pine needles out of her hair. When she got close, he introduced her to Dale. She shook Dale's hand, stroked Pancho's neck, and looked Soldier over before turning her attention to Kerney.

"You made quite a find here, Chief," Melody said.

"How so?"

"We've recovered a pelvis and some bones from the lower extremities. Femurs, fibulas, and feet. The pelvis strongly suggests it was a female. I'd guess she's been dead about a year. Maybe less."

"The skeleton is incomplete?"

"So far. There are some tool marks on the bones. From the looks of it, I'd say the body was sawed or cut up."

"Was she killed here?"

"That's hard to say. Maybe not."

"Was she dismembered here?"

"I don't know. We're looking for trace evidence now. If we find fibers, hair, or bloodstains, we'll have a clearer picture. But don't count on anything: weather probably washed it all away. I'll take the usual soil samples for analysis. Maybe we'll get lucky and some foreign matter will turn up."

"Did you find the scrap of fabric and the comb?"

"We did indeed. It's bagged and tagged."

"Do you have anything that points to the cause of death?"

Melody laughed. "Dream on, Chief. I've got bones here, not a body. Some have been chewed on. But I can't wait to take a closer look at them under a microscope. I think the killer knew how to butcher a carcass."

"Any ranch hand worth his salt knows how to butcher," Kerney said.

"Don't I know it," Melody said.

"You've found no garments or personal items?"

"Nothing other than what you discovered. I'd say whoever did this didn't want the victim to be identified."

"Find the rest of the skeleton," Kerney said.

Melody looked out over the mesa. "It could be scattered anywhere. There's a lot of ground to cover here, Chief."

"I know it. Bring in additional help. I want a full sweep of the mesa."

Melody smiled. "Sergeant Gonzales said this is your land."

"It is," Kerney replied as he remounted. "Welcome to the neighborhood."

Melody smiled. "It's beautiful. I can think of better

ways to spend a weekend in this country than scraping up soil samples."

"Me, too, and that's exactly what I intend to do."

Melody waved and watched the two men ride away, thinking Kerney looked very hunky on horseback.

"That's a nice-looking woman," Dale said, when they were out of earshot.

"Yes, she is," Kerney said, pointing Soldier toward the windmill.

"She sure seems to like her job. I never heard anybody sound so damn cheery about a butchered murder victim."

Kerney laughed.

"What did I say?"

"Nothing."

Dale trotted Pancho until he was even with Soldier. "What?"

"If I remember correctly, you don't like puzzles."

"Never did," Dale said. "When we were kids, you always figured the damn things out before I could."

"Melody likes puzzles."

"That's not all she likes," Dale said.

"Meaning?"

"Meaning you."

"Get serious."

"That was a thousand-watt smile she gave you when we showed up. Did you know that a lot of relationships nowadays start in the workplace?"

"Is that a fact?" Kerney said.

"That's a fact. You should take advantage of those opportunities when they come along."

"Since when have you become an expert on relationships?"

"I read about it somewhere."

Kerney laughed again. "I thought so."

"But I've been living with women for over twenty years. A wife and two daughters can teach a man a lot about how women operate, how their minds work."

"I defer to your experience."

"That'll be the day. Think you have a chance of finding the killer?"

"There's always a chance."

They passed the stock tank and rode south through a thicket of big sagebrush that spread across the grassland. They found the second windmill and tank, both in good working order, with no recent sign of cattle milling at the water source. Unless forced to move, cows stayed near water, trampling the ground bare and sterile.

The mesa rose gradually and seemed to run hard up against the Sangre de Cristo Mountains. They crossed a brake of cholla cactus, moving carefully around the long, spindly branches that could dig clusters of thorns into a horse and rider, and entered another large sweep of open country.

All Kerney saw told him the range had been well rested. New grass was greening up nicely among the unforaged, knee-high blue grama. His mind started racing with all that needed doing to put the land into production. Maybe the cabin—the only structure on the ranch—could be shored up to serve as temporary quarters. He would need to get inside and inspect it. But a place to stay wasn't the half of it: a barn, stables, corral, shipping pen, a loading chute, and new fences to segregate pastures were essential to put the land to use. Then he had to buy livestock.

Reality hit: starting up a ranch wasn't going to be cheap. It would take a big mortgage to get things underway, and Kerney had no idea if he could swing a large bank loan. The thought that he might not be able to pull it off put a knot in his stomach.

"Deep thoughts?" Dale asked, as he rode alongside.

"You could say that," Kerney answered, nodding at the stand of ponderosas that defined the far edge of the mesa. He didn't want to talk about his newfound worries. "Let's see what's on the other side of those trees."

They followed a game trail into the woods, tall pines cutting the afternoon sun to half-light, and reached a treeless, rocky shoulder that jutted out over the backside of the mesa. The Sangre de Cristo Mountains, austere and vast against the skyline, stood a close two ridgelines away.

Below, in a small defile at the edge of a narrow valley, a forty-acre swath of trees had been clear-cut. Only stumps, dead branches, and slash remained. An alluvial fan of gravel and sand spread out from a small occasional stream that ran through the defile. Erosion had begun in the sandy soil; water-filled down-cut troughs twisted around tree stumps at the edge of the stream.

"Jesus," Dale said, "who would do something like that?"

"Good question," Kerney said, trying to contain his anger. He nudged Soldier ahead and the horse picked his way carefully down the slope.

In the defile they scoured the area and found tire tracks that petered out on a rocky Jeep trail that climbed up the adjoining mesa. A hundred feet in, they discovered a cut barbed-wire fence and a discarded motor oil container.

Kerney had started the weekend with no intention of doing any police work. He was totally unprepared to collect or document evidence. He left the container where it was, staked it with a tree branch, and noted its location. Back in the defile, they inspected the tree stumps. The absence of weathering pointed to recent harvesting.

"What do you think?" Dale asked, as he picked out some burrs that had galled Pancho's flank.

"I think we've got a poacher who sells firewood for a living. Someone who knows his way around the area."

"He sure picked a spot to cut where he wouldn't be seen."

"Exactly."

"You're going to lose this acreage to erosion if you don't act fast. About the best you can do right now is slow it down and keep it from spreading. It's gonna take a chunk of money and a lot of hard work to save it."

"I know." Kerney looked up at the mesa. The tips of the ponderosas were tinged gold by the afternoon sunlight. "We need to get started back."

"Do you think the poaching and the murder are connected?"

"Could be. You never know."

"Barbara and the girls aren't going to believe a word of this when I get home."

"Don't start polishing up your story yet. The weekend isn't over."

"What else can happen?"

"Just about anything," Kerney replied.

They rode back to the crime scene. Another chopper was on the ground and additional techs were busy field searching an expanded area. He could see Melody Jordan in the distance at another grove of trees. She turned and waved, but she was too far away for Kerney to tell if she had a thousand-watt smile on her face.

He found Sergeant Gonzales and filled him in on the wood poaching.

"Do you want me to jump on it right away, Chief?" Gonzales asked.

"How far along are you here?"

"Nothing more has turned up. We'll be back out in the morning."

"Do you think Officer Thorpe can pick up some evidence and photograph tire tracks without your supervision?"

"He should be able to handle it."

"Send Thorpe in the chopper. Loan me your notebook and I'll sketch the scene for him."

Gonzales pulled a notebook from his pocket and held it out. Kerney drew a rough map of the defile, noting the location of the tire tracks, the cut fence, and the empty oil container.

"Have Thorpe bring back a sample of the cut barbed wire," Kerney said. "We might get a good tool mark to use as evidence."

"Will do," Gonzales said.

"Stay with it, Sergeant."

"We'll be here until last light."

The chopper carrying Officer Thorpe took off soon after Dale and Kerney left. They watched it rise in the distance and turn toward the poaching site. Enough daylight remained for the two men to follow the south end of the mesa back to the cabin. They dropped off the crest and skirted around a sheared bluff that resembled a poorly chiseled arrowhead. A ranch road plunged down the mesa in a series of switchbacks, and faded into ruts that followed a fence line.

They made the turn around the mesa and joined up with the county road. Dead ahead, barely visible in the growing dusk, stood the cabin, truck, and horse trailer. Before they reached the cabin, Kerney could hear Shoe barking. He dismounted to the clamor of the dog scratching at the metal floor of the horse trailer. The mutt was trying to dig his way out of captivity. When Kerney spoke to the dog, it stopped scratching and sat expectantly, eyes fixed on Kerney.

"You'll have to wait a few minutes," Kerney said.

Shoe's tail flapped in response.

Dale got busy with dinner and Kerney tended to the horses, watering them at the stream and feeding each a bag of grain. Then he hobbled them nearby for the night on some good grass where they could graze.

As he walked back to the trailer, rotor noise cut the stillness. He watched the lights of the helicopters pass out of the valley, let Shoe out of the trailer, and tied him to the bumper. The dog rolled on his back, and lifted his front paws in the air. Kerney gave him a tummy scratch.

When dinner was ready, Dale found Kerney in the truck with the cab light on, studying a plat map.

"According to this map, Nestor Barela owns land that parallels mine on the backside of the mesa," Kerney said, taking the plate from Dale's hand.

Dinner consisted of steak, a baked potato, and a large slab of homemade apple pie. He got out of the truck and followed Dale to the campfire. Two camp stools had been set up. He sat down, balanced the plate on his knees, and cut into the steak with a knife.

"He might be worth talking to," Dale said.

"He holds the grazing rights on my property."

"He sure hasn't been using them."

"Maybe he went into the wood cutting business instead." Kerney took a bite of steak. "This is good."

"Homegrown range-fed beef. Can you pay the taxes on this place?"

"I'm trying not to think about it. The appraisal is due next week. I don't have a clue what the inheritance tax will be."

"It will be a pretty penny."

"Yeah, and it'll take a huge mortgage to cover the taxes and make the improvements the place needs."

"I've been yearning for some high-country summer grazing land."

"What are you saying, Dale?"

"This land is like a grass bank waiting for cattle that need fattening up. I've got yearlings that will add two hundred pounds easy in a summer up here."

"Do you want to buy me out?"

"I had a partnership in mind: your land, my beef. I'll take out a loan each year to make the tax payments, and you give me half interest in the property. You carry the bank note for the improvements. That way we share the load."

Kerney shook his head. "I won't let you borrow against your land on my account. It's too risky."

"You're one stubborn son of a bitch."

"I know it."

"Well, think about it. It might work."

"I didn't know being land rich could be so damn frustrating."

"If you want to ranch, you're going to have to use somebody else's money to do it."

"I guess that's true. Hold off until I know what the taxes will be. Okay?"

"Okay."

"Did Barbara bake the pie?"

"She did, and sent it along with her love."

"Save your steak bone for Shoe," Kerney said.

"It's already got his name on it."

The dog, still tied to the bumper, flapped his tail, drooled, and kept his eyes fixed on the two men.

In the morning, it was Kerney's turn to cook. At first light, he fixed enough chow to insure leftovers for the dog. After cleaning up the dishes, he fed Shoe, put on the makeshift collar and leash, and took him for a walk.

Dale laughed as Kerney led the dog away. Shoe seemed perfectly content to be on a leash, and after sniffing around for the right spot, he did his business. The dog still limped. Kerney hoped that some weight gain and exercise would correct the problem.

Sergeant Gonzales arrived in a four-wheel drive pulling a horse trailer, followed by a Game and Fish truck, with another trailer, and several patrol units. Kerney questioned him about the crime scene search, and Gabe reported that nothing more had been found. Gonzales, his team, and the Game and Fish officer were all dressed in riding gear.

"Have the techs work the site one more time," Kerney said.

"They're on the way," Gonzales said. "We'll cover the mesa on horseback. If anything else is there, we'll turn it up."

Kerney saw Gonzales and his team off, tied Shoe to the bumper of the trailer, borrowed Dale's truck, and promised to return in a hour. He wanted to pay a friendly visit to Nestor Barela and see what kind of neighbor he had inherited.

The ranch road leading to Barela's place was an expensive piece of work. Graded, crowned, and topped with packed base course, it was far superior to the poorly maintained county road. The headquarters sat in a horseshoe canyon about a hundred acres deep and half as wide. From the last cattle guard into the headquarters, the road was asphalt.

Kerney stopped before he crossed the cattle guard and looked the place over. The most prominent building was an indoor arena near a large horse barn. Expensive white pipe fences enclosed cooldown areas, exercise rings, show jumping gates, and corrals. Two smaller

outbuildings, a hay shed, and a loading pen were sheltered at the side of the canyon.

Across a pasture, tucked on the other side of the
canyon, was an adobe house with a half-story attic
framed with battens, a pitched roof, and a row of cottonwoods along the windward side. Laundry flapped on
a clothesline steps away from a side porch.

The main residence dominated high ground at the
back of the canyon where the winds would swirl and
bluster. It was enormous, and obviously positioned for
the view rather than for protection from the elements.
Built in a symmetrical H with pitched roofs, the house
had a deep veranda running across the core of the structure that connected the two lateral sides. A chimney
protruded in the center of each distinct roof line. A low
wall with white-picket gates confined some shade trees
at the front of the house. A free-standing three-car
garage built in the same style stood below and to one
side of the residence.

All in all, it looked like Barela had sold the place to
somebody with a hell of a lot of money, who had converted the cattle operation into a horse ranch.

Erma's lawyer and executor, Milton Lynch, who lived
in the southern part of the state, had only been able to
provide sketchy information about Barela. Kerney had a
name, a post office box number, what Barela paid for his
lease, and the location of the ranch, all which could easily be out of date.

He stopped at the horse barn, where several trucks
were parked. A hand-crafted sign above the doors read
HORSE CANYON RANCH. He could hear the sounds of men

and animals inside the barn. He called out and a middle-aged Anglo man, thick through the chest, wearing a stained felt cowboy hat, a plaid snap button shirt, jeans, and a pair of work boots caked with manure and straw, walked out to greet him.

Kerney introduced himself by name only. "Is the foreman here?"

"I'm the ranch manager," the man said, pulling off his work glove to shake Kerney's hand. "Emmet Griffin." His voice carried a trace of a brush-country Texas accent as he rolled his words together. "What can I do for you?"

"I'm looking for Nestor Barela," Kerney answered.

"Barela sold out three years ago and moved to town," Griffin said.

"I understand he leases the Fergurson land."

Kerney's statement raised Griffin's interest. "He does, but he doesn't really use it. He puts a few cows on it each spring, fattens them up, and slaughters them for his freezer. It keeps Fergurson's taxes down and fills Barela's stomach."

"That's a pretty expensive way to fill a freezer."

Griffin laughed, showing his teeth below his mustache. "It sure the hell is."

"Do you think Barela would be willing to consider a sublease?"

Griffin shook his head. "I've tried that. He won't sublease it, and the Fergurson woman won't sell. My boss would love to buy that property as a buffer. A lot of the big spreads east of here are being carved up and sold in five- to twenty-acre tracts. She doesn't want that kind of development along her boundary. She likes her privacy."

"Is your boss here?"

"Nope. She should be back in a day or two."

"What's her name?"

"Alicia Bingham."

"What breed of horses is she training?"

"We breed and train. Dutch Warmblood and English Anglo-Arab, for dressage and show jumping. We sell to an international market. Our buyers are mostly top-flight competitors."

"Do you know how I can contact Barela?"

"Not really. One of his sons and a grandson go up to the mesa now and then to check on their lease holding. But I don't know where they live, exactly. I heard the old man moved his whole family onto one piece of land."

"Thanks for your time."

"Hell, I'd rather talk to you than muck out stalls. Good luck with old Nestor Barela. You'll need it."

Back at the cabin, Soldier and Pancho were saddled and ready to go, and Shoe was caged inside the horse trailer working on a steak bone. He wagged his tail when Kerney called his name.

Dale had pulled the wood off the cabin door and was nowhere to be seen. Kerney found him inside, knee-deep in rotting hay. Thick cobwebs hung down from the log rafters, which had been nailed and tied with bailing wire to the bond beam that ran along the top course of the stone walls. The tin roof was rusted through in spots, and one of the logs that spanned the ceiling had decayed and broken apart.

"You might as well knock this damn thing down and

start over from scratch," Dale said. "You've got vermin droppings and black widow nests everywhere."

He held out a yellowed, chewed-up piece of stationery.

"What's this?"

"Part of a love letter from Erma Fergurson."

"To whom?"

"Can't tell."

Kerney studied the faded handwritten letter. It spoke of a starry night on the mesa, not liking the idea of sleeping alone, and bodies entwined. It carried Erma's signature and had no date.

"Good for her," Kerney said with a smile. "I hope she had a lot of fun with him, whoever he was."

"Want to look for more letters?"

"We'll let Erma's affairs of the heart stay where they are for now." He dropped the piece of stationery on the moldy hay.

"Did you see Barela?"

"Barela sold out and moved to town three years ago. I haven't talked to him."

"So, no arrest is pending?"

"Not yet."

"That's disappointing."

"Don't fuss, Dale. You've got Erma's love letter to add to your adventures, once you get home." Kerney stepped outside. "Let's go. I want to find out how those poachers hauled that wood away. There has to be an outlet from the valley through the next ridgeline. Let's see if we can find it on the north side. We haven't covered that stretch of land yet."

"Lead the way," Dale said, striding to Pancho.

They rode off Kerney's land toward the mountains where the country road veered toward San Geronimo. An unimproved dirt track sliced into a canyon along a small stream, showing signs of recent vehicle travel. At the junction where two small creeks converged, snow covered the ground. Fresh tire tracks forked up the side of the foothills. They topped out to find a high mountain meadow, wedged between a small mesa and the mountains.

The meadow was fenced, and a locked gate and NO TRESPASSING signs barred their passage. Halfway in the meadow stood a new timber-frame house with a blue metal pitched roof. A child's bicycle leaned against the covered porch. No motor vehicles were present.

A rectangular greenhouse had been erected at the far end of the meadow, a good distance from the house. Built with concrete blocks and rough-cut lumber, the roof joists were covered with thick translucent plastic panels.

"They sure are tucked away in here," Dale said. "Are we going in?"

"We haven't been invited," Kerney said. "How about I buy you lunch in Las Vegas?"

"It's a little early to eat."

"It won't be after I track down Nestor Barela and talk to him."

"We're packing it in?"

"As far as the trail riding goes." Kerney pointed to a dip in the tree line where the horizontal line of a mesa showed through. "If I'm oriented correctly, that's my property over there. The defile should be just a little to the south and east. We may have found a neighbor who just might know something about the poaching. I'll pay him a visit when he's home."

"Then why go see Barela?"

"Because he may know something the neighbor doesn't."

"Makes sense," Dale said. "You really do think like a cop."

"It's habit forming."

Shoe sat in the back of the extended cab on a jump seat, panting quietly, as they made the short fifteen-mile trip to Las Vegas, New Mexico. The city, situated on the edge of the high plains with Hermit's Peak and the Sangre de Cristo Mountains looming in the background, had its boom days late in the last century when the arrival of the railroad turned it into a major transportation center.

With almost a thousand historic buildings dating from early in the century and before, Las Vegas was staging a comeback. A number of the old buildings that ringed the plaza and spread down Bridge Street had been renovated, new businesses had opened, tourism had picked up, and newcomers were moving in.

They stopped at the police department on a corner of the plaza. Kerney went in, introduced himself to the shift commander, flashed his credentials, and asked a few questions. The officer knew Barela, and Kerney got directions to Nestor's house.

Barela lived just outside the city limits on land along the Gallinas River that he'd turned into a compound for his extended family. It consisted of four manufactured homes on concrete pads lined up in a row facing the highway.

A wrought-iron portal arched over the driveway, with the words *Los Barelas* spelled out in cursive writing. Beneath the lettering was a fabricated cutout of a cowboy on horseback twirling a lasso. A fenced pasture dipped down to the river where a young man was cleaning out the inside of a four-horse trailer at the side of a barn.

Six quarter horses in the pasture looked up at the sound of Dale's truck on the dirt driveway, swished their tails lazily, and went back to grazing. There were eight cars and trucks of various makes parked in front of the house, none of them more than two or three years old.

The front door to a house swung open as they drew near, and a stocky man in his late thirties with reddish brown hair and a neatly trimmed beard walked off the porch to greet them.

Kerney waved, got out after Dale slowed to a stop, and limped to meet the man halfway. His right knee, shattered by a bullet in a gunfight, ached from his time in the saddle.

"I'm looking for Nestor Barela," he said.

"Are you here about the horse we have for sale?" the man asked.

"No, I'm here about the Fergurson lease."

"We're not giving up that lease until it runs out."

"When is that?" Kerney asked, knowing full well the lease expired at the end of the year.

The man thought about answering, shrugged it off,

and nodded at the house where an elderly man stood framed in a doorway. "Talk to my father. He's home."

Kerney reached the porch step and smiled at a sinewy man somewhere in his late seventies. His legs were bowed from years in the saddle. The back of his hands carried the scars from a lifetime of hard physical work. He had a full head of gray hair and sharp, clear brown eyes.

"Mr. Barela?" Kerney asked.

"Yes," Barela answered suspiciously.

Kerney decided not to give too much away. "My name is Kevin Kerney." He nodded in the direction of the truck, where Dale waited. "My friend and I are interested in buying your grazing rights on the Fergurson land for the summer."

Barela's expression soured further. "I'm not interested."

"I'd be willing to pay a premium for it."

"I don't keep it to make money," Nestor replied.

"Mind telling me why you do keep it?" Kerney asked. "It hasn't been put in production for some time, as far as I can tell."

"You've been on the land?"

"Just for a quick look. I'd heard you weren't grazing it."

"It's posted. Stay off."

"I'd like to talk to the owner."

"You can't. She's dead."

"Do you think the land will come up for sale?"

"Everything is for sale at the right price."

"Are there woodcutters working in the area?"

"Why do you ask?"

"I saw a truck hauling logs out this morning."

"That's normal. Since the Forest Service started limiting permits, some of the private land owners have been selling woodcutting rights."

"Anyone in particular that you know of?"

"Osborn and Patterson, I've been told."

"Is anyone cutting wood on your leasehold?"

"Nobody cuts wood on that property."

"You're sure?"

"I would know."

"Who bought your ranch?"

"An Englishwoman owns it. I never met her. She lives in Los Angeles. A local attorney handled the sale for her. You ask a lot of questions."

Kerney smiled and shrugged off the comment. "I'd really like to find some land where I can summer over my cattle. I've heard there is a high meadow north of the mesa. Would that serve?"

"It's a small parcel on a bad road. You couldn't run more than five cows on it. A family from California bought it. The man used to teach college, or something like that."

"I'm sorry I've taken so much of your time, Señor Barela."

"Stay off the property," Nestor said. "It is still under my care." He closed the door in Kerney's face.

Kerney made a quick stop at the state police office where he found the district commander on duty. Capt. Victor Garduno briefed him on the continuing search of the mesa. Additional skeletal remains had been found about a mile from the original crime scene, including parts of the spine, ribs, and an arm bone. But no skull.

"We're still looking," Garduno said. A lean, big-shouldered man, the captain had a self-contained, confident manner.

Kerney switched gears and gave Captain Garduno a brief rundown on his conversation with Nestor Barela, and his hunch that the wood could have been trucked out through the meadow.

"I'd like to learn more about Nestor, his family, and the owner of the timber-frame cabin," he added. "Barela said the guy who built it moved here from California."

"That won't be a problem," Captain Garduno said.

"Can you get me crime statistics for the San Geronimo area?"

Garduno wrote a note to himself. "Consider it done, Chief. Sergeant Gonzales has asked for a records search on missing women over the last ten years. You should have the report on your desk when you get back to your office."

"Good deal. Has Melody Jordan reported in?"

"She's back at headquarters, examining the bones. Sergeant Gonzales would like to remain the primary officer on the case, Chief."

"Are you recommending him?"

"He spent five years in criminal investigations before he made his sergeant stripes. I use him as an investigator whenever I can't get an agent assigned out of Santa Fe."

"Can you get along without him for a while?"

"A senior patrol officer can cover his duties."

"Give him the green light."

Kerney got back to the truck and Dale groused at him for taking so long, and complained of being hungry. Kerney bought lunch at a Mexican place on the plaza. Dale packed away the food while Kerney watched cars pull up in front of the Plaza Hotel. The hotel, a prominent city landmark, was a three-story brick structure with Gothic Revival columns, overhangs, and windows.

Dale ate and listened while Kerney repeated the gist of his conversation with Nestor Barela.

"So Barela wouldn't tell you squat," he said between bites. "That's pretty suspicious. But I don't think that old man cut and hauled that wood away by himself. Just eyeing him from the truck, he looked pretty much worn down to me."

"Maybe it's a family affair." Kerney picked at his meal. "He has strong backs to help him. They could haul a lot of wood in that four-stall horse trailer that was parked down at the barn, without raising any suspicion."

"I guess I just don't think like a cop." Dale wiped his chin with a paper napkin and dropped it on his empty plate. "I'm gonna have to bring Barbara and the girls up here for a vacation."

"Any time," Kerney said, as he motioned for the check. "I'll fix up my cabin for you."

Dale snickered. "I said vacation, Kerney. That means a nice hotel with clean sheets every day, dinners out, and with three women, shopping. Lots of shopping. Since I can't afford Santa Fe, I'll bring them here."

"Sounds like a plan," Kerney said as he paid the bill and left the tip. "Are you ready? I've got some work to do."

"More cop stuff?"

"Yeah."

Dale pushed his chair back and stood up. "What a yarn I have to tell when I get home. And it doesn't need a bit of exaggeration."

"I'm glad you had a good time."

"Did I ever."

In the truck, Dale popped a George Strait tape into the cassette deck and cranked up the volume. Kerney groaned quietly. County and western was his least favorite music.

Shoe crawled out of the backseat, sat on Kerney's lap, and stared at him with serious eyes. Either the dog didn't smell bad anymore, or Kerney was getting used to him.

He was without a doubt the hairiest beast Kerney had ever owned.

3

Kerney's apartment was a furnished one-bedroom guest cottage in the south capital neighborhood, within a short walk to the Santa Fe plaza. Although bland and boxy, it had a fireplace, reasonably decent furniture, and a small enclosed patio. Kerney liked the neighborhood with its old houses, narrow streets, and mature trees that gave a small-town feeling to the area. His landlord, Leo Dunn, was a retired cop who had built the cottage at the rear of his property solely for the rental income.

Over the years, most of Leo's tenants were officers going through divorces or just starting out in law enforcement. Leo knew firsthand how poorly cops were paid, so he kept the rent reasonable.

Kerney stopped at Leo's house, an older, pueblo-style single story with a long veranda, to introduce Shoe to his landlord. He got provisional permission to keep the dog as long as it didn't crap on the rug, chew up the furniture, or bother the neighbors.

Before leaving for the office, Kerney got Shoe settled,

and left the patio door open to the small backyard so the dog could do his business outside. Since Leo was around most of the time to keep an eye on things, a burglary was highly unlikely. On top of that, Kerney didn't really have much worth stealing.

At the state police headquarters, a building complex that included the Department of Public Safety and the New Mexico Law Enforcement Academy, Kerney found Melody Jordan in the laboratory.

She looked up from the microscope and smiled when Kerney approached. "Great timing, Chief. I was about to ask dispatch to track you down."

"What have you got?"

"Several facts that may help. The body was dismembered while clothed. I found minute fibers embedded in the bones—denim and wool. We might be able to match that fabric scrap you found with the maker. And we may get lucky with the wool fibers."

"Do you have any hunches?"

"The victim wore high-end apparel, Chief. Not the kind of clothing bought at discount stores. But we'll have to wait for our fiber expert to confirm it."

Melody swung her stool to face Kerney. "More good news: We may not need the skull to make an ID. The left humerus shows a severe old break, about a third of the way down. It isn't the kind of injury that would go unattended."

"That is good news. Have the bones told you anything else?"

"Tentatively. Remember, we have to factor in the weathering of the bones, but I'd give the victim's age between twenty and thirty years, based on the microscopic examination of the fibula we found."

"The victim's race?"

"Probably Anglo or Hispanic, based on the size of the pubic bone. Find the skull and I can narrow it down further. If you do, I'll have a facial reconstruction made."

"What's next?"

"I want to see if I can match up the saw marks to various types of hand or power tools. That will take some time. I'll also do an X-ray examination to see if I can discover any foreign or metallic objects. I still don't have a clue how the woman was killed."

"You do good work, Ms. Jordan." Kerney turned away and started for the door.

"Thanks." Melody pushed her hair away from her forehead and stood. "Was that a mustang you were riding on the mesa?"

Kerney paused at the door and looked back. "You know your horses."

"Do you ride a lot?" The thousand-watt smile Dale had noticed on the mesa lit up Melody's face.

"Not as much as I'd like. I don't have the time."

"I have two quarter horses, a mare and a gelding. I stable them at a friend's place. I think you'd like the gelding. I've been looking for somebody who can give him a good workout. He needs a firm hand. Interested?"

Kerney pushed back the appealing thought of a day in the saddle accompanied by an attractive woman, and chose his words carefully. "I don't see how I can fit it into my schedule. Thanks again for the good work."

Melody's smile faded. She returned to the stool, lowered her head over the microscope, and spoke without looking up. "I'll have a follow-up report for you as soon as possible."

Kerney waited a beat for Melody to say more. She kept her eye glued to the microscope, picked up a pencil, and started writing. He left thinking there were a lot of drawbacks to being a boss.

Sgt. Gabe Gonzales arrived at the district office after dark to find a pile of paperwork waiting for him. He thumbed through it quickly. It contained a note from his captain assigning him full-time to the murder investigation, a preliminary report of Melody Jordan's examination of the skeletal remains, a copy of the most recent crime statistics for the San Geronimo area that had been faxed to Chief Kerney, and a list of missing persons reports on women who had disappeared in northern New Mexico during the past ten years. Clipped to the paperwork was a note indicating that investigative reports on the targeted missing women had been received from various law enforcement agencies and could be accessed by computer.

Gabe read Melody Jordan's report first before scanning the computer files on the ten women reported missing from northern New Mexico. He found no medical information on a woman with an old fracture to the upper left arm. It didn't surprise him: that kind of detail usually didn't surface in a preliminary missing persons report.

He scrolled the computer files again. Eight of the missing women were residents of the state, and two were tourists passing through. Only three fell within the age range Melody had established. He would work those three as a short list before moving on to the others. If nothing promising materialized, he'd access the National Crime Information Center data bank on missing persons and see what popped up.

He checked the time and grimaced. Since his divorce last year, getting home at a reasonable hour had become important to Gabe. He had one child from the marriage, Orlando, who lived with him, attended the local university, and worked part-time.

Both were busy, but when Gabe worked the day shift he liked to get home early and fix dinner for the two of them.

Tonight that wasn't going to happen.

He called home, got the answering machine, left Orlando a message, and started organizing his field notes for his report. It would take a good two hours to do the write-up, make fresh crime scene sketches, and mount the photographs on exhibit forms. Deputy Chief Kerney expected the report on his desk first thing in the morning, and Gabe wanted to make sure it got there complete and on time.

He sat back in his chair, rubbed the back of his neck, and thought about Kerney. He was an outsider who had been quickly elevated to deputy chief, but his reputation as an investigator was outstanding. In short order, Kerney had personally cleared two major cases, a multimillion-dollar Santa Fe art theft and the murder of a small-town cop. But he was also an old friend of the state police chief, Andy Baca, which kept the issue of cronyism alive among the department gossips.

Gabe decided not to waste his time worrying about whether or not Kerney was a good boss. That question would be answered as Gabe learned more about how the chief operated. He picked up the crime statistics report for San Geronimo that Kerney had requested. During the last year there had been two incidents of cattle theft, two reports of illegal wood harvesting, and three acts of vandalism to cabins, along with eight burglaries to summer homes.

Gabe got out the two prior-year statistical reports and paged through the property crimes information. Up until last year, San Geronimo had been virtually crime free. He made a note to check with the county sheriff for an update on recent criminal activity in San Geronimo. If the rising crime trend had continued into the new year, that would be very interesting information.

He put the reports away, turned to the keyboard, and began typing. Tomorrow started his two days off, but he'd be back on the mesa at first light. They hadn't found the dead woman's skull yet, and Gabe wasn't about to stop searching until every inch of ground had been covered.

Before heading home, Kerney made a quick stop at a supermarket where he bought everything he needed to care for a dog. In the apartment he found Shoe on his feet, wagging his tail, with one of Kerney's sneakers clasped in his mouth. Three more shoes had been brought from the bedroom and scattered around the living room floor.

"Quite a collection you got there," Kerney said, as he extracted the sneaker from the dog's mouth. Wet with slobber, it had chew marks on the heel and tongue and some of the padding had been gnawed away. "I guess it's yours now, boy."

He dropped it on the floor in front of the dog. Shoe snatched it up and gave it a shake.

The other shoes the dog had fetched were only slightly damaged. Except for the mate of the shoe he'd given to the dog, Kerney put the rest away with a reminder to himself to keep the bedroom closet door closed in the future. He spent an hour brushing tangles out of Shoe's matted coat, sprayed him again, cleaned up the dog hair on the carpet, and fed the mutt.

As Shoe ate, Kerney eyed the result of his efforts to groom the dog. Salt-and-pepper hair dangled from his hindquarters and belly, and his tail was a twisted knot that needed clipping. The mutt still looked pretty ratty.

Kerney picked up and fanned through Saturday's mail, looking for a letter from Sara Brannon. He'd written to her last week. Given the distance his letters had to travel, he didn't expect a rapid reply, but occasionally their correspondence crossed in the mail. This time there was nothing. He hoped Sara hadn't changed her mind about coming to Santa Fe when her tour of duty ended.

All of the mail was junk, except for an envelope from Erma Ferguson's personal representative and executor of her estate. He opened the envelope and read Milton Lynch's letter. The appraisal had come in at two thousand dollars an acre. The land was worth almost thirteen million dollars. The final appraisal report would be mailed to Kerney within the week.

He stared at the amount in stunned silence before calling Lynch's home phone number. Lynch answered on the third ring.

"I thought I might be hearing from you," Lynch said.

"How in the hell can that land be worth thirteen million dollars?" Kerney asked.

"I haven't seen the complete report, but it seems that some of the ranchers in the area have sold out to high bidders, or are subdividing their land. Five years ago, ten sections might have gone for eight or nine hundred dollars an acre, but not any more."

"Doesn't the land qualify under the farm-use value reduction provision of the tax code?"

"The two-thousand-dollar-per-acre figure is the reduction. Subdivided five- to twenty-acre tracts are selling at four to six thousand dollars per acre."

"What will the taxes be?"

"You'll be taken to the cleaners, I'm afraid. The Taxpayer Relief Act defines a qualified heir as either a family member materially involved in the operation of the ranch for five of the last eight years, or an employee with ten or more years of employment prior to the decedent's death. You don't qualify for the one-point-three-million-dollar taxable estate exclusion. You'll pay taxes on the full value, less seven hundred thousand dollars."

"How much will I owe?"

"Federal taxes will exceed six million dollars. I haven't factored in the state tax bite."

"How soon do I have to pay?"

"Nine months after Erma's death."

"Is that a firm date?"

"The tax forms are due then, but I could file a six-month extension for payment on your behalf."

"Is there anything I can do to avoid selling the land?"

"Installment payments to the IRS are possible. The estate can spread the cost out over fourteen years. But the IRS will charge interest—four to six percent."

Kerney did some quick mental calculations. "That amounts to over four hundred thousand dollars a year, plus interest."

"That's right."

"Who did the appraisal?"

"I believe I've secured the lowest possible appraisal on the property."

"I'm sure you have. I need the appraiser's name for police business."

Lynch paused. "Hold on."

After a minute, he came back on the line and read off the information. A Santa Fe firm had done the appraisal.

Kerney scribbled down the name and address. "Do you know who sold Erma the land?"

"She bought it from Nestor Barela in nineteen-sixty. Don't ask what she paid for it. It would only depress you. May I say something, Mr. Kerney?"

"Please do."

"Erma's estate is quite considerable. Not only did she inherit a sizable amount from her parents many years ago, she invested it wisely, and added to her net worth as the demand for her art drove up the price of her paintings. Except for the land she willed to you, the remainder of her estate will become an endowment to the university art department."

"I understand that."

"Erma wanted you to be able to keep all of the land. She knew how much it would mean to you. I advised her to establish a trust in your name, and she directed me to do so, with the proviso that I encumber sufficient resources in the trust to pay the inheritance taxes on the property. Her death occurred a week before the trust was to be established."

"I see."

"If you want to keep at least part of Erma's gift, let the estate sell some of the property for taxes. You'll still own a sizable chunk of land. I'm no rancher, but it seems to me you would have enough acreage left to start a small cattle operation."

"I'll think about it."

"You'll need to make a decision fairly soon," Lynch said.

"I know it."

"Let me know what you decide, Mr. Kerney. Remember, you stand to come out of this very well-off."

"I'm aware of that."

Kerney hung up in a foul mood, realizing he had no call to be so abrupt with Milton Lynch; he was a good man doing a good job. Erma had picked her executor wisely.

What grated Kerney had nothing to do with the windfall inheritance, although the amount of his net worth on paper staggered him. The thought of giving up thirty-two hundred acres felt like fate slapping him down again. As a child, he'd watched his parents lose the ranch on the Tularosa to the army when White Sands expanded. Now, he faced losing half of the best, and perhaps only, opportunity he would ever have to return to ranching. It felt like a bad dream or a sick joke coming back to haunt him.

He was glad he'd resisted Dale's offer to come in as a partner. With a tax bite in the high seven figures, it was totally out of the question.

For now, he didn't know what the hell to do, other than mull it over and think about options.

Shoe was at his feet, head resting on the sneaker, his eyes locked on Kerney. He reached down, picked up the sneaker, and tossed it through the archway into the living room. Shoe got up and fetched it back, his tail wagging.

"Let's see what else you can do." Kerney tried some common commands, and Shoe promptly obeyed each of them.

"Smart dog." He fed the dog a treat. Shoe dropped down on the floor and ate his biscuit.

Seconds before the doorbell rang, Shoe raised his head and let out a long howl.

"So you're a watchdog, are you?" Kerney said as he pulled himself upright.

Shoe followed him to the front door, the sneaker firmly clasped in his jaws, and sat. Kerney opened it to find Sara Brannon smiling at him from the front step.

"Good God, what are you doing here?"

"The army took pity on me and sent me home early. You have a dog, Kerney," she said. "Does it have a name?"

"His name is Shoe," Kerney said, grinning in delight.

"I can see why. He's pretty mangy looking."

"He's had a rough time of it. But he's smart; he can come, sit, fetch, roll over, and stay. He just moved in."

Sara knelt and scratched Shoe under the chin. The dog dropped the sneaker and gave her a kiss. "Do you have any other roommates I need to know about?"

Kerney shook his head. "None."

She held out a bottle of wine as she stepped inside. "Can I buy you a drink?"

Kerney took the bottle from Sara's hand. "I think I need one."

"Don't you like surprises?"

"This one I do."

She slipped out of her coat and dropped it on the arm of a sofa that faced a corner fireplace and a patio door. On one side, an archway opened onto a kitchen that contained a small café table and two chairs. Opposite the kitchen, on the wall next to an open bedroom door, hung a small watercolor of a herd of horses moving through a snowstorm. It was the only personal touch in the room.

Sara inspected the watercolor. "That's very nice."

"Fletcher Hartley did it. I wrote you about him. I think you'll enjoy meeting him."

"From what you've told me about him in your letters, he sounds like quite a character." She turned back and gestured at the bottle in Kerney's hand. "Are you going to open the wine, or not?"

"You bet."

"Well, let's get started celebrating this reunion."

Sara sat at the kitchen table while Kerney searched for wineglasses and a corkscrew. He took his time doing it, glancing at Sara out of the corner of his eye. He had a snapshot of her, but it didn't convey the full impact of her physical presence. Her strawberry blond hair was a bit shorter now, further accenting the sensual line of her neck. Her green eyes sparkled with a hint of something Kerney couldn't quite decipher. Even in blue jeans and a mock turtleneck pullover, Sara look stunning.

He brought the glasses to the table, sat across from her, uncorked the bottle, and poured the wine. "Cheers."

Sara touched her wineglass to Kerney's and took a sip. "So tell me, Kerney, have you slept with many women since I've been gone?"

"How would you define 'many women'?"

"More than one," Sara answered.

"Then I have not slept with many women."

"Only one?"

"One."

"Tell me about her."

"Her name is Karen Cox. She's a lawyer, an ADA. Divorced. Two children. She lives in Catron County."

"Attractive?"

"Very."

"Are you still seeing her?"

"No. I got a note from her recently. She's hooked up with a ranch foreman."

"She likes cowboys."

"So it would seem."

"That shows good taste. Any regrets?"

"No. And you?"

"I've been a very good girl, which hasn't been easy. Will Andy let you take some time off?"

"He's out of town for the week at a convention in Florida. He left me in charge."

"That simplifies matters. I've really never spent much time in Santa Fe. Will you tour me around?"

"Of course."

"Well?"

"Well, what?"

"Start the tour," Sara said, putting down her wineglass. "I'd love to see your bedroom."

With her head on his shoulder and her leg draped over his thigh, Sara gently scratched Kerney's chest with her fingernails. The heat from her body felt like a long warm ember against Kerney's skin.

"That was a lot of fun," she said.

"It was my pleasure, Major Brannon."

"It's Lieutenant Colonel Brannon."

Sara's statement surprised Kerney. He had spent one tour in Vietnam late in the war as an infantry lieutenant and knew that only a remarkable circumstance would accelerate a very junior major to light colonel. "Congratulations. How did that happen?"

"I'll tell you about it later."

"Why so secretive?"

"I'm not accustomed to telling war stories. Have you ever wanted to be a father, Kerney?"

"I always thought I would, some day."

"Still interested?"

"I'm too long in the tooth."

"Not at all."

Kerney pulled back his head.

"Are you staring at me in the dark?" Sara asked. Her fingers traveled down to the gunshot scar on Kerney's stomach. She rubbed it lightly and felt the rough texture of the skin and the hard abdominal muscle underneath.

"I have excellent night vision."

Outside the closed bedroom door, Shoe whined quietly in dismay. "Your dog wants to come in," Sara said, moving her fingers down to Kerney's hip.

"Don't change the subject. Are you thinking of having a baby?"

"I'm putting a stud book together, just as a possibility. Your name is on the list."

"I'm honored to be considered. But you'd be taking a chance. I've never sired any offspring."

"You seem to have the necessary enthusiasm for the task."

Kerney laughed. "Is this something you're serious about?"

"I'm not sure."

"How many names are in your stud book?"

"I'm not telling." Sara's hand traveled below Kerney's hip to his crotch. "Now, that's very interesting."

She rolled on top of Kerney, and for a very long time conversation ceased.

Carl Boaz saw hoofprints in the snow at the gate when he got back to the meadow late Sunday night. He unlocked the gate, moved the truck through, relocked the gate, and drove to his cabin, wondering who in the hell had been snooping around. He made a quick tour outside with a flashlight, looking for any sign of trespassing. Everything appeared okay.

Inside, Boaz kept his coat on while he lit a kerosene lamp and fired up the wood stove. Off the power grid, the cabin had no electricity other than what a gasoline generator supplied. Boaz rarely used electricity in the cabin; it was much more important to reserve the power for the greenhouse and the well pump.

He left the cabin and walked to the greenhouse. From the gate at the top of the meadow, the greenhouse looked like a cheap, thrown-together structure. But hidden from view on the south side, a row of solar panels fed power to a bank of batteries that ran fans and heating coils. The system was so efficient Boaz only needed to use the backup generator after three or four consecutive cloudy days.

He circled the greenhouse, checked the door locks, looked for fresh tracks, found nothing, and walked back to the cabin. Boaz smiled as he passed the child's bicycle propped against the porch rail. Wanda the bitch had left it behind when she moved out with her bratty eight-year-old son to return to L.A. He had found the bicycle in the toolshed and decided to use it to give the place a homey, family kind of look.

The cabin had warmed up nicely. Heavily insulated, it consisted of a large room with two sleeping lofts, a small bathroom off the downstairs kitchen area, and an attached room at the back of the cabin Boaz had built for Wanda to use as a pottery studio. With Wanda gone, Boaz had converted the room into a woodshed. It easily held three cords of dry firewood.

He shucked his coat, put a tea kettle on the propane stove to heat up coffee water, and turned on the battery-powered shortwave receiver. He liked listening to the BBC Sunday night broadcasts.

At the table, Boaz studied his sketch of a cornfield that he would plant after the last spring frost. He would move new nursery stock to the cornfield, use the corn to shield the marijuana, and start another greenhouse crop of grass right away. That would more than double his yield in one season.

In the morning he would dig up the cactus plants in the greenhouse that Wanda had transplanted from the mesa, and start some more marijuana seedlings. There were only twenty cactus plants, but they took up valuable space. He couldn't believe he'd let the bitch talk him into starting a little cactus garden.

The teapot whistled and Boaz got up and made his coffee. A BBC newsreader was reporting on a New Zealand woman who grew rare nineteenth-century roses in her garden. He turned up the volume, listened to the batty old lady ramble on about her roses in a down-under accent, and started working on his finances.

Money was tight, and he wouldn't see a profit until he could market his product. Every dime he'd made from dealing at colleges in Southern California had gone into his enterprise. The land, the cabin, the greenhouse, the move last year to New Mexico, had cost a lot of money. But if he could make it through the next six months, and get half a dozen more crops in, he would be a rich man.

Then he would finish his novel.

He stared at his piece-of-shit Ph.D. diploma from UC Santa Barbara that was nailed to a joist supporting the sleeping lofts. All those years in school, for what? A shitty teaching assistant position in some backwater philosophy department with no hope for a tenure-track appointment. Worthless.

A truck horn blared from the locked gate—two short beeps. Boaz grabbed his coat and went outside. A full moon and a clear sky made it easy for him to see Rudy's truck. The headlights were off and the motor was running. It was about time Rudy showed up to pay him some money. He was weeks overdue.

"Where have you been, man?" Boaz asked as he climbed over the gate and approached the driver's door.

"Working," Rudy replied through the open truck window.

"You want to come in?"

"Can't stay."

"Did you bring my money?"

"Yeah," Rudy said, as he raised the pistol from his lap and blew a third eye through Boaz's forehead.

4

Up early, Gabe Gonzales made coffee, and sat at the kitchen table reviewing his completed reports. It was much too soon for Orlando to be awake, and the house was quiet.

Theresa, his ex-wife, had forced Gabe to buy out her equity in the house, a Victorian built by his grandfather on a street behind the Las Vegas Public Library. It took Gabe a second mortgage to do it, and he was still paying on an earlier loan used to renovate the house after his grandfather had sold it to him.

He had his eye on a lieutenant's vacancy that would ease some of the monthly pressure to pay bills. Orlando was on a full scholarship at the university and worked a part-time job to cover his personal expenses, so having him living at home wasn't much of a burden. But Gabe still walked around most of the time with a nearly empty wallet.

He looked at the clock on the kitchen stove, picked

up the cordless phone, and called Officer Russell
Thorpe at home.

"Wake up, rookie," Gabe said when Thorpe answered.
"I need you to run some paperwork down to Chief
Kerney in Santa Fe. Pick it up at my place."

"Then what?"

"Since you've just volunteered to work on your days
off, call me when you get back. We'll do one more
sweep of the mesa. I still think we may have missed
something."

"Ten-four."

Thorpe picked up the reports, departed, and Gabe
headed out. He took the paved road past the county
detention center and followed it to where the pavement
ended. Several miles in on the dusty dirt road he passed
through San Geronimo.

Once a prosperous ranching community, in the late
nineteenth century the village had spawned *Las Gorras
Blancas*, the White Caps. It was a secret militant organization of Hispanic ranchers determined to drive out
the Anglo settlers who had encroached on the old Mexican land grant with the help of corrupt politicians.

Wearing white hoods to conceal their identities, *Las
Gorras Blancas* raided at night, burning barns and
haystacks, ripping down fences, and shooting the land
grabbers' livestock. They staged midnight rallies on the
Las Vegas Plaza, circulated petitions to the citizens, and
even had a leader elected to the territorial legislature.
But they couldn't stop the bleeding away of the land to
the Anglo newcomers, and by the turn of the century
much of it was gone forever.

Gabe thought about the recent rise in property crimes and wondered if, a century later, a modern version of *Las Gorras Blancas* was riding again. It was worth thinking about; land prices were climbing and the few old Hispanic families left in the valley were having a hell of a time paying their property taxes. Maybe somebody had gotten pissed off enough to start ripping off the latest wave of Anglo immigrants.

The morning sky changed from hot pink to flat gray as the sun broke above the horizon and disappeared behind a low, thick cloud.

Chief Kerney had asked Gabe to check out the owner of the cabin to the north of his property. He turned onto the dirt track that led to Carl Boaz's cabin in the meadow. Finding out about Boaz had been easy. His property had been added to the fire department response grid map after the cabin had been built. Supposedly, Boaz lived there with a girlfriend and her young son.

If Gabe hadn't been driving a 4 x 4 state police Ram Charger, he would have stopped and walked in—the road was that bad. He made the last turn near the top of the hill and saw two crows sitting on the top of a steel gate. Above, several more circled lazily at low altitude. He looked at a mound on the ground, and looked again.

He got out, walked to the mound, and bent over it. A dead man looked up at him with blank eyes. Cold nighttime temperatures had left the body covered with frost. The bullet hole in his forehead was perfectly round, and his face was tattooed with pinpoint hemor-rhages from powder burns.

He'd been shot at very close range. Gabe put on a pair of plastic gloves, tilted the body slightly, searched the back pockets for a wallet, found it, and looked for a driver's license. Issued by the state of California, it iden-tified the dead man as Carl Boaz.

Gabe stayed low, keyed his hand-held radio, and called in the crime. The crows didn't move from the gate until he returned to the vehicle. Then they hopped away a few yards and perched on the top strand of the wire fence.

He crouched behind the open door and scanned the meadow with binoculars. Approaching the cabin would be risky. He would have to cover at least a hundred yards of open space from the gate to the cabin. There might be an armed hostage taker barricaded inside one of the structures with captives.

He saw no movement, but stayed put for a few min-utes before getting a tarp out of the back of the 4 x 4 and covering the corpse. He didn't want crows feasting while he waited for backup.

He called for assistance, positioned himself at the rear of the vehicle where he had the most protection, and kept scanning the cabin and greenhouse. All the preliminary work—photographing, measuring, and evi-dence collection—could wait until he was sure the area was secure.

The crows flapped lazily off the wire, circled above him, and cawed. There would be no free lunch for them today.

• • •

Kerney's bedroom phone rang. He reached for it and checked the time: it was seven o'clock. He listened to the dispatcher's report, asked for a helicopter to stand by, and hung up.

"What is it?" Sara asked as she sat up in the bed and pulled the sheet up over her breasts.

"Cold?"

"No, modest."

"I don't think so."

"Are you going to tell me or not?"

Kerney looked at Sara, wondering how she could look so sexy on such little sleep. They had stayed awake and talked through most of the night, catching each other up. Kerney now knew about the firefight in the DMZ that had led to her meritorious promotion, and the Distinguished Service Medal. Kerney thought the honors were richly deserved.

"A homicide at a cabin near my property," he said. "Want to go with me?"

"Doesn't that sound romantic?" Sara said as she stretched out and put the pillow over her head.

"Is that a no?"

Sara muttered something.

"What?"

Sara took the pillow off her face. "I'll pass. I'm going back to sleep and then I'm going shopping. I haven't bought any new clothes in almost two years, and I need a few things to wear. Besides, I drove straight through from Cheyenne yesterday, just to get here last night."

"Do you want me to find you another tour guide for the day?"

"Are you trying to pawn me off to somebody else so soon?"

"No way." Kerney sat up and swung his legs to the floor. "I'll leave you a key and be back in time to take you out to dinner."

"Pick a nice place to eat; I plan to be dressed to kill. Are you in a hurry to leave?"

"The chopper will wait for me."

Sara kicked off the bedcovers.

"Not sleepy anymore?"

"Not that sleepy," Sara replied. "Come here."

Kerney saluted and followed orders.

Several hours into the preliminary investigation of Carl Boaz's murder, Gabe saw the chopper carrying Chief Kerney come over the mesa and land in the meadow. From the porch he watched Kerney walk toward him. He limped badly for a few steps before smoothing out his gait.

Gabe knew Kerney's knee had been shattered in a gunfight with a drug dealer. It had happened some years ago when Kerney was with the Santa Fe PD. It wasn't the only time the chief had used deadly force. In high-risk situations, the man knew how to keep his cool and survive.

In his twenty years as a cop, Gabe had never been under fire. He wondered how he'd stack up if he had to put it on the line.

Gabe had assigned Russell Thorpe the job of receiving evidence and recording the personnel entering the crime scene. He watched Thorpe intercept Kerney halfway across the meadow and hold out a clipboard with a sign-in sheet. Kerney signed it and spent a minute talking to the officer before moving on.

Down at the greenhouse, Ben Morfin, the district narcotics agent, was conducting an inventory of marijuana plants. He was at one thousand and counting.

"Bring me up to speed, Sergeant," Kerney said when he reached Gabe.

"Carl Boaz, age thirty-five, died last night from a single gunshot wound to the head, fired at close range. There are no wants or warrants on the victim and no record of any arrests. Boaz held a doctorate in philosophy from a California university. Seems he dropped out of academia and went into organic gardening, specializing in the commercial cultivation of marijuana."

Kerney raised an eyebrow. "How much?"

"When the tally is done, I'm guessing it will exceed two thousand plants. It could be a seven-figure cash crop."

"Is there any tie-in between Boaz and the skeleton on the mesa?"

"Just the dog so far, Chief. There's a snapshot in the cabin of Boaz, his ex-girlfriend, her son, and the dog you found on the mesa. Want to know the dog's name?"

"Tell me."

"Buster."

Kerney laughed. "Are you making this up?"

"No way."

"I guess every kid should have a dog named Buster, no matter who he lives with. Tell me about Boaz's ex-girlfriend."

"Her name is Wanda Knox. She moved back to California about a month ago, and started writing Boaz letters telling him he was a self-absorbed asshole. She also wanted him to ship Buster and her son's bicycle out to the coast. Boaz kept a journal, Chief. He sold drugs at Southern California colleges before he decided to go into the production end of the business. I've got a list of his dealers and his contacts."

"DEA will like that."

Gabe nodded in agreement. "Boaz also noted in his journal that somebody by the name of Rudy owed him four hundred dollars. No last name. I think Rudy may be a local; the entry was made six weeks ago. There's an earlier entry from last September showing that Rudy paid Boaz the same amount."

"For what?"

"Unknown, but I have my suspicions. I found the route the poacher took to haul the wood out. It comes right through the meadow. I think Boaz gave the poacher access to the clear-cut area and got paid for it."

"Boaz didn't cut the wood himself?"

"His truck tire tracks don't match up with any of the impressions we found on the route. Also, there is no evidence that he hauled wood out to cut and split here—no chips, no sawdust, no bark. At least not in quantity."

"So we need to find Rudy."

"Do you want me to start canvassing?"

"Not yet. Give me Wanda's current address before I leave. I'll ask the California authorities to locate and question her. Maybe she knows who Rudy is, and how to find him."

"Can I give you some questions for Wanda to pass along to the California police?"

"Sure thing."

"I'd like some help, Chief, if you can spare the manpower."

"Two agents will be up from Santa Fe in the morning, and I've already cleared it with your captain to assign the district narcotics officer to work with you. They're yours as long as you need them."

"Thanks. Do you want the tour?"

"I do."

"There's something I want to show you in the greenhouse. Boaz had a little cactus garden, separate from his marijuana crop. Just a single, small variety of twenty plants. I've never seen it before. Neither has the narcotics agent. We think it might be used to produce some exotic type of hallucinogenic."

"Lead on," Kerney said.

By noon Sara was completely burned out on the frilly, fringed, beaded, cutesy, embroidered western fashions she'd seen in virtually all of the downtown boutiques near the plaza. The streets were filled with late-season skiers, clumping around in their boots and parkas with half-day ski passes dangling from jacket zippers, busily shopping Santa Fe.

Several blocks away on a side street in a lovely old

brick Victorian house, she found a clothing store that had what she wanted: simple, elegant silk tops in earth-tone colors, a wonderful full-length, long-sleeved brown dress with a high neckline that looked very sleek when she put it on, and new designer jeans that made her look equally slinky. After so many months in starched fatigues and tailored military uniforms, the fabric felt satiny and sensual against her skin.

She didn't wince at all when she paid the bill, although the prices were outrageous. It was her treat to herself for two years of doing without in South Korea. She asked the sales clerk where she might buy some sexy lingerie, and got directions to a nearby store along with a knowing smile.

"You've got that right," Sara said as she picked up her bags and walked away. The woman's laugh followed her out the door.

At the lingerie shop, she took her time and came away with some tasty little items that were comfortable to wear yet decidedly provocative. She made her beauty salon appointment just in time, and spent a wonderful hour letting Patrick somebody-or-other pamper, condition, and trim her hair.

Back at Kerney's apartment, Shoe met her at the door, sneaker firmly in his mouth, tail wagging, still looking mangy as hell. She gave him a scratch under the chin, and he followed her into the bedroom. She dumped the packages on the bed and checked the alarm clock on the nightstand. Kerney wouldn't be back for hours.

Sara looked at Shoe and decided the dog needed

some TLC. She fanned through the Yellow Pages and found a pet grooming business that could take Shoe right away. She got directions to the shop, grabbed the new leash and collar Kerney had bought, and loaded the dog into her Jeep Cherokee.

"Come on, Shoe," she said, as she backed out of the driveway. "Let's get you cleaned up. That way we can both knock Kerney's socks off."

After taking the tour of the crime scene, Kerney pitched in and gave Sergeant Gonzales a hand. He spent several hours helping Gabe systematically search the cabin, which yielded further information on Wanda Knox and her son. He now had a very good photograph of the woman, plus a small address book Wanda had left behind with the names and addresses of friends and relatives in Southern California.

Back at state police headquarters in Santa Fe, Kerney prepared a brief summary of the known facts pertaining to the Boaz murder case, typed up questions for Wanda Knox, and photocopied the address book. According to the letters sent to Boaz, Wanda currently lived in Arcadia, California. Kerney checked her address against a map. Arcadia was close to Pasadena, and many of the entries in the address book showed friends and family living either in Arcadia, Pasadena, or surrounding communities.

He called the Arcadia PD, talked to the chief, told him what he needed, and got quick agreement to have a detective follow up as soon as Kerney faxed the information.

"If Ms. Knox can't positively identify a man named Rudy, ask your officer to do an Identi-Kit," Kerney said. The kit was used to produce a facial likeness of a person based on verbal descriptions furnished by a witness.

"That's no problem," the chief said. "Anything else?"

"A list of names of anyone else she knew or met in New Mexico would be helpful."

"You've got it. How's the weather out there?"

"High fifties, windy, and blue skies," Kerney answered.

"Jesus, what I'd give to see blue skies again. We've had solid smog for two months."

Kerney faxed the information to Arcadia, cleared some paperwork off his desk, and checked the wall clock. If he hustled he could get to the real-estate appraisal company before closing time.

Capital City Land Survey and Appraisal was located on De Vargas Street in a building that faced the Santa Fe River Park. The window in Donald Preston's office gave a nice view of the park and the cluster of buildings across the way that defined the downtown city core. Preston sat behind a map-covered desk. On the floor were an assortment of surveying instruments and two metal field satchels.

Somewhere in his forties, Preston had a prominent nose, thick lips that he rubbed together before speaking, and a florid complexion.

"I just did the valuation assessment on your property," Preston said. "We're working up the final report to send to the estate executor this week."

"I'm really here on a different matter," Kerney said. He showed Preston his shield and sketched out the facts of the skeleton discovered on the mesa.

Preston's eyes widened. "I walked right by that grove of trees."

"When did you do the appraisal?"

"The week before last. I went out with my land surveying team."

"Were you with them all the time?"

"No, only the last day. The team was on-site for a good three or four days before I got there."

"Who was on the team?"

"Bill Kemp, Johnny Nelson, and Jude Mondragon."

"Did they mention seeing anyone during the survey?"

"If they did, I didn't hear about it."

"Did you see anybody while you were on the property?"

"Not a soul."

"Did you see a dog?"

"I didn't see a dog."

"Did you come across any old campsites, discarded clothing, or litter?"

Preston shook his head. "I saw nothing like that."

"Did you see any woodcutters or loggers on the road?"

"No, but I sure saw the clear-cut area in the canyon on the west boundary. I'm including it in my report."

"Did you inform Mr. Lynch?"

"No. It's not unusual to find logging on private property, although whoever did the cutting sure chewed up the area."

"Have you done other appraisals in the valley recently?"

"Three, as a matter of fact. The Horse Canyon Ranch owner bought some parcels contiguous to her property. Each was about three hundred acres."

"Was there any woodcutting on those parcels?"

"Nope."

"Are Mondragon, Kemp, and Nelson here?"

"They should be in the back room."

"Do you mind if I speak with them?"

"Not at all."

Brief conversations with Preston's employees resulted in no additional information about the crimes. As a matter of personal interest, Kerney asked to see the surveys of the parcels bought by Alicia Bingham, the Horse Canyon Ranch owner. Except for the Boaz cabin property and the National Forest land on the west boundary, his ten sections were surrounded by Bingham's holdings.

Already late for this dinner date with Sara, Kerney thanked the men for their assistance and drove home in a hurry. He entered the house and stared at Shoe in disbelief. The dog was almost unrecognizable. His hindquarters had been clipped, his belly shaved, his paws and legs trimmed, and his coat glistened. Only the sneaker in his mouth identified him.

The door to the bedroom was closed and Sara was nowhere in sight.

"What did you do to my dog?" Kerney called out.

"He got a shampoo, a cut, and a pedicure," Sara said, stepping out of the bedroom. "He's a handsome brute, isn't he?"

Kerney found it hard to answer. Sara wore a long brown dress that covered her from ankle to neck and revealed every curve of her body. "Both of you look fantastic."

"I'm glad you noticed. Change your clothes, Kerney, and take me to dinner. I'm hungry."

The Canyon Road restaurant was in a low adobe building tucked behind some expensive condos. The maître d' met them at the door in a finely tailored suit, greeted them in a Swiss German accent, and led them through the small antechamber into the dining area. The interior was painted an austere white, and a few understated weavings on the wall were accented by recessed lights. The tablecloths were linen, the glassware was crystal, and the place settings were silver. The customers were nicely dressed and the hum conversation in the room was muted and subdued.

The maître d' took them through the front dining area to a smaller, more intimate room. He seated Sara and Kerney at a corner table near a fireplace while a waiter dressed in a crisp white server's jacket and black slacks stood nearby.

Kerney wore a raw silk oatmeal-colored sport coat, a charcoal linen shirt buttoned at the collar, dark gray wool dress slacks, and a pair of black alligator cowboy boots. He looked distinguished and handsome.

Two women dining at a nearby table gave Kerney the once over. Sara smiled sweetly at them until they turned away.

"Did you catch any bad guys today?" Sara asked, as

the busboy poured water and the waiter stood by with the wine list.

"Not a one."

"When do I get to see your ranch?"

"It's hardly a ranch, at this point," Kerney said. "And I can't see how I'm going to keep it."

"Taxes?"

Kerney nodded. The waiter discreetly interrupted with the wine list and asked for a drink order.

After the waiter left with the order, Kerney filled Sara in on the money he'd have to pay in taxes, and how Erma's instructions to give him the land free and clear hadn't been executed before her death.

"How sad," Sara said. "But I'm sure Erma had no intention of dying."

"No, she was enjoying life too much. I guess I just have to accept the fact that it's the thought that counts."

"Does it?" Sara asked.

"Somewhat."

"My parents have been selling sections of the ranch to my brother and me so we can avoid the heavy inheritance tax, plus giving us the maximum tax-free gift each year in land. We'll be half owners within the next five years."

Kerney had visited the Montana sheep ranch with Sara. It covered a hundred thousand acres that encompassed three lush valleys and some beautiful high country.

"Do you plan to return to the ranch after you retire from the army?"

"To visit, not to live. I'll let my brother and his wife

buy me out as they can. They're the ones putting the blood, sweat, and tears into it."

"When will you retire?"

"I'm thinking in about ten more years. I like my career, but it's hell on any kind of personal life. I'll be forty-two if I retire with twenty years of service. If I stayed in any longer I'd just hit the glass ceiling. There's only a handful of women in the army who wear stars."

"You could be one of them."

"That would be nice."

"You're only two ranks away from brigadier general."

"Those are two very long steps. After lieutenant colonel, very few officers make the cut."

Their waiter brought the wine and menus, explained the house specials in great detail, and motioned for the busboy to bring a basket of fresh breads and rolls.

After they moved away from the table, Kerney lifted his wineglass to Sara. "Perhaps you'll be the first woman to command a combat division."

Sara raised her glass in reply. "Now, that might be worth staying in for."

"Seriously?"

"What a coup that would be. It would be hard to pass it up."

The waiter returned, took their orders, complimented them on their selections, and departed.

"This is turning into a lovely evening, Kerney. I think I'm going to have to put a star after your name in my stud book."

"Along with appropriate remarks on my performance?"

Sara smiled coyly. "Of course. Do you know what I'd like to do after dinner?"

"What's that?"

"Show you my new lingerie."

"More research for the stud book?"

"Exactly."

In the late evening darkness, Gabe Gonzales stood at the open gate watching the district narcotics agent, Ben Morfin, load the last of the marijuana plants into a truck. The crime scene techs had left, the medical examiner had come and gone, Boaz's body had been removed, and Russell Thorpe was on his way to the district office with all the evidence that had been collected during the search.

It had been a bitch of a day. The discovery of the marijuana necessitated expanding the crime scene investigation to encompass the entire meadow and all the buildings. Gabe and the team had gone over, under, and through everything. They had even moved the firewood stacked in a room of the cabin, stick by stick, to make sure nothing had been missed.

At the greenhouse, the truck headlights flashed on and the engine kicked over.

Morfin drove to the gate, stopped, and spoke through the open window. "That's it."

"You've got it all?"

"Exactly two thousand six hundred and seventy-eight plants," Morfin said. "Boaz just missed a big score.

He was four weeks shy of a seven-figure harvest."

"I'll see you in the morning," Gabe said.

As Morfin drove off, Gabe closed and locked the gate and walked down the hill. The moon rose above Hermit's Peak, spreading a pale velvet light over the mountain and the valley. It made everything look deceptively peaceful.

A patrol unit at the bottom of the dirt track blocked access to the cabin. The officer inside the cruiser would spend a mind-numbing night on-site, guarding the crime scene.

He stopped, told the officer he would be at home if needed, got in the Ram Charger, called in his destination and ETA, and drove away.

It was too late to think about fixing dinner. He would get a pizza on the way home, spend a few minutes with Orlando, and then start in on the paperwork.

"Mom called," Orlando said, licking his fingers and reaching for another slice of pizza. "She wants me to spend spring break with her in Albuquerque."

"I thought you'd be working over spring break," Gabe said.

"Yeah, most of the time. I told her I'd come down for a couple of days."

"She'll like that." The pizza tasted bland. Gabe pushed the box in Orlando's direction. "I'm probably not going to be home much for a while anyway."

Gabe watched as Orlando nodded and chewed at the same time. He was a good-looking boy, two inches taller than Gabe, who'd inherited his mother's dark eyes and even features.

"What's up?" Orlando finally asked.

"I'm working two murder cases in San Geronimo. A drug grower and an unidentified female."

"No shit? Were they killed at the same time?"

"No. All we've got on the woman are some bones that were scattered on a mesa."

"No identification?"

"Not yet."

"Where did you find the bones?"

"Near Nestor Barela's old ranch."

Orlando wiped his hands on a paper towel. "Think you'll be able to find the killers?"

"It's too early to say."

Orlando stood up. "How come you keep doing this kind of work? Don't you get sick of it? Murder and all."

"You sound like your mother," Gabe said.

"Retire, Dad. You've earned it."

"Too many bills."

"Sell the house," Orlando said, picking up his day-pack. "I'm not going to stay in Las Vegas after I graduate from college anyway."

"You've been saying that for the last year. Why is living in your hometown so bad? You never used to feel this way before."

"I just want to get out and see the world, okay?"

"Okay, but the house stays in the family. You can have it when you get sick of seeing the world and move back home."

"I'm not coming back."

"That's what you say now," Gabe said. "You may feel differently later on."

"I don't think so." Orlando dropped his crumbled paper towel in the empty pizza box. "I've got to go study."

"You feeling all right, champ?"

"Just tired."

Gabe nodded toward the kitchen door. "Go hit the books. I've got my own homework to do."

Orlando left and Gabe worked until his eyes gave out and his mind was fuzzy. He left his paperwork on the kitchen table and climbed the stairs with the ornate carved banister. At the end of the long hallway he could see light shining under the door to Orlando's room.

Except for Orlando's possessions, Theresa had taken most of the furniture when she'd moved out. Gabe had been replacing it a piece at a time, as he could afford to. He had a television and a couch in the downstairs front room. But the dining room was empty, as was the library, except for the collection of his grandfather's old books. His bedroom contained one double bed, a reading lamp clipped to the headboard, and a dresser he'd picked up at a garage sale. He needed to buy a rug or a picture to hang on the wall.

In the bathroom he brushed his teeth, stripped down to his underwear, and dumped his clothes in the laundry hamper. The alarm clock was on the floor near his bed, next to the telephone. He set it, got under the covers, and was asleep within minutes.

• • •

After dinner, Kerney and Sara went back to his apartment. Kerney got the fireplace going, exiled Shoe to the patio, lit some candles, put a Brahms piano concerto on the stereo, and poured some brandy.

They never made it to the bedroom.

"Chilly?" Kerney asked later.

"Just a bit."

He padded into the bedroom. Lean with a small butt, a slim waist, square shoulders, and a nice chest, Kerney looked very sexy naked.

Their clothes were scattered on the furniture and the floor. They'd certainly been in a hurry; the brandy hadn't been touched.

He came out of the bedroom holding a robe and a heavy flannel shirt. "Your choice."

Sara took the shirt, slipped it on, picked up her brandy glass, and stretched out on the carpet in front of the fireplace. She felt delightfully ravished and a little weak in the knees.

Kerney joined her on the carpet.

"Take me camping, Kerney," she said, reaching for Kerney's hand. He had perfectly proportioned fingers.

"Are you burned out on Santa Fe already?"

"I need to wake up to the smell of pine needles and the sight of a New Mexico sunrise."

"Did you bring your gear?"

"It's in the Cherokee."

"Where do you want to go?"

"Take a guess."

Kerney nodded. "Give me the morning to get a few things done."

"That's fine with me. Plan on being late for work."

"Again?" Kerney asked with a grin.

"Oh, yes."

5

Kerney arrived at his office to find a phone message from a detective at the Arcadia PD waiting for him. He called back and spoke to Det. Sgt. George Broom.

"I wish all my assignments were this easy," Broom said. "The address you gave us for Wanda Knox turned out to be a residential treatment center for addicted mothers. They call it a therapeutic community. It specializes in working with women and their children. It's one of those places that's run sort of like a commune. Kids, pets, and toys everywhere; everybody does chores and goes to group therapy. That sort of stuff."

"What kind of drugs does Wanda Knox use?" Kerney asked.

"Cocaine. She says Boaz got her started. She's twenty-eight and still a looker, Chief. She used to be a cheerleader in high school. She worked as a secretary in the philosophy department at the university where Boaz was a teaching assistant. That's where she met him. She and the kid started living with Boaz about a year before they pulled up stakes and moved to New Mexico. She didn't act upset when I told her Boaz had been murdered. I guess the romance soured."

"Did she ID Rudy?"

"She doesn't know his last name. She said Rudy paid Boaz to give him access to the land where he cut the wood. Does that kind of shit really go on out there? Poaching and stuff like that?"

"All the time. Did you get a description of Rudy?"

"That, and a composite drawing. Rudy is Hispanic, in his mid-to-late thirties, clean shaven, about five foot ten. He's stocky—weighs in at between two-twenty and two-forty pounds—and has brown eyes and brown hair cut long below the ears."

"That's helpful."

"Do you want something even better?"

"Are you holding out on me, Sergeant?"

Bloom laughed. "I couldn't resist, Chief. Wanda's kid is a miniature toy car nut. You know, those Hot Wheels you can buy just about anywhere. Lane—that's the kid's name—is eight years old. He told me Rudy drove a dark blue, three-quarter-ton, long-bed Chevy pickup truck, with a winch on the front bumper, and a hydraulic lift mounted in the bed. The kid really knows his vehicles."

"That narrows the field."

"You want the license number?"

"Does your sense of humor get you in trouble, Sergeant?" Kerney asked.

"All the time." Broom read off the numbers and letters for the license plate. "According to the kid, the truck has permanently installed wrought-iron side railings that extend above the cab. He even drew me a picture of the truck."

"Fax everything you've got to me."

"It's on the way. That question you had about those cactus plants you found in the greenhouse?"

"What about them?"

"Wanda said she found them in the canyon where Rudy was woodcutting and transplanted them to the greenhouse. She was going to give them as presents. I don't think you've stumbled on a new hallucinogenic."

"Thanks, Sergeant."

"What do you want to do with Wanda? From what she told me, you can have her arrested for conspiracy to commit a felony."

"I take it she was cooperative?"

"You bet."

"Let's cut her a break, unless something more develops."

"Good deal."

Melody Jordan stood in the doorway of Kerney's office. He waved her inside as he hung up the telephone.

"Here's your copy of my follow-up report, Chief," she said, placing the file folder on his desk. "Do you want a summary?"

"Please," Kerney replied.

"We found no trace evidence or foreign matter. Soil samples revealed nothing to suggest the body had been moved, but that doesn't mean anything. X rays of the bones showed nothing other than the old fracture to the upper arm. It was impossible to match the saw marks to a specific cutting instrument. We don't have a complete catalogue of hand or power saws. Nobody does; there are just too many of them. The comparisons we could make came up negative."

"Fiber samples?" Kerney asked.

"The denim we were able to identify. It's either one of two labels marketed by the same maker. The fibers embedded in the bone turned out to be a wool and cashmere blend, light brown in color. There's no way to tell what type of upper garment it was."

"Do you still think the victim's clothes were expensive?"

Melody nodded her head. "It's the kind of clothing I'd like to wear if I could afford it. I've got a question about the old fracture to the left humerus. The way the bone was set looks odd to me."

"How so?"

"Either the doctor who did the job wasn't very good or there was a considerable period of time before the victim received medical attention. I'd like to consult an outside expert."

"Whom do you have in mind?"

"There's a physical anthropologist from Indiana University in residence at the School of American Research, on a sabbatical. He's also a medical doctor. I attended one of his seminars on human remains identification. He's top-notch in the field. I'd like to get his opinion."

"How soon can you set it up?"

Melody's cheeks colored slightly. "I've already spoken

with him. He can see me this morning. He'll do the examination gratis."

Kerney wondered what the blush on Melody's cheek was all about. "Keep me informed."

Melody hurried out and Kerney went to the fax machine, where the last pages of Sergeant Broom's report were spilling onto the tray. As he waited, he asked the office secretary to run a motor vehicle check on the license plate Broom had provided. He picked up the loose sheets, returned to his office, and started reading through the material. The last page was a handwritten letter from Wanda's son. It read:

Dear Chief Kerney,

Sgt. Broom said that I could rite to you. If you find my dog Buster please send him back to me. He's mostly black with some brown and white on his legs and tummy. He has realy long hair. He ran away the day my Mom and I left New Mexico.

I love Buster very much. He is the best dog in the hole world.

I hope you find him. Thank you.

LANE KNOX

He looked up to find Charlotte Flores standing in front of his desk.

"Here's the motor vehicle report you wanted, Chief," Charlotte said.

Kerney took the papers from the secretary's out-stretched hand. He scanned it, put Lane Knox's letter to one side, and gave Charlotte the rest of Broom's report, along with the file he'd received from Melody Jordan. "Fax everything to Sergeant Gonzales at the Las Vegas office. Give it top priority."

Charlotte studied Kerney's face. Usually the chief was cordial and polite. Today he sounded abrupt and distracted. "Are you feeling all right, Chief?"

Kerney forced a smile. "I'm fine."

Charlotte gave him a quizzical look and left.

Kerney went to the window and watched traffic on the Old Albuquerque Highway. Across the road, the huge American flag at the entrance to the new car dealership flapped and billowed in a gusty wind. Spring winds in New Mexico often rose up without warning, drove dust along at gale force, and threw a brown haze into the sky. He could barely see the foothills below the Sangre de Cristo Mountains, and all the shiny new vehicles lined up in rows were dulled by a coat of sand. A truck passing down the road had a huge tumbleweed pinned against its grille. The tumbleweed broke free, bounced against the truck windshield, and rolled across the highway, where it landed against a chain-link fence.

Lane Knox certainly deserved to have his dog back. But sending Shoe, or rather Buster, off to California wasn't a happy thought. Kerney really liked that mutt.

In the small conference room at the Las Vegas district state police office, Gabe Gonzales thumbed through and rearranged the multiple copies of his case files, thinking he must have been really hammered with fatigue the night before. He'd gone to bed sure that everything had been sorted the way he wanted it for the presentation to his team. He'd made copies for each officer before discovering that Melody Jordan's preliminary forensic report was out of order in the packet.

He corrected the error in each packet, held one copy back for Ben Morfin, and passed the rest out to his team. "Look this over and then we'll talk," Gabe said.

Gabe's team consisted of Russell Thorpe, Ben Morfin—who was off meeting with a botanist at the university—and two agents sent up from Santa Fe, Robert Duran and Frank Houge.

Gabe didn't speak until the men finished reading the material. "Let's get started," he said. "Technically, we have four different crimes. A homicide of an unknown female, the murder of Carl Boaz, the illegal production of a controlled substance, and wood poaching. Ben Morfin will handle the narcotics case."

"Where is Ben?" Frank Houge asked. Houge was a thick-bodied man with a bit of a gut, and a high nasal voice.

"He went to Boaz's greenhouse to get the cactus plants we found. Then he's meeting with a botanist at New Mexico Highlands University to have them identified."

"What's Ben going to be doing after that?" Robert Duran asked. The opposite of Houge, Duran was small in stature. He stayed lean by running in long-distance and cross-country races.

"He'll spend today back at the Boaz crime scene with the lab techs, and then start probing Boaz's drug contacts on the West Coast, through the Drug Enforcement Agency."

"Where do you want us?" Duran asked.

"I need a man on the mesa looking for more bones. We've got some good initial findings from forensics, but I'd be a whole lot happier if we could complete the skeleton."

"I'll take that," Duran said.

"Good. I've put together a grid sketch of the areas that have already been covered. Don't go over old ground. You can use the Dodge four-by-four to get up on the mesa. I've marked a county map that will take you to the site."

"What do you have for me?" Houge asked.

"I want you to work a short list of missing women. Forensics reports that the upper left arm bone suffered an old fracture. That, along with the age estimate of the victim and the fiber analysis, may help us make an ID."

"I'll contact the victims' families, get medical records, and double-check what the women were wearing at the time of their disappearance," Houge said.

"Don't get the families' hopes up," Gabe said.

Houge nodded in agreement.

"Thorpe will help me develop a list of area woodcutters and firewood sellers," Gabe said, getting to his feet. "We spend today—and today only—on information and evidence gathering. We've got enough right now to suspect that the man who killed Boaz is the wood poacher. Maybe Ben can turn up Rudy's last name with a second search, or the California authorities will come through with more information from Wanda Knox. But with or without it, tomorrow we go looking for Rudy."

Houge waved his paperwork at Gabe. "From what

you've got here, Rudy could be the key to all these felonies."

"Wouldn't that be a nice early Easter present?" Gabe replied.

Gabe held Thorpe back after Houge and Duran left. "I want a complete search of newspapers, city directories, and telephone books. Get me names, addresses, and numbers of all the firewood sellers and woodcutters you can find from Santa Fe to Las Vegas."

Although it was not what he had hoped to do on his first criminal investigation assignment, Thorpe nodded.

Gabe read the young officer's disappointment, and was about to react to it when Captain Garduno walked in.

"You'll want to see this stuff right away, Gabe," Garduno said, dropping some pages in front of Gonzales. "It just came in from Chief Kerney's office."

"Thanks, Cap," Gabe said as Garduno left the room. He scanned the material in order, passing each page to Thorpe as he finished.

When Russell handed the last sheet back, Gabe asked, "What information would you act on first?"

"According to Motor Vehicles, the registered owner is Joaquin Santistevan. His driver's license photo doesn't match with the composite drawing of Rudy, and Wanda Knox's physical description is way off in terms of height, weight, and age. She said Rudy is in his mid-to-late thirties. Santistevan has a date of birth that makes him twenty-seven."

Gabe nodded. "What else?"

"Well, the kid got the truck right. The make and model of Santistevan's vehicle corresponds with his description."

"What would you do with this information?"

"Find and talk to Santistevan," Thorpe replied.

"Why?"

"Eyewitnesses aren't always reliable. Maybe Santistevan and Rudy are one and the same person, maybe not."

"And if they're not?"

Thorpe shrugged. "It could mean anything. Maybe Santistevan is just a pal or a relative who lent Rudy his truck. Maybe he's Rudy's partner in the poaching. Maybe Santistevan sold his truck to Rudy, who never bothered to register it in his name."

"Those are all good questions that need answers," Gabe said, holding up his hand to cut Thorpe off.

Thorpe smiled. "Did I pass the test, Sergeant?"

"Don't get cocky on me, rookie," Gabe said. "Every day you're on the street, you'll be tested. You start independent patrol next week, and I want you to survive it."

Thorpe coughed into his closed fist to hide his embarrassment. "Sorry, Sergeant."

"No harm done," Gabe said, handing Thorpe the motor vehicle report on Santistevan. "Get me a location for this guy. He's got a rural route address in the county. Do you know how to do that?"

"Through the post office," Thorpe said as he got to his feet.

"What else should you do?"

Thorpe studied the report. "Run Santistevan's Social Security number, date of birth, and vehicle registration through NCIC."

"That's right. If you get any hits, wants, or warrants, call the reporting department and get specifics." Gabe held out Melody Jordan's follow-up report. "Have dispatch pass this along to Houge."

"Yes, Sergeant." Thorpe took the file and turned to leave.

"Hey, Thorpe," Gabe said.

"Sergeant?"

"I think you're going to work out okay."

Thorpe nodded his thanks for the compliment, but Gabe didn't see it. His head was buried in the papers on the table.

After Thorpe closed the door, Gabe looked up and smiled. Coaching rookies was a lot like raising kids. The analogy made Gabe think about little Lane Knox in California, who was nuts about toy cars and trucks. At Lane's age, Orlando collected baseball cards. For years, Orlando had dragged him off every chance he got to buy more cards. He had been crazy about them. There were shoe boxes full of the damn things that Orlando had spent hours poring over, memorizing players' statistics.

Those were good years.

He opened the phone book, turned to the listings for firewood sellers, and started compiling a contact list, which he would give to Thorpe to finish as soon as the rookie returned.

At twenty-six, Agent Ben Morfin looked a good five years younger than his age. When he'd graduated from the academy at twenty-one, his youthful appearance won him a special assignment as an undercover narcotics agent at an Albuquerque high school. During the year he spent back in public school, Morfin had busted a number of pushers and street dealers, which earned him a departmental citation.

After wrapping up his testimony in the court trials on the cases, Morfin put in almost four years as a patrol officer before returning to narcotics. Assigned full-time to the Las Vegas district, he'd been back in plainclothes for six months and loving it.

He parked behind the physical science building at New Mexico Highlands University and gave dispatch his location. Gabe Gonzales came on the horn and gave him a quick update on the information received from the Arcadia PD.

Ben signed off, scribbled some notes, got the flat of cactus plants out of the backseat of his unmarked unit, and walked across the parking lot.

In the heart of Las Vegas, the campus was situated on a small hill bisected by city streets containing row after row of Victorian houses and cottages. With brick facades, flat roofs, and low parapets, most of the campus buildings had a territorial appearance.

Morfin found Professor Ruth Pino's office, put the tray containing the cactus on a hallway chair, and knocked on the door.

Professor Pino opened the door and looked Ben up and down. "I'm sorry, but I only see students during normal office hours," she said, "unless it's an emergency. I don't believe you're in any of my classes."

"I'm not," Ben said, showing his shield and ID. "I'm

Agent Morfin with the state police. I called you earlier this morning."

"You don't look old enough to be a policeman," Pino said as she turned away and walked toward her desk. "Come in."

"I get that all the time," Ben said as he picked up the container of cactus plants and followed Pino inside. A petite, middle-aged Hispanic woman no more than five-two, Professor Pino wore blue jeans, hiking boots, and a lightweight sweater that didn't detract from her still-youthful figure.

"So, you have some plants you think might have hallucinogenic properties," Professor Pino said.

"I'm hoping that's what you can tell me." Ben put the plants on her desk.

Ruth Pino turned, looked at the plants, and gave Morfin a startled glance. "Where did you get these?" she asked sharply.

"At a marijuana grower's greenhouse."

Pino made a closer inspection. The clustered stems were about an inch tall, the spines about a half-inch long, and the fruit was green. She reached for her handbook of rare endemic plants and paged through it. "Do you know where these were harvested?"

Morfin caught the excitement in Pino's voice. "In a canyon near San Geronimo."

"Who collected them?"

"A woman who lived with the marijuana grower."

Pino studied a page in the handbook and looked at the cactus plants one last time. "I need exact information on the location, Agent Morfin."

"Wait a minute, Professor. Back up. What has you so excited?"

"The common name of this plant is Knowlton's cactus. It's on the federal biologically endangered species list. There is only one known area in northwestern New Mexico where this cactus has ever been found."

"Ever?"

"In the world. The Nature Conservancy owns the land. It's on a secret preserve."

"A secret preserve for cactus?" Ben asked.

Professor Pino nodded. "Probably no more than three thousand plants exist in the wild. It's a variety treasured by collectors. One cactus can bring up to hundreds of dollars, depending on its size. The Knowlton's cactus has been reduced to near extinction. It's illegal to harvest it. If these truly came from a second site, you've made a very significant discovery."

"Are you saying I don't have a plant that produces any mind-altering substances?"

"That's exactly what I'm saying. How soon can you get me a specific site location?"

"It may take a while."

"That won't do. Who can I talk to about giving my request priority?"

"The sergeant in charge of the case and my captain."

"Give me their names," Professor Pino said, reaching for a pen.

"Sergeant Gonzales and Captain Garduno." Ben picked up the tray of cactus plants.

"Leave those with me please," Ruth said.

"They're evidence in a criminal investigation."

"I understand that. But I don't think you know how to care for those plants, and I won't have you negligently harming them." Ruth Pino smiled. "Tell you what: I'll give you my husband and firstborn son as hostages in exchange for the Knowlton's cactus."

Morfin shook his head in mock disbelief. "I guess I could transfer them to your custody for further analysis."

"I'll care for them lovingly."

"You'll have to sign some paperwork. Are you always so hard-nosed, Professor?"

Ruth Pino laughed. "I'm the toughest instructor in the department, Agent Morfin, and proud of it."

"I just got off the phone with my wife's first cousin," Captain Garduno said when Gabe walked into his office. "She teaches at the university."

"Would that be Professor Ruth Pino?"

"Morfin called in the information to you, I take it."

"He left out the part about your family ties."

"He didn't know. Ruth is hot to visit the site where the cactus was found. She's even cancelled her classes for the day to do it. Didn't you send Thorpe over there to collect evidence?"

"I did."

"Can you spare him to show Ruth around?"

"Sure."

"Good. I'll let her know. What do you have on Santistevan?"

"He's got a clean record. No wants, warrants, or

arrests. No military service. One speeding ticket in the last three years. He paid the fine. His mail is delivered to a neighborhood postal box in San Geronimo."

"Is there any evidence that Santistevan is tied to the crimes?"

"Not yet. All I've got is an eight-year-old kid's description of a truck, a license plate number, and a composite drawing along with a physical description of Rudy that doesn't correspond to Santistevan at all," Gabe said.

"That's a start."

"Maybe. But we're not lacking for evidence, Cap. The ballistics report came in a few minutes ago: a thirty-eight caliber bullet killed Boaz. Also, the lab lifted a clean fingerprint from the oil container found at the poaching site. The print isn't in the computer, but the lab can match it when we find the perp. We've got a good tool mark from the barbed wire samples we collected, and some good plaster-cast tire impressions. The tread marks left at the cabin gate and the clear-cut area are identical."

"So, go arrest somebody," Captain Garduno said jokingly, knowing full well that solid evidence without a suspect was always a frustrating dilemma.

Gabe cracked a small smile. "I'll get right on it."

Melody Jordan timed her departure from work to allow for a quick change of clothes before her scheduled meeting with Dr. Campbell Lawrence at the School of American Research. She switched to a pair of dress slacks and a top that fit just tightly enough to give an understated suggestion of her breasts. She would change back again before returning to work.

Campbell Lawrence was a good-looking man in his late thirties who didn't wear a wedding ring. At the conclusion of his seminar last fall, Lawrence had joined Melody and some of the other students for drinks. She had found him witty, charming, and—she liked to think—more than passingly interested in her.

Now Lawrence was back on a year's sabbatical. She had seen him only once since his seminar, when he spoke at a noontime colloquium at the school. Time didn't permit more than a brief exchange after his presentation, but Lawrence had seemed genuinely pleased to see her again.

She checked her hair, flew out the door of her house, and drove hurriedly to the campus. She eased into a parking space, gathered up the X-ray envelope and the box of bones, and walked down the crushed gravel path toward the Indian Arts Research Center.

The school, located on the grounds of an old estate near the historic Canyon Road and Acequia Madre district, was a lovely collection of adobe buildings behind high walls, spread over beautifully landscaped grounds. The compound contained a library, administrative offices, cottages for scholars in residence, an artist studio, and a priceless collection of Native-American arts and crafts housed in a high security building.

The school had been started early in the century as an archaeological field research facility, long before most colleges offered courses in the subject. It soon earned a prestigious reputation as a renowned anthropological and humanities research and study center, and nowadays drew visiting scholars to the campus on a year-round basis. It even had its own publishing house.

Melody found Campbell Lawrence in the small lab inside the Indian Arts Research Center.

"Thanks for seeing me on such short notice," she said.

"You caught me at a good time," Campbell said with a smile as he shook Melody's hand. "Show me what you've got."

Melody handed Campbell the X-ray envelope and started placing the bones on an examination table. Finished, she turned to find him studying the X rays on a wall-mounted fluoroscope.

While Campbell concentrated on the X rays, Melody looked him over. He had a full head of curly brown hair cut short and a neatly trimmed mustache. His hair line, low on his forehead, drew attention to his gray eyes. He was, Melody thought, very attractive.

"This break is old," Campbell said. "I'd say it happened in childhood and wasn't properly immobilized after the bone was set."

"That's highly unusual," Melody said.

"Only if you're applying Western standards of medicine. I think the injury was treated as a break, not a fracture. Whoever did it may not have had access to any equipment or facilities. It may not have been treated by a physician. I would imagine the victim probably had some chronic pain as a consequence."

"With impaired mobility of the arm?" Melody asked.

"Possibly. But what interests me most is the slight

deformity here." He pointed to the joint end. "That's not from getting hacked up. Let's take a look at the bones."

Campbell walked to the table and picked up the long bones. "There's the deformity again. Just the slightest bit of bowing in the humerus and femur. Run a phosphorus and calcium test on the bones. If the results show deficiencies, I'd say your victim had rickets as a young child."

He picked up the pelvic bone. "A female, certainly."

"Any guesses on race?" Melody asked, hoping Campbell would confirm her own assessment.

Campbell measured the humerus and the femur. "I wish you had more of the skeleton for a comparison. But if we estimate her height at five feet, four inches, which I think is a good guess, then I'd say her legs were a bit shorter than normal. Not much, but a bit."

He put the tape measure down. "It can't be anything more than speculation, but from what I've seen, I'd say this young woman was of mixed race, Hispano-Indian, probably from the southern part of Mexico or Central America. She suffered from poor nutrition, vitamin deficiency, and woefully inadequate medical care."

"That's very helpful, doctor," Melody said.

"Please, it's Campbell."

"Are you and your family enjoying your time in Santa Fe?" Melody asked as she repacked the bones.

"I'm divorced."

Melody tried to look sympathetic. "Oh, I didn't know."

"I'm fully recovered from it."

She turned her attention to gathering up the evidence and repacking it. "Have you gotten out to see the sights since you've been here?"

"Not as much as I'd hoped to. Do you have any suggestions?"

"I can give you a year's worth of ideas. If you're free, we could discuss it over dinner tonight. I'm a fairly decent cook."

"I'd like that very much," Campbell said.

Melody gave him her address, directions to her house, and a thousand-watt smile.

Post office records showed that a second individual, Isaac Medina, received mail at Santistevan's rural delivery address. Gabe stopped at the first occupied house in San Geronimo and asked the elderly woman who came to the door for directions. The woman pointed out a dwelling on a small hill behind her house. A pickup truck was parked in front of the house and smoke drifted from the chimney.

"Isaac lives there," she said. "But Joaquin Santistevan moved away some time ago. You have to go through the village to get to Isaac's driveway. Turn right at the old store. You'll see his gate halfway up the hill."

Gabe called in his location before he entered Medina's driveway and drove toward the house slowly, scanning it as he approached. No one was in sight.

He parked and waited a minute before getting out of his vehicle. The dwelling had a slanted tin roof that covered an enclosed porch with a row of waist-high windows. Through the windows, Gabe could see a line of upright freezers and refrigerators, all different shapes and sizes. On the ground in front of the house were a dozen or more old washing machines, clothes dryers, and dishwashers, some scavenged for parts and some intact.

He knocked hard at the porch door and called out. A stocky, unshaven man with gray hair stepped out of the house and opened the porch door.

"What do you want?" the man said.

"Isaac Medina?" Gabe asked.

The man nodded.

Gabe showed his shield and ID. "I'm looking for Joaquin."

"He doesn't live with me anymore."

"Can you tell me where to find him?"

"Is he in trouble?"

"No."

"What do you want to ask him?"

"I want to talk to him about his truck," Gabe said.

"You mean the accident?"

"That's right," Gabe said.

"Come," Medina said as he pointed to the side of the house. "I'll show you. He told me he wasn't going to report it to the police because his insurance rates would go up."

Gabe followed Medina to the back of the house where a three-quarter-ton Chevy truck with a caved-in front end and smashed windshield was parked.

"What did Joaquin tell you about the accident?" Gabe asked as he walked around the vehicle. No winch, no hydraulic lift in the bed, no wrought-iron side rails, and the truck was gray in color, not dark blue.

"He didn't have to tell me nothing; I was with him. We hit a deer. See for yourself. There's still blood, skin, and fur on the grille and bumper. It happened a mile from the house. We walked home, got my truck, towed the Chevy here, and then we butchered and dressed the deer. I still have some venison steaks in the freezer."

Gabe looked and saw blood splatter, flakes of hide, and small strands of fur embedded in the grille. "When did the accident occur?"

"Late October, last year."

"Where's the license plate?"

"Joaquin took it off the truck."

"How can I contact Joaquin?"

"You're not here about the accident," Medina said.

"His license plate was reported by a witness to a crime."

"Joaquin is no criminal. What kind of crime?"

"Wood poaching."

Medina laughed, showing a row of crooked lower teeth. "He doesn't need to steal wood from anybody. His father owns the biggest woodlot in the county."

"You know that for a fact?"

"Sure I do. I'm his uncle. His mother is my sister."

"What's the name of his father's company?"

"Buena Vista Lumber and Supply."

"Why was Joaquin living with you?"

"He was separated from his wife for almost a year. Now they're back together."

"What's his wife's name?"

"Debbie."

"Is she one of the Romero girls?"

"No, her maiden name was Espinoza."

"Where can I find Joaquin?"

"He works at the woodlot for his father, Philip San-tistevan."

"Thanks, Mr. Medina."

"Does this have anything to do with the gringo who got murdered at the cabin?" Medina asked.

"That's a completely different case," Gabe said, quite sure that Medina would be on the phone to his nephew as soon as he drove away.

At midmorning, the U.S. Attorney called Kerney from Albuquerque. She wanted a face-to-face afternoon meeting on a joint task force bribery and conspiracy operation involving Social Security Administration employees and Motor Vehicle Division workers who were under investigation for selling driver's licenses and Social Security cards to illegal, undocumented aliens.

There was no way Kerney could refuse. He hung up, called Sara, explained the situation, and told her their camping trip would have to be delayed.

"There's no need to apologize," Sara said. "We'll simply do it some other time."

"I should be home early in the evening." Silence greeted Kerney's comment. He waited for a response and none came. "Sara?"

"This conversation is starting to sound much too domestic," she said.

"What does that mean?"

"Nothing."

"Am I missing something here?"

"Everything's fine."

"It doesn't sound that way to me."

"Stop it, Kerney. I'll see you when you get off work."

Kerney hung up the receiver, wondering what in the hell was going on. He waited a minute, dialed his home number again, and got a busy signal.

There wasn't time to brood over it. In five minutes he would be taking a phone call from a newspaper reporter about the early morning discovery of an elderly woman who had been raped and murdered at a remote farmhouse in southeastern New Mexico.

The department's public information officer had set up the call. Kerney buzzed him and asked for the fact sheet on the case.

The lieutenant came in, gave Kerney the sheet, and sat.

Kerney read it quickly. "In other words, we've got nothing so far."

"What we've got is heat, Chief. I just got off the phone with the county sheriff. The victim was the grandmother of the chairman of the county commission. The sheriff wants the department to offer all possible assistance."

"Has he talked to the newspapers about it?"

"Of course he has. He's a politician. He'll do his best with the limited resources available. But without the department's help—you know the rest of it."

Kerney nodded. Laying off responsibility to the state police for major case investigations was standard procedure for sheriffs who had limited budgets, few personnel, and no technical specialists.

"I've got a TV reporter and another print journalist

standing by to speak to you after this interview is finished. They're covering the same story."

"Don't schedule any more for me," Kerney said.

"I'll handle whatever else comes in." The lieutenant glanced at his wristwatch. "Your first call should be happening right about now."

The phone rang and Kerney picked it up.

Buena Vista Lumber and Supply, ten miles south of Las Vegas on a state road, contained hundreds of cords of dry and green split firewood, stacks of peeled vigas used for roof beams in Santa Fe–style homes, and virtually every type of fencing material imaginable. A chain-link fence enclosed the lot.

Gabe drove to the office trailer in front of a large metal storage building and parked. He found Joaquin Santistevan inside the trailer at a desk, giving a telephone quote to a customer. On the desk was a framed photograph of a young, pretty Hispanic woman.

Santistevan finished the call and turned to Gabe. He had the same lean build as Orlando and looked to be about the same height. "What can I do for you?"

Gabe showed Santistevan his credentials. "I'm looking for a woodcutter who drives a dark blue, three-quarter-ton Chevy with a winch on the front bumper, side rails, and a hydraulic lift in the bed."

"I see trucks like that in and out of here all the time. Do you have a name?"

"Rudy."

"That's it?"

"That's it," Gabe said, handing Santistevan the composite drawing. "Does your father have an employee named Rudy?"

"No." Joaquin looked at the drawing and gave it back.

"Maybe he does contract woodcutting for your father."

"I handle that end of the business. Nobody who looks like that cuts wood for us."

"What did you do with the license plate from the truck you left at your uncle's place?"

"Why do you want to know?"

"It was reported to be on a vehicle used in a crime."

"Somebody needs glasses." Santistevan stood up. "We've got a wall of old license plates in the storage building. I added it to the collection. It's been there for months. Want to see it?"

"I do," Gabe said, following Joaquin out of the office.

The license plate collection ran the length and width of two frame walls of a corner office. It included plates from the 1930s right up to the present, in chronological order.

"It's right there," Santistevan said, pointing to his plate. "The tag doesn't even expire until August. What kind of crime are you investigating?"

"Wood poaching. You wouldn't knowingly buy firewood that's been illegally harvested, would you?"

"I can account for every cord in the yard, either by Forest Service permit or a contract with a private landowner."

"Thanks for your time."

Gabe left, parked down the road where he could see traffic leaving the woodlot, and tried to figure out what in the hell was bothering him. It was something about the photograph of Santistevan's wife and her maiden name. Isaac Medina had said it was Debbie Espinoza.

Shit, he knew the Espinoza family, he thought to himself. He pulled out the composite drawing and studied it. It was Debbie Espinoza's brother, Rudy.

He called dispatch. "Go to Channel two," Gabe said. Channel 2 was the secure broadcast frequency not picked up by police scanners.

"Ten-four," the dispatcher replied, switching over.

"Run a check on Rudy Espinoza. Keep it local. I busted him about four years ago for driving under the influence."

After a long wait, the dispatcher came back on the air.

"He's done six months' probation for a second DWI since then, and he was booked and released for lack of evidence on a breaking-and-entering charge."

"Where?"

"San Geronimo, last summer."

"When was the DWI bust?"

"June of last year."

"What was he driving?"

"Hold on."

Gabe could hear the dispatcher's keystrokes as she entered the search into the computer.

"A nineteen-ninety-four Chevy three-quarter-ton pickup, blue in color. Tags are expired. Plate number Two-six-six CJR."

"Got an address?"

"Anytime you're ready."

Gabe took down the information, signed off, and made contact with Duran, Houge, and Morfin on Channel 2 as he pulled onto the highway and started rolling toward the interstate.

"I've got a possible suspect in the Boaz murder," he said as he hit the switch to the overhead lights and floored the unit.

"Go," Duran said.

"Rudy Espinoza. He matches the information supplied to us by Boaz's ex-girlfriend and son. So does his vehicle. I may have tipped my hand."

"Is he running?" Houge asked.

"Could be. Look for a dark blue Chevy three-quarter-ton with side rails, front-end winch, and hydraulic lift in the bed. Plate number Two-six-six CJR, tags expired."

"Where?" Morfin asked.

"Ojitos Frios. ID any other moving vehicle that looks suspicious."

"Armed and dangerous?" Duran asked.

"Roger that," Gabe said. "Run Code three, lights only, and stay on the air. Give me locations and ETAs."

"I'm at Boaz's cabin," Morfin said. "Five minutes to Ojitos Frios."

"Ten to fifteen minutes," Houge said. "I'm on the interstate proceeding south past the cutoff to Villanueva State Park."

"I'll play catch up," Duran said. "I've got to get off this stinking mesa first."

"I'm on Highway Eighty-four, five minutes from the Romeroville interstate ramp," Gabe said. "Give me sixty-second microphone checks—two clicks each."

The dispatcher came on. "This channel is cleared of all other traffic. Additional units are responding; SP 218, SP 376, and SP 101."

"SP 218 take state road 283."

"Ten-four."

"SP 376, ETA to Highway 84?"

"Three minutes."

"Patrol Eighty-four south of Buena Vista Lumber."

"Ten-four."

"SP 101."

"Go," said Captain Garduno.

"Are you assuming command?" Gabe asked.

"I'm along for the ride, Sergeant."

"ETA?" Gabe asked as he reached the overpass to the interstate.

"I see you crossing the bridge now," Garduno said. "One minute."

"Ten-four. Join up."

"Give me your fucking car keys," Rudy Espinoza said as he hung up the phone.

"Use your own truck," Angie said. "I've got to go to town later."

Rudy dumped the contents of Angie's purse on the kitchen counter, found the keys, and pulled all the cash out of her wallet.

"What the hell is wrong with you?" Angie asked, grabbing for her purse.

"Nothing," Rudy said as he pushed her away and walked into the bedroom. "If the cops come, you haven't seen me."

"I don't know why I ever took you back," Angie yelled at him.

"You're no fucking prize yourself," Rudy said, sticking the thirty-eight and a handful of folded bills in his jacket pocket. "I'll call you later."

"Don't bother."

He got in the Mustang, fired it up, and peeled out of the driveway. Angie stood on the front step giving him the finger as he swung onto the county road.

If the cops were looking for him like Joaquin said, it was time to go south.

Ben Morfin topped the hill into Ojitos Frios and saw a car throwing up a dust cloud on the county road at the far end of the valley.

"Someone is coming your way, Sergeant," he said into the microphone. "I'm too far back to ID it, but he's moving fast."

"Location?" Gabe snapped.

"About a mile outside Ojitos Frios."

"Shut down your Code Three and close up."

"Ten-four."

Gabe keyed his hand microphone again, slowed his unit, and killed the overhead lights. "SP 101."

"I'm on your tail," Garduno said.

"Block the road behind me."

"Roger."

"I'll join with SP 101," Houge said. "ETA five minutes."

"Ten-four. All other units, stay on station," Gabe said. "Let's see what we've got."

"We've got a tan Mustang," Ben Morfin said. "Can't read the plate. He's spewing up so much dust he can't see me. I've got him clocked at seventy-five."

"Lights and siren, Ben. See if he stomps it."

"He just goosed it."

"Fall back and give him some slack," Gabe said. He swung his vehicle into the center of the road where the shoulders fell off sharply, unracked the shotgun, and called dispatch.

"Go ahead, SP 126."

"SP 126 will be attempting a traffic stop of an unknown vehicle speeding on County Road A-twenty."

"Traffic stop. CR A-twenty. Ten-four. Fourteen-twenty-three hours."

He put one round in the chamber, got out of the unit, and walked to a tree twenty feet off the shoulder of the road. He could see the dust spreading into the canopy of the trees, and could hear the harsh sound of Morfin's siren closing in.

The Mustang tore into view, suspension bucking over the washboard road. Gabe watched as the driver stood on the brakes, overcorrected his steering, went into a skid that spun the vehicle like a top, and put it nose first into the deep shoulder.

He could hear the hiss of radiator steam and the squeal of metal as the driver opened the car door. Through the dissipating dust, two hands emerged and grasped the roof of the car. Legs followed, feet found the ground, and Rudy Espinoza pulled himself out of the Mustang.

The lights from Ben Morfin's unit cut through the

haze twenty feet down the road. Ben was crouched behind the open door of his unit with his weapon at the ready.

"Rudy," Gabe called, raising the shotgun to his shoulder. "Walk toward me with your hands over your head. Do it now!"

Hands raised, Espinoza moved sluggishly up the embankment and started walking across the road.

"Stop," Gabe called when Rudy reached the middle of the road. "Lock your hands at the back of your head and drop slowly to your knees. Do it now."

Espinoza sank to his knees and started to lower his hands.

"Hands up," Gabe yelled. "Now."

"I can't," Rudy said. "Something is wrong with my head." He raised his left hand and fell facedown on the ground with his right arm concealed under his body.

"Bring your right hand out where I can see it," Gabe ordered.

Rudy didn't move.

"Do it!"

"Kiss my ass," Rudy said as he rose to his knees and pulled out a pistol.

"Gun!" Morfin hollered as Gabe pulled the trigger.

Gabe heard the crack of Ben's nine millimeter as the blast of his shotgun echoed in his ears. Rudy jerked under the impact, rocked back on his heels, and fell forward on his face.

Gabe racked another shell into the chamber while

Morfin circled behind Rudy, kicked the pistol away, and checked the body.

"He's dead," Ben said as he holstered his weapon.

"The stupid son of a bitch," Gabe said, lowering the shotgun. He held it tight to keep his hands from shaking.

6

After hanging up on Kerney, Sara tried without success to reach Susie Hayes at home. Susie, her best friend at West Point, was now a civilian living in Tucson. She thought about calling Susie at work, but took Shoe on a long walk instead, wandering for several hours through quiet neighborhood streets. Overhanging trees thick with buds about to blossom into leaves lined row after row of a charming mixture of older homes. Some were Victorian, some were flat-roof adobe casitas, and others were California mission style. Sprinkled throughout the neighborhood were red-brick cottages that had been turned into apartments, and midwestern farmhouses with pitched roofs that looked as though they had been magically transported to Santa Fe from Kansas wheat fields.

Very little else on the walk registered with Sara. She spent the time chiding herself for acting like such a brainless schoolgirl with Kerney. Where did all her silliness come from? She'd never intended to come to Santa

Fe and talk about babies and keeping a stud book. Kerney seemed to take it all in jest, which was almost as troubling. He was the only man she'd ever mentioned the possibility of making babies with, and she wondered if he'd caught her serious undertone. But did she really want a baby? Did she really want Kerney to be the man in her life?

She returned to Kerney's house and let Shoe off the leash. He went directly to the kitchen, drank his water bowl dry, and curled up on the vinyl floor with his chin resting on the sneaker.

She refilled the water bowl, sat at the kitchen table, kicked off her shoes, and looked at Shoe. He was such a sweet dog. He eyed her shoes with interest. She decided to ease up on herself. She needed to decompress and get the last two years behind her. Her virtual isolation in South Korea, immersed in a male-dominated, combat-ready unit had taken its toll. The rewards had been satisfying. But sublimating almost every feminine feeling had been more emotionally expensive than she'd realized. Maybe being with a sexy man after so long without any healthy lovemaking had opened up her hormonal floodgates, and her confusion was nothing other than a readjustment to a more normal life.

Feeling less unsettled, she got to her feet, snagged her shoes before the dog could pounce on them, and walked into the living room, glad that her first attempt to reach Susie had been unsuccessful. All she would have done was blabber. Now, at least she had her head screwed on somewhat straight.

She found her address book, looked up Susie's work number, and dialed it. When Susie answered, she told her a fraction of what was going on inside her head, and asked if she could come for a visit.

"Get your butt down here, girl," Susie said. "We've got some serious talking to do."

"I'll be there sometime tomorrow."

"Call me when you get into town."

Sara hung up. She would wait for Kerney to return before leaving. He deserved some sort of explanation, but she wasn't sure exactly what it would be.

Word of the Espinoza shooting cut short Kerney's meeting with the U.S. Attorney in Albuquerque. He made the 120-mile drive to Las Vegas in good time, using his radio to stay updated on the situation. Three hours after the shooting, no evidence had been developed linking Espinoza to the Boaz murder—no Chevy truck, no murder weapon, and no matching fingerprints.

A large number of police vehicles were parked in front of the district office, including a crime scene van and the unmarked unit assigned to the headquarters shooting team supervisor, who was responsible for investigating all deadly force incidents.

Kerney killed the engine and gave himself a minute to push down his worry about Sara. She had been snappish on the telephone, and while he'd toyed with the idea that she was merely disappointed about the postponed camping trip, he didn't really believe it. Sara wasn't one to pout or get testy about trivial matters, and she knew firsthand that the demands of police work often screwed up a personal life.

He shrugged off his anxiety and walked into the building where a dozen or so officers, agents, and technicians filled the reception area. Some were busy writing reports while others waited to give statements to the shooting team. In a corner of the room, Officer Thorpe sat with a petite, attractive Hispanic woman dressed in jeans, a sweater, and hiking boots. There was a backpack at her feet and she was writing notes in a journal balanced on her knees. Kerney had no idea who the woman was. Captain Garduno, Sergeant Gonzales, and Agent Morfin were nowhere in sight.

As he crossed to the reception desk, Thorpe approached him.

"Chief, Professor Pino would like to speak with you." Thorpe nodded his head in the direction of the woman.

"Who?"

"Professor Pino. She's a plant specialist—a botanist—who teaches at the university."

"What does she want?"

"She found a rare plant on your property. It's called Knowlton's cactus. It has her really pumped."

"Can she wait?"

Thorpe nodded. "I told her you might be busy for a while."

"Good enough."

Kerney smiled at the woman as he passed by, wondering what was going on. He filed the thought as a question for Captain Garduno and found him in his office.

"Chief," Garduno said, gesturing at the empty chair in front of his desk.

"How far along is the shooting team?" Kerney asked as he sat. Both Gonzales and Morfin would be treated as murder suspects until cleared of the charges by the DA and a grand jury. Only a finding of justified homicide in the death of Rudy Espinoza would allow the officers to remain with the department. If the shooting wasn't legal, both faced the possibility of felony convictions and prison time.

"They're finished with Gonzales and are interviewing Morfin now," Garduno said. "It looks good. Both Gabe and Ben used voice-activated recorders to tape the traffic stop. They fired in self-defense; there was no other way to stop the action."

"When will the report go to the grand jury?"

"Three days. I've put both men on paid administrative leave, effective immediately."

"Has Espinoza been positively made as Boaz's killer?"

Garduno wrinkled his nose. "Not yet. But Wanda Knox identified Espinoza from the mug shot we faxed to the Arcadia PD. The call just came in."

"So, for now, we've got a dead suspect whose only known crimes were trespassing on private property, illegal woodcutting, and speeding."

"It was a righteous use of deadly force, Chief. Espinoza pulled a gun on Gonzales."

"I'm not questioning that, Captain. But the press could decide to hound us until we have clear proof that Espinoza was a murderer and not some petty crook who got gunned down by an overly aggressive state police officer during a routine traffic stop."

"Agents Duran and Houge will start the legwork on Espinoza tomorrow," Garduno said. "We'll find the evidence."

"Houge and Duran will be in southern New Mexico, working a rape-murder case of an elderly woman."

"That scuttles the investigation for the next three days."

"I'll find a way to keep it going. Officer Thorpe has a botanist waiting to see me. What's that about?"

"Ben Morfin took the cactus plants found in Boaz's greenhouse to Professor Pino for an identification. She got real excited and asked to conduct a field survey to determine where the plants had been collected. I sent Officer Thorpe along with her. According to the professor, you've got only the second known distribution of Knowlton's cactus growing on your property."

"In the state?"

"In the world, Chief. Ruth Pino can tell you all about it."

"Where is Gabe Gonzales?" Kerney asked, getting to his feet.

"Sequestered in the conference room."

"I'd like to see him."

"Go on in."

Kerney found Gabe Gonzales tapping his fingers on the conference table. "How are you holding up, Sergeant?"

"I've seen a lot of dead people over the years, but this is the first time I ever had to put somebody down."

"It's not the same, is it?"

"Not even close."

"Are you all right with it?"

"I will be. I know it was a clean shooting."

"How far did you get before the shooting team pulled you in for a statement?"

"Not very. Angie Romero, Espinoza's girlfriend, swears the only vehicle Rudy normally drove was the Toyota pickup parked in her driveway."

"Is she playing it straight?"

Gabe shrugged his shoulders. "Who knows? She drinks her breakfast straight out of a whiskey bottle. She's half-blasted most of the time. Ben Morfin searched the truck and found nothing. I'm pretty sure Espinoza's brother-in-law, Joaquin Santistevan, tipped him that he was about to get busted. Otherwise, Espinoza had no reason to run. But the phone company has no record of a call made from the wood yard to Espinoza, or from Angie's house to Santistevan. Frank Houge is checking with cellular providers now."

"We need to find that Chevy truck," Kerney said.

"And the murder weapon. Maybe Houge and Duran will score while I'm cooling my heels for the next three days."

"That's not going to happen. They're both reassigned to another case effective tomorrow."

"That sucks, Chief."

"I know it does. Can I make a suggestion?"

"Sure."

"You need a couple of days out in the fresh air. Meet some new people, take scenic drives, poke around and explore, visit new places. It's a pretty time of year."

"Am I hearing you right, Chief?"

"It depends on what you want to hear, Sergeant."

Gabe rubbed his chin and gave Kerney a long look.

"It's your call, Sergeant. I can't order you to violate department policy."

"Who would I report to?"

"Me alone. No one else."

Gabe grinned. "I like the idea."

"I was hoping you would," Kerney said, handing Gonzales his business card. "On the back you'll find my private office and home telephone numbers. Use those numbers to reach me or leave messages."

Gabe took the card. "You were pretty sure I'd go along with this, weren't you?"

"I pulled your personnel jacket, Sergeant. There was enough in it to convince me that you don't always go by the book."

"I've heard that said about you."

"I guess that make us members of the same club. Nail Espinoza to the Boaz murder."

Ruth Pino contemplated the man who limped into the interview cubicle and sat at the small table across from her. Since he looked intelligent, Ruth decided he might be capable of understanding the important points that needed to be made.

Kerney listened as Ruth Pino explained the rarity of the Knowlton's cactus, its value to collectors, and the importance of the discovery of a new habitat on the alluvial apron at the bottom of the mesa. She spoke with intensity, in clipped sentences, and Kerney could imagine her in the classroom putting fear into the hearts of easily intimidated undergraduates.

"Whoever destroyed the trees along the watershed should be shot," Pino said, spreading out her field sketch on the small table in the interview cubical. She turned it so that Kerney could read the neat lettering and symbols.

Kerney held back from telling Pino her hopes had been realized.

"The tire tracks from the vehicle alone destroyed over a hundred plants." Pino's finger traced the line of destruction. "I can't even begin to estimate how many more were eradicated during the woodcutting."

"But some remain," Kerney said.

"Yes, but heavily threatened. The habitat has been altered, and unless the erosion along the alluvial apron is stopped, the entire distribution could be wiped out by the end of the rainy season."

Pino's finger poked the sketch in two places. "The cactus still thrives here and here, at the downstream points away from the clear-cutting. I estimate the total surviving population will exceed two thousand plants, with a very high ratio of mature specimens. Had the site been left undisturbed, the total would have probably exceeded eight to ten thousand. What happened is a travesty."

"Can the cactus be protected?"

"With your cooperation and some very substantial financial resources," Pino said.

"Cooperation I can give, Professor, but my resources are fairly limited right now."

"It must be done."

"I don't disagree," Kerney said. "Tell me how I can help."

"Give me unlimited access to the site. I'll bring in a team of graduate students from the university. We need to do a thorough mapping, a complete census, and some immediate, temporary erosion control."

"Of course."

"Once the distribution range has been clearly established, the tract must be fenced and possibly even guarded from poachers."

"Who would know about the site?" Kerney asked.

"Harvesting has already taken place, Mr. Kerney. It cannot be allowed to happen again."

"From what I've been told, the woman responsible for the harvesting had no idea the cactus was an endangered plant."

"That may well be," Pino said with a shake of her head. "But Knowlton's cactus was persistently collected in northwestern New Mexico until the Nature Conservancy stepped in and bought the land. European collectors have been known to pay over two hundred dollars for a mature plant, sometimes more. Any word of a new discovery will bring out the poachers. They're no different than pot hunters who violate the Federal Antiquities Act."

"How much fencing will be needed?"

"That's impossible to say at this point. I've had less than a day to conduct a spot field analysis. If other viable distributions are found, each will require protection."

"Let me know what you come up with, Professor."

"You will help us save this site, won't you?"

"I can't even promise you that I'll be able to retain ownership of the land, Professor. But I'll do what I can while I can."

With her eyes locked on to Kerney, Ruth Pino held up a hand. "What exactly does that mean?"

"The land is still in probate, and the tax bite is rather large. I may have to sell off a part of it."

"I see. Would you mind if I brought a few outside experts into the loop?"

"Who might they be?"

"Representatives from organizations who can help me develop a restoration plan for the site. It won't cost you any money."

"By all means."

"Have you ever seen a Knowlton's cactus?"

"I doubt it."

"It isn't a very dramatic or exotic specimen, but it deserves to continue to exist on the planet."

"I agree. I'll help you build the fences and pay for what I can, Professor. I don't like what was done to the land any more than you do."

Ruth Pino assembled her map and notes, tucked the papers inside her leather-bound journal, and gave Kerney an agreeable smile. "I may have to revise my opinion of police officers."

"Why is that?"

"It seems that not all of them suffer from authoritarian personality disorders."

Kerney smiled as he stood. "Can you say the same about university professors?"

"Occasionally."

● ● ●

Emotionally and physically drained from the events of the day, Gabe arrived home to find a car parked next to Orlando's subcompact in the driveway. He left his unit on the street, entered through the side door to the kitchen, dumped his briefcase on the table, and sank down on a chair. From upstairs he could hear music and the sound of male voices coming from Orlando's room. He wondered who was visiting his son.

He rubbed the back of his neck where the muscles felt like corded knots, twisted his torso to relieve the strain in his back, stared at the wall, and thought about his day. The image of Rudy Espinoza reeling under the impact of the shotgun blast kept spinning though his mind.

Gabe walked to the refrigerator. There wasn't much inside. Dinner would have to be canned soup and grilled cheese sandwiches. He got busy preparing the meal, his thoughts turning to his conversation with Chief Kerney. Having the chief's permission to continue to work the case might not mean squat in the final analysis. He could still get written up for violating departmental policies. That would surely torpedo his chances for promotion. It wasn't a pleasant thought. But the important issue was getting Orlando through his degree program at the university, and successfully launched. If he had to remain a patrol sergeant and continue to pinch pennies to do it, so be it.

He heard footsteps on the stairs and turned to find Orlando and Bernardo Barela, Nestor's grandson, standing in the doorway.

"Hey, guys," Gabe said. "What's up?"

"Just hanging," Orlando said.

"How are you, Bernardo?" Gabe asked.

"Fine, Mr. Gonzales," Bernardo said, flashing a smile.

Bernardo's smile had always struck Gabe as smug and insolent. He had his thumbs hooked in the pockets of tight blue jeans that broke at the heel of his cowboy boots. He kept his eyes locked on Gabe.

"I haven't seen you in a while," Gabe said.

Bernardo shrugged. "I've been busy working and stuff."

Smaller in stature than Orlando, Bernardo had a narrow face that ended in a pointed chin. He pushed his hair away from his forehead.

"Still working for your grandfather and uncle?"

"Yeah, I'm out at the new ranch."

"Are you two heading out?" Gabe asked Orlando.

"Yeah," Orlando said. "We'll grab a burger and a beer somewhere. Want me to bring you back something?"

"No thanks." Gabe nodded at the stove. "It's grilled cheese and soup for me." He nodded at Bernardo. "Say hello to your family for me."

"Sure thing."

"Have a good time," Gabe said.

The boys left and Gabe settled in front of the television with his cup of soup and sandwich. With the lights off, the almost empty room seemed less uninviting. The TV, a big screen model, had been Gabe's only expensive purchase since Theresa's departure. Since he wasn't dating, wasn't partying with the divorced and single officers in the district, and wasn't doing the bar scene, the television had become his single source of entertainment.

He stared at the screen as he channel surfed and ate his sandwich. Orlando and Bernardo had been friends ever since they'd played varsity baseball in high school. Gabe hadn't seen much of Bernardo over the last year, and Orlando hadn't said anything about a falling out. He hadn't asked any questions about Bernardo's absence in Orlando's social life. But he'd been glad when the relationship seemed to fade. Bernardo had always made Gabe a little uneasy with his macho attitude and tough guy posturing.

He took a sip of soup, locked the channel in on a basketball game, and reminded himself to talk to Nestor Barela in the morning. Maybe the old man knew something about Rudy Espinoza and Carl Boaz.

He finished eating, stretched out on the couch, and before the station broke away for a commercial, he was sound asleep.

Shoe met Kerney at the door, tail wagging, with the sneaker clamped in his teeth. He scratched the dog's ear and found Sara in the bedroom packing her suitcase.

She looked up and gave him a vague smile. "I'm glad you got here before I left."

"Where are you going?"

"Tucson, to visit an old friend."

"Are you all right?"

"Fine. I know I sounded bitchy on the telephone. It had nothing to do with you."

"What was it about?"

"It's not something I want to get into right now."

"Did I say something, do something?"

Sara's smile tightened. "It's not you, Kerney. I've got some thinking to do. Just call it bad timing on my part. I never should have barged in on you unannounced."

"I'm glad you did."

"Well, it's been fun." Sara picked up the suitcase and her coat.

"Wait a minute, Sara. Tell me what's up."

"It isn't your problem."

Kerney could sense her reserve. It felt like a huge gap between them. "It will be if you leave this way."

"I'm not leaving because of you."

"This isn't about bad timing, is it?"

Sara bit her lower lip. "No."

"Or stud books."

Sara hesitated. "Not really."

"Give me a hint."

"I'm not ready to discuss it. Give it a rest for now, okay?"

"Okay."

"I'm sorry."

"About what?"

"Leaving this way." She walked past Kerney into the living room.

"Maybe we should talk this out," Kerney said.

"I do need some talk, Kerney. Good, old-fashioned girl talk. That's why I'm going to Tucson. My best friend from West Point lives there."

"Are you coming back?"

Sara's eyes searched Kerney's face. "Am I invited back?"

"You bet."

"I'll call you from Tucson," Sara said as she opened the front door. She gave Kerney a quick kiss and a fleeting smile. "You've done nothing to upset me."

"I hope that's true."

Sara dropped to one knee and scratched Shoe's chest. He dropped the sneaker and licked Sara's chin.

"Take care of your dog, Kerney," she said as she stood up. "He's a sweetheart."

"I'll do that."

"See you soon."

"Yeah."

Kerney stood at the door and watched Sara load her bag in the Jeep and drive away. She waved once before she passed out of sight.

"What was that all about?" he asked the dog as he closed the front door.

Shoe gave the sneaker a vigorous shake and trotted off to the kitchen. Kerney tagged along, wondering what nuances he'd missed, what mistakes he'd made, and whether he'd completely turned Sara off.

He hoped she was leveling with him and that her sudden departure wasn't prompted by something he'd done. The thought didn't relieve the hollow feeling in his gut.

The dog leash was on the kitchen table. Kerney picked it up. There was still time to get to one of the shopping malls and buy a travel cage for Shoe. In the morning he'd make arrangements to have the dog shipped to the Knox boy in California.

Shoe saw the leash in Kerney's hand, let go of the sneaker, and jumped up on Kerney in eager anticipation.

"So, you're ready to leave, too, are you?"

Shoe dropped down on all fours and headed straight for the front door.

Orlando Gonzales sat at a table by the window of the Rough Rider Bar. Across the street stood the old Fred Harvey Hotel and the train station. A slow freight moving south along the tracks rumbled like a low bass note in harmony with the Tex-Mex CD playing on the stereo behind the bar.

He took a pull on the long neck beer and started at Bernardo. "You wanted to talk. About what?"

"We need to catch up," Bernardo said, flashing a smile.

"I thought the plan was we weren't going to hang together anymore."

"Did you read the story in the newspaper about the bones the cops found on the mesa?"

Orlando's hand froze as he reached for his beer bottle. "Jesus. Was that her?"

"Part of her. I spread the body around. Some parts here, some parts there. The cops will never be able to ID her."

"You cut her up?" Orlando asked in a choked whisper.

"Yeah."

"Why didn't you tell me this before?"

"Because you couldn't handle it."

"We should have just let her go."

"Yeah, straight to the police. Listen, we both raped her."

"I know that. But you killed her."

"In the eyes of the law, both of us did. You should know that, being a cop's son and all. It's called murder during the commission of a felony."

"I know what it's called," Orlando hissed.

"You're still all fucked up about it, aren't you?"

"Keep your voice down."

Bernardo looked over his shoulder. A few *viejos* sat at the bar in front of an enlarged photograph of Teddy Roosevelt and members of his Rough Riders, many of them New Mexican cowboys, taken at the top of San Juan Hill. A middle-aged couple played a video game at the back of the room where pictures from the old Rough Rider reunions once held in Las Vegas were hung on the wall. Nobody was within earshot.

"Listen, the bitch was a Mexican who was never reported missing. I checked it out."

"You did what?" Orlando asked.

"I talked to the dude who manages my grandfather's old ranch. He told me Luiza went back to Mexico. End of story."

"You couldn't keep your mouth shut, could you?"

"At least I'm not letting this shit eat me up."

"We did something wrong."

Bernardo shrugged. "Just keep me posted on what your old man and the other cops are doing with the case."

"Is that what you wanted to talk to me about?" Orlando shook his head. "You can't be serious."

"I am. We're in this together."

"What good would it do?"

"Maybe keep our asses out of prison. We don't need any surprises."

Orlando studied Bernardo suspiciously. "Can you be connected to the girl in any way?"

"Chill, *boto*. I met her one time, that's all. I already told you that."

Orlando thought back to the night they'd picked her up. He'd been too drunk to remember anything clearly, but he couldn't shake the feeling that Bernardo's version of how he talked Luiza into the truck was a little screwy.

"You're sure?"

"Why would I lie about that?" Bernardo replied.

Orlando picked up his beer, clenched the bottle until his first turned white, and took a swallow.

"Well?"

"I'll see what I can find out."

"That's better," Bernardo said, reaching for his brew. "Relax, dude. Drink up."

"Relax, shit. I feel like puking. I never wanted her dead."

"Shit happens," Bernardo said.

"It doesn't bother you, does it?"

"Not really. I can't make it go away. Neither can you. Besides, lots of murders never get solved."

"You're cold, Bernardo."

"I just want to keep everything cool."

"Including me?"

"I worry about you."

Orlando made a face and stood up. "I can live with it."

Bernardo chuckled.

"What?" Orlando snapped.

"Can you?"

"I have for a year. Give me a ride home."

"It's early. Drink another beer."

"I'll walk."

Bernardo slapped his empty bottle on the table and got to his feet. "I'll take you home, *mano*. You're no fun to drink with anymore, anyway."

7

Bernardo pulled into Orlando's driveway. The living room curtains were open and a flickering television glowed through the window. Orlando had kept his head turned away on the drive home, gazing out the passenger window of the car, saying nothing.

Bernardo killed the engine. "You got something on your mind, bro?" he asked.

"Everything's cool," Orlando replied as he opened the door.

Bernardo placed his hand on Orlando's arm. "You sure?"

Orlando peeled Bernardo's fingers off his arm. "What's with you?"

"Nothing. We just have to be straight with each other, that's all."

Orlando got out of the car. "You want straight? I'll give you straight. I don't want to see you or talk about this shit again."

"Mano." Bernardo leaned across the passenger seat to look at Orlando.

"What?"

"You call me if you learn anything."

"Yeah."

"I mean it."

Orlando nodded sharply and walked toward the house.

Bernardo drove away, thinking he'd made a mistake asking Orlando to check out what the cops were doing with the investigation. It had just shaken him up and bummed him out. He wondered if Orlando might crack under the strain.

He thought back to the night of the murder. They'd been cruising together in his grandfather's truck, drinking beers, and shooting the shit, both with a major buzz going, when Bernardo had spotted Luiza walking along the road from Ojitos Frios.

It had been Bernardo's idea to pick her up and screw her. Orlando was too drunk to argue, too drunk to care. He passed out just before Bernardo turned the truck around and went back to get her. He pulled up alongside her with his pistol in hand, and told her if she didn't get in he'd kill her. She didn't resist or argue.

After finding a secluded spot away from the road, Bernardo waited until Orlando came to and gave him first crack at Luiza. Still drunk, it didn't take him long to finish, and when he crawled away to puke his guts out, Bernardo took his turn.

Luiza held herself rigid while he fucked her, eyes filled with hate, and Bernardo knew he was going to kill her. When it was over, he pinned her to the ground and smashed her skull with a rock.

He wrapped her body in a tarp and went to Orlando, who was sitting under a tree, his eyes wide with disbelief.

"You killed her," Orlando said.

"She was going to turn us in for rape."

"You said she wanted to get it on with us."

"She changed her mind."

"What are we going to do?"

"I'll take care of it," Bernardo said.

And he did. After taking Orlando home, he returned, cut up the corpse like he was butchering a steer, and hid part of the body on the mesa and the rest in an arroyo twenty miles away. Then he washed out the bed of the truck and got home before anyone was up.

Bernardo coasted to a stop in front of his parents' house. He stayed in the car and lit a cigarette. His parents wouldn't let him smoke inside.

He'd lied to Orlando about not knowing Luiza. He'd met her when she came up from Mexico to work as a housekeeper at the Box Z Ranch that bordered his grandfather's new spread.

Luiza had been a complete turn-on: a great looking piece of ass, with a tight body, full tits, a small waist, long black hair, and shy dark eyes. He put some moves on her that Luiza had brushed off, treating him like some little kid.

When she changed jobs and started working at the Horse Canyon Ranch, Bernardo couldn't stop thinking about her. He would see her occasionally, but she'd have nothing to do with him. Once he'd offered her a ride when she was walking along the county road. But she just blew him off and kept walking, making him feel like a fool. After that, Bernardo started to think of ways to teach the dick-teasing bitch a lesson.

Raping and killing Luiza had been a spur of the moment thing, but it opened up a whole new world for Bernardo. If his luck held and the cops couldn't identify Luiza's remains, the next time he would plan things more carefully. He had just the girl picked out. The image of Jessica Varela, the gringo chick with the Spanish name who worked at the hardware store, popped into his mind, and a pleasant feeling of anticipation ran through him.

He pushed the image aside and thought about Orlando. He could ruin everything, and Bernardo wasn't about to let that happen. He would have to keep an eye on him.

He crushed out the cigarette in the ashtray, got out of the car, and went into the house.

In his room, Orlando undressed and got into bed, trying to convince himself that Bernardo was right and there was nothing to worry about. But ever since the rape and murder, Orlando knew he would be caught and sent to prison—maybe even executed.

For a year he'd kept trying to pretend it never happened. But talking with Bernardo had brought it all back, like a hammer inside his head.

It had been Bernardo's idea to see if Luiza wanted to get it on. If Orlando hadn't been drunk, he never would have done it. But a lame excuse didn't count for shit. What could he say? That he didn't mean for it to happen? That he never wanted to see her hurt or killed? Lame.

He'd thought a lot about suicide, but he didn't have the balls for it. Time and again, he'd thought about telling his father, and he didn't have the balls for that, either. If he could hold on for just a little more than a year, he would have his degree and then he could split. Get away from it all and go somewhere new. Put this shit behind him.

Downstairs in the living room, his father was asleep on the couch with the television on. His briefcase sat on the floor next to the kitchen table. Orlando thought about sneaking down to look through it. Instead, he started to cry softly into his pillow.

After an uneasy night with little sleep, Kerney kicked off the bed covers, pulled on his jeans, stood up, and stumbled over Shoe in the dark. The dog yelped and scurried out of the bedroom. Kerney found him hiding under the kitchen table.

He glanced at the pet cage he'd bought the night before. With Sara gone he didn't like the idea of sending Shoe away; it would just make the place feel all the more empty. He squelched the thought before it turned into a gloomy feeling and made himself a bowl of instant oatmeal.

By the time he was out of the shower and dressed, Kerney had decided to handle the mesa murder case himself, at least for a few days. It would keep the investigation from stalling, and give him something to think about besides Sara's abrupt departure.

He made some phone calls and found an air freight company that could ship Shoe from Santa Fe and deliver him to the treatment center where Wanda Knox and her son resided. Then he called the treatment center in California and confirmed with a staff member that Shoe would be welcomed at the facility.

He asked the woman to tell Lane Knox his dog would be there sometime during the day, packed Shoe's sneaker and all the pet necessities he'd bought in the cage, leashed the dog, put him in his unit, and drove to the air freight office, where Kerney paid the charges and the freight agent put Shoe in the cage. Shoe immediately started scratching to get out. He gave Kerney a sad look as the freight agent carried him away.

Kerney hesitated, almost called the man back, then turned and walked out of the building, knowing he would miss that dog.

At his office, he pulled the mesa murder file and read it through in detail. Melody Jordan had updated her report with the findings from her meeting with Dr. Lawrence. Lawrence's assessment wasn't hard evidence, but narrowing the possibility that the murder victim might be either a Central American or Mexican national could prove helpful.

The work Frank Houge had done before being pulled off the case was inconclusive. None of the three missing women who matched the victim's age had suffered an old fracture to the left arm, nor had any of the others from the remaining open cases.

Kerney skimmed the missing persons printout from the National Crime Information Center, came up empty on any matches, and decided it was time to get out and do some old-fashioned legwork. It would also give him a chance to meet some of his new neighbors.

His ride across the mesa with Dale replayed through his mind as he drove out of Santa Fe. It was a beautiful piece of land Erma Fergurson had left to him. He tried to visualize it through Erma's artistic eye. He could see the crowns of the tall ponderosas in the heavy timber at the rim of the mesa with the stark face of Elk Mountain splitting the horizon, and the rich rangeland, thick with grasses bent by the weight of heavy seeds sparkling like pale white jewels in the breeze.

He wondered where Erma had gone with her brushes and her canvas to paint, and how many landscapes she'd produced during her summer retreats on the mesa. She'd left one of her paintings to him, but he hadn't seen it, and wouldn't until he had a chance to get down to Las Cruces. He knew he would love it. Maybe it would be a landscape of the mesa.

The pessimistic thought that he wasn't going to be able to keep all the land washed over him. He slapped his hand hard against the steering wheel to drive the thought away.

Gabe reviewed the background checks on Nestor Barela and his family that had been requested by Chief Kerney. On paper Nestor, his three sons, their wives, and the grandchildren were all law-abiding citizens with no criminal records. Nestor had served in World War II as a tank commander and his oldest son, Roque, had been in Vietnam with the Ordnance Corps.

Nestor's three sons, Roque, Lalo, and Elias, all had clean slates. Roque, the oldest, had retired from the state highway department and now ran the family ranch. Lalo, the middle son, was a medical technologist at the local hospital, and Elias worked as an independent plumbing contractor.

Lalo's boy, Fermin, was a career marine assigned to embassy duty in the Philippines. The other grandchildren consisted of two boys—Bernardo and Gerald—offspring of Nestor's youngest son Elias, and Roque's three girls, who were still in high school. Both Gerald and Bernardo lived at home.

Gerald worked in the business office at a regional vocational school and was engaged to be married in June. Bernardo worked with his Uncle Roque on the family ranch south of Las Vegas that Nestor had bought with part of the proceeds from the sale of Horse Canyon.

Nestor had one great-grandchild, a two-year-old girl born out of wedlock to Bernardo and his former high school girlfriend, who lived in Denver. Under a court order, Bernardo paid child support of three hundred dollars a month, and his payments were up to date.

Nestor's wife had died several years before he'd sold Horse Canyon. He'd built the family compound on the Gallinas River to have his sons, their wives, and the grandchildren close to him, deeding a house and five acres to each of his boys, and keeping one parcel and a home for himself.

Gabe approved of Nestor's old-fashioned yet modern scheme to keep his extended family together. Too many Hispanic families had scattered as land changed hands and children moved away.

None of the information about the Barelas surprised Gabe. He'd grown up with Elias Barela and knew the family fairly well.

Nestor's truck was parked in front of his house, but there wasn't an answer when Gabe knocked at the door. He turned the corner of the house, saw three men leading saddled horses from the barn to a stock trailer, and walked down to meet them. When he got close, he recognized Nestor, Roque, and Bernardo.

He nodded a greeting to Bernardo. "Did you have a good time with Orlando last night?"

"Yeah, we drank a few beers and hung out for a while."

Gabe shook Roque's hand. "Working hard, Roque?"

Roque smiled. "Always. My father treats us like peons."

Nestor laughed. "You tell such stories, Roque." He eyed Gabe's civilian attire. "What brings the state police to see us?"

"To ask a few questions. Did you know Carl Boaz?"

"I didn't even know his name until I read it in the paper," Nestor said.

"How about you?" Gabe asked Roque.

"I knew him by sight," Roque replied. "But not to talk to."

"How about Rudy Espinoza?"

"We all knew Rudy," Roque said. "He was nothing but trouble."

"Do not speak unkindly of the dead," Nestor said.

"I heard a rumor that you shot him," Roque said, "for cutting wood and speeding."

"Did Rudy have your permission to enter the Fergurson property?" Gabe asked, sidestepping the remark.

"Never," Nestor answered. "I give no one permission to go on that land."

Gabe turned to Bernardo. "Did you ever see him driving a three-quarter-ton dark blue Chevy long bed?"

"If I did, I don't remember it. We don't spend much time at the mesa."

"That's right," Roque added.

"You said Rudy was trouble. Did he cause you any?"

Roque shook his head. "Not personally."

"A gringo came here on Sunday," Nestor said. "A tall man with a limp. I don't remember his name. He was with another man in a pickup truck. He wanted to buy out my lease on the Fergurson property. He asked about Boaz."

Gabe knew of the chief's visit to Barela and decided to keep it to himself. "Did he ask for Boaz by name?"

"No," Nestor said.

"Did either Boaz or Rudy ever give you cause to be suspicious?"

"Rudy just drank a lot," Bernardo said.

"He couldn't keep a job," Roque added.

"That's it?"

"Rumors," Roque said.

"Rumors?"

"That he was maybe breaking into some of the summer homes in the valley," Roque said.

"Who told you this?"

"I don't know where I heard it."

"Do you think he killed the woman you found on the mesa?" Bernardo asked.

"I don't know," Gabe replied. Bernardo's eager tone of voice struck him as somewhat odd. "What do you think?"

Bernardo shrugged his shoulders. "Well, if he was so bad, why not?"

"That's an interesting theory. Do you know who Rudy hung out with?"

"Not me," Bernardo said.

Both Roque and Nestor echoed Bernardo's comment.

"But I heard he got fired from Horse Canyon Ranch," Roque added.

"When?"

"About a year ago. He worked there a short time."

"Do you know why he got canned?"

"I have no idea. Emmet Griffin, the ranch manager, can tell you."

"Thanks," Gabe said. He shook hands with the men and walked up the gentle incline toward the compound.

Nestor waited until Gabe was out of earshot before turning to Bernardo. "Unsaddle my horse, *Jito*, and put him in the pasture."

"You're not going to the ranch with us?" Roque asked.

"No, I'm going to the mesa."

"What for?" Bernardo asked.

"To see for myself what damage has been done."

"You shouldn't go alone," Roque said.

Nestor looked sharply at his son. His reaction brought a quick, acquiescent nod from Roque. His gaze moved to Bernardo, and he raised his chin to point at the trailer containing the three mounts. "*Jito*, get my horse and put him back in the pasture."

Bernardo moved off.

"Well, be home before dark," Roque said, still unable to mask his concern over Nestor's plan to go to the mesa by himself.

"Stop always worrying about me, Roque. You make me feel old, and I am not ready to welcome such a judgment." He patted his son on the arm. "I'll be back before you get home."

On the road through Ojitos Frios, Nestor Barela found himself behind a slow-moving white van with a state government license plate. There were few places safe to pass on the dirt road, but he did so when the driver of the van opened the window and waved him around. He waved back at the woman and the passengers as he drove by. Soon the vehicle was out of sight in his rearview mirror.

He grunted in annoyance as he approached the old cabin. The gate to the property stood open and the scrap wood that had been nailed over the cabin door had been pulled off. He wondered if the police had entered the old building searching for clues.

Before he could take a look the white van appeared on the road. It slowed, turned, rattled over the cattle guard, and stopped next to his truck. Nestor approached the woman behind the wheel. Painted on the side of the vehicle was the logo of the state university.

"This land is posted," he said to the woman. The six passengers with her all looked very young. "No trespassing."

"I have the owner's permission," Ruth Pino said.

"The owner is dead," Nestor replied.

"The new owner is very much alive," Ruth replied, studying the man. He was about her father's age, perhaps a few years older, and his voice conveyed the tone of a man who expected to be obeyed.

"Who is the new owner?"

"Kevin Kerney. He inherited the property from Erma Ferguson."

The name registered with Nestor. "Does he walk with a limp?"

"Yes, he does."

"And you are sure he is the owner?"

"I doubt that Mr. Kerney would lie to me," Ruth replied. "He is the deputy chief of the state police. Would you mind telling me who you are?"

"I hold the lease on this property," Nestor said, concealing his surprise about Kerney and his profession. Why had the man not told him who he was?

"Then you must be Nestor Barela," Ruth said.

"I am."

"You can't deny us entry," Ruth noted.

"Why are you here?"

"Fieldwork, Mr. Barela. There is a very rare plant on this land, and it must be protected."

"What kind of plant?" Nestor asked.

"A cactus," Ruth said. She described it in detail.

"I have seen it."

Ruth's eyes widened in expectation. "You must show us where."

"I have no time to hunt for plants," Nestor said. "Where did you find this cactus?"

"At the wood poaching site," Ruth answered, "on the west side of the mesa."

"How much timber was taken?"

Ruth shook her head sadly. "Far too much."

"I will go with you," Nestor said. "I wish to see what has been done."

Ruth smiled. "We'll follow you."

It was midmorning when Susie Hayes took Sara's call in her Tucson office. After listening to Sara, Susie decided to take the rest of the day off and spend it with her friend. She had never heard Sara sound so pensive.

She asked where Sara was calling from, gave her directions to her townhouse, and beat her home by twenty minutes. When the doorbell rang she opened it to find Sara smiling apologetically.

Susie gave her a hug and pulled her inside. "You look wiped out, girl. Did you drive straight through?"

Sara nodded. "Thanks for putting up with me."

She laughed and took Sara into the living room. "I owe you a bushel full of favors. I wouldn't have made it through the academy if it hadn't been for you always telling me to finish what I started."

"Maybe I didn't do you a favor."

Situated in the foothills, Susie's townhouse had excellent views of the mountains to the east and the city below. She got Sara settled on the couch that faced a large picture window and sat next to her.

"Yes, you did, Colonel."

Sara looked surprised. "You heard about that?"

"I may have left active duty, but I'm still tied into the grapevine. You did a hell of a job on the DMZ. Congratulations."

"Thanks."

"Now, tell me about this cop you're in love with."

" I never said anything about being in love."

Susie stifled a laugh with her hand.

"What?" Sara demanded.

"Oh, do you talk about having a baby with every man you sleep with?"

Sara looked at her friend. Susie's gray eyes smiled back at her.

"I like him a lot," Sara said. It sounded defensive.

Susie ran her hand through her chestnut hair, put her feet on the cushions, and wrapped her arms around her knees. "Let's have it, Sara, and I mean full disclosure. We've got all day, tonight, and tomorrow, if needed."

Gabe stopped by the county sheriff's office and got fresh crime statistics for the first quarter of the new year. Thefts and break-ins in San Geronimo had continued to rise, and none had been cleared. Somebody was having a hell of a lot of success ripping people off in the valley.

At home Gabe worked the phone. Connecting the dots between Rudy Espinoza and Joaquin Santistevan proved more difficult than he'd expected. He'd assumed that the phone company would be able to verify a call from the woodlot to Angie Romero's residence about the time Gabe had left, but no such call was made.

Gabe tried the cellular providers, hoping either Rudy or Joaquin were customers with one of the companies. He came up empty with the local companies, worked the out-of-town providers, and struck out again.

The exercise took him the better part of the morning. He left the house wondering how in the hell Joaquin had gotten in touch with Rudy. Without confirmation that Joaquin had tipped Espinoza, Gabe didn't want to make any premature moves.

He decided to stake out Buena Vista Lumber and Supply to see if Joaquin left the office for lunch. If so, he would do a little snooping and talk to the employees.

He found a good spot where he wouldn't be noticed and settled down to wait. The lunch hour came and went, and Gabe was about to call it off when Santistevan's truck appeared and turned onto the highway, traveling south. Gabe wondered where Joaquin was headed. There wasn't much along the state road for a good thirty-odd miles—certainly no place to grab a quick lunch.

He drove into the lot half-expecting to be recognized, but the two employees on duty were not people he knew. One man was busy checking out a customer's load, while the other worked at a large pile of wood chips, bagging the material in burlap sacks.

He parked and made a show of inspecting fencing materials before wandering over to the worker bagging chips, where the odor of fresh-cut, green piñon wood greeted him.

"You need some help?" the man asked, as he tied off a bag and tossed it to one side. Anglo and in his mid-thirties, the man had long hair that was skinned tight against his head and tied in a bun at the nape of his neck.

"Not really," Gabe said. "Do you sell that stuff or give it away?" he asked, nodding at the mound of chips.

"Sell it," the man answered as he kept working. "Texans buy it to use in their fireplaces. They don't have much piñon to burn and they like the smell of it. Put a few chips in with the logs and it gives a nice aroma."

"You're kidding."

"It's true. A trucker hauls three or four semiloads a year to Lubbock, Amarillo, even Dallas."

"A local trucker?"

"Yeah, Lenny Alarid, from Anton Chico, does the hauling."

"How well did you know Rudy Espinoza?"

The man stopped working and looked directly at Gabe. "What's it to you?"

Technically Gabe had no official powers while on administrative leave, so there was no need to identify himself as a cop. "Rudy's family isn't happy with what happened. I'm looking into it."

"Wasn't that something? Yeah, I knew Rudy. He worked here for a while until the boss fired him."

"Joaquin?"

"No, Philip. Rudy had sticky fingers."

"He was stealing?"

"Yeah, little crap. Hand tools, fence posts, partial rolls of leftover wire—stuff like that."

"When did he work here?"

"Last summer. I think he got the boot in August."

"What was his job?"

"Yard worker, just like me."

"Who did he hang with?"

"Nobody, really. Joaquin, a little bit. You know, the brother-in-law thing."

"Do you remember the truck he drove?"

"A beat-up Toyota. Piece of shit."

"Nothing else?"

"That's all I ever saw him in. Is Rudy's family gonna hire a lawyer and sue the shit out of the cops for shooting Rudy?"

"Possibly."

"Nobody should get wasted for just being a thief."

"You're not wrong," Gabe replied.

Approaching Ojitos Frios, Gabe hoped the rumors circulating about the Rudy Espinoza shooting hadn't reached Angie Romero. He didn't want to face an angry, uncooperative drunk with an attitude.

Serious drinkers sweated booze out of every pore, and Angie's front room stank with the sickening smell of alcohol-laced perspiration.

"Who was the son of a bitch who shot him, Gabe?" Angie asked.

"I can't tell you that," Gabe replied, looking for a place to sit down that wasn't totally foul. He decided to remain standing.

"Rudy was a good man when he wasn't drinking."

"I'm sure he was."

Gabe knew the Romero family fairly well. The oldest of the three sisters, Angie had transformed herself from a bubbly teenager into a worn-out alcoholic and a family embarrassment. The house she lived in belonged to her grandfather, the Mustang she drove was registered to an uncle, and the money she lived on came from her father, a vice president at a local bank.

"We were going to get married," Angie added, as she sat on the soiled divan and sipped her whiskey from a coffee mug.

Her narrow face seemed completely asymmetrical, her lips and fingernails were painted blueberry, and she wore a wrinkled pair of black jeans, a black turtleneck sweater, and no shoes. Her dull, watery eyes looked sunken against the contrast of her rouged cheeks. Gabe figured Angie had dressed—as best she could in an alcoholic daze—to be a lady in mourning.

"Do you know who called Rudy just before he left the house?"

"No, he answered the phone and then said he had to leave. When do I get my car back?"

"Soon."

"It better not be wrecked."

"There is very little damage. Was Rudy working anywhere?"

"Not since last summer."

"How did he get money?"

"Odd jobs."

"What was he doing?"

"He didn't say."

"Not a word?"

Angie shrugged her shoulders. "He had money. I didn't ask where he got it."

"A lot of money?"

"I don't know if it was a lot. He borrowed some from me before he took the Mustang and left."

"Did he say where he was going?"

"No."

"Was he tight with Joaquin?"

"What are you getting at?" Angie asked as she got up and went to the kitchen. She returned with a full mug. "All these questions. Rudy got killed by a cop, that's all I know."

"Something made him run."

"Who wants to be hassled by cops?"

"I'm trying to find out what happened. Was Rudy tight with Joaquin?"

"He was his brother-in-law."

"But not good friends?"

"They got along."

"Did he ever talk about Joaquin?"

"Only to say that Joaquin had some woman problems."

"With his wife, Debbie?"

"Her, and with some other girlfriend, while he was separated."

"Does the girl have a name?"

"I didn't pay any attention. Are you finished? I have things to do."

"Take care of yourself, Angie."

"Just leave me alone, okay?"

• • •

Kerney did a house-to-house canvas of San Geronimo and the surrounding countryside, asking questions about a young Mexican woman who had either lived or worked in the area. Not surprisingly, no one recalled a woman who matched the description Kerney had compiled from the information supplied by Melody Jordan's analysis.

What Kerney did find surprising was the number of new homes in tucked away places. Aside from upscale vacation cabins and summer homes sprinkled throughout the valley, there were houses of year-round residents in several rural subdivisions and on small parcels of land adjoining some of the large ranches.

Very few people were home. But from the number of swing sets, sandboxes, and basketball hoops outside it was clear that working couples with children were migrating to the once remote, rural setting.

North of San Geronimo, above Mineral Springs in the pine forest at the edge of Johnson Mesa, he questioned caretakers at three youth and church summer camps, and came up empty again.

The afternoon wore on as he stopped at the larger ranches in the valley before looping back through San Geronimo and picking up the county road that paralleled the mesa.

He couldn't quite think of the mesa as his land. Not yet. Maybe not ever.

The old stone cabin came into view with a pickup truck parked inside the open gate. He turned in and recognized Nestor Barela walking toward the cabin.

Barela heard the sound of Kerney's vehicle and reversed his direction.

"So, it is the policeman who now owns the Fergurson land," Barela said when Kerney approached. His tone wasn't friendly.

"Mr. Barela," Kerney replied.

"I do not like being made to a seem a fool," Barela said. "You came to my house under false pretenses."

"I saw no need at the time to tell you who I was."

"Because you suspected me of wrong-doing?"

"The thought crossed my mind."

"And now?"

"I haven't reached any conclusions," Kerney replied.

"I would never spoil this land."

"I'm not saying you did. Why are you here, Mr. Barela?"

"To see for myself what was done." Barela gestured at the cabin. "The wood covering the door must be replaced, and the gate must be locked."

Kerney shook his head. "Not until the police investigation is concluded. When it is, I'll close the cabin up, buy a lock for the gate, and give you a key."

"When will that be?"

"It could be days, maybe a week."

"Make sure you do as you promise," Barela said, turning away abruptly.

Kerney watched as the old man got into his truck, wondering why Barela even cared about a worthless structure on the verge of collapse.

He closed the cabin door, got a CRIME SCENE warning placard out of his unit, and taped the warning on the door. He taped another placard to the gate and closed it before leaving.

• • •

Emmet Griffin opened the door to the Horse Canyon Ranch foreman's residence holding a bowl of stew in one hand. Kerney displayed his shield, identified himself, and asked for a few minutes.

"I thought you might be a cop," Griffin said as he motioned with his head for Kerney to enter.

"What gave me away?"

Griffin padded across the hardwood floor in his stocking feet. A pair of cruddy work boots were carefully placed on some newspapers by the door.

"I used to talk the talk, and walk the walk. Spent five years as a deputy sheriff in Texas before deciding working with animals was a hell of a lot safer." Griffin sat in a worn wicker armchair with a matching ottoman, pulled the ottoman close, placed the bowl of stew on it, and started eating.

"No lunch," he said between spoonfuls. "You don't mind?"

"Not at all."

Besides the chair and ottoman, the only other furniture in the room consisted of a small TV on a low table and a floor-to-ceiling pole lamp with three light canisters that was right out of the 1950s.

"One of your officers stopped by earlier," Griffin said. "A Sergeant Gonzales. He was asking about Rudy Espinoza."

"What did you tell him?"

"That I had to let him go because he wasn't worth a damn. About a week after he started, we began losing things." Griffin paused to wipe his mouth on a shirtsleeve. "I didn't pay much mind to it at first. Stuff can get misplaced. But when a couple of good saddles turned up gone, I fired him."

"Did he admit to taking the saddles?"

"No."

"Did you report it to the sheriff's office?"

Griffin laughed. "A lot of good that did. The deputy came out and took a report. End of story."

"Did you ever actually catch Espinoza stealing?"

"Nope. But I knew the rest of my crew wasn't doing it. They've been with me since I moved over to this job."

"Where were you working before?"

"The Box Z down on the Conchas River."

"Did Espinoza cause any other problems?"

"Not with me."

"With somebody else?" Kerney asked.

"The housekeeper didn't like him. He kept pestering her. She complained to the boss."

"What was he doing?"

"Making excuses to go up to the house, trying to get alone with her—at least that's what she said." Griffin dropped the spoon in the empty bowl. "He wasn't the only one to show interest in her. Luiza attracted men. Cute little thing. Real pretty in a shy sort of way."

"Can you describe her?"

"She was about five four, in her mid-twenties. Dark hair, dark skin. Her left arm was skinnier than her right arm. She said she broke it when she was a kid."

"Do you know her full name?"

"Luiza San Miguel was her Spanish name. But she was mostly Indian."

"You talk about her in the past tense."

"Yeah, she quit and went home to Mexico. She was from somewhere in Chiapas, the southernmost state, on the border with Guatemala."

"You knew her fairly well?"

"Not really. But my old boss at the Box Z gave her a good recommendation when she came to work here." Griffin took his bowl into the kitchen, returned, brushed the dirt off his boots, and pulled them on.

"Did you work with her at the Box Z?"

Griffin shook his head. "Nope, she didn't start there until after I left."

"When did she quit working here?"

"Soon after I fired Espinoza. Sometime in April last year."

"Did she give a reason for leaving?"

"Not to me. Maybe the boss knows."

"Where is your boss?"

"Santa Fe," Griffin said as he reached for his work jacket. "Won't be back until late tonight."

"What about tomorrow?"

"She'll be here all day, far as I know," Griffin replied. "I can't say I liked Rudy much, but I sure didn't wish him dead. You boys are taking some shit about that shooting."

Kerney held out a business card. "Please give Ms. Bingham my card. Tell her I'll stop by to speak with her in the morning."

"I'll do that." Griffin took the card and stuck it in his jacket pocket.

• • •

Kerney inserted his card key in the electronic lock and walked down the empty corridor past silent offices. The majority of the civilian workers and headquarters staff was gone for the day, but lights were on in the vestibule to the crime lab. He thought about checking in with Melody Jordan—if she was still working—but decided he had no reason to do so, and walked up the stairs to his second-floor office.

Kerney often worked late to compensate for his totally nonexistent social life. Tonight he was even less inclined to go home. The place would only seem more empty than usual with the departure of Sara and the dog.

A message that Andy Baca had called from Florida was taped to the handset of his telephone. He called Andy, who was about to leave for a cocktail party at the convention center, and enlightened him on the events of the week.

He rang off after reassuring Andy that everything was under control, and started in on the paperwork. He was halfway through a proposed plan for a narcotics raid when his telephone rang.

"Good, you're there," Melody Jordan said when he answered. "I've got something to show you, Chief."

"Come up."

"See you in a minute."

Kerney's attempt to refocus on the plan failed as his gaze kept wandering to the open office door. He thought about asking Melody to join him for a drink.

Since he did not directly supervise Melody, it would not violate policy to do so.

Why not? Kerney thought. He was a free man with no obligations, and the company of a pretty woman might be the right tonic for his blues.

Melody walked in just as he forced his attention back to the text. She wore a black V-neck top under a waist-length lightweight jacket and a short pleated skirt that accentuated her trim figure.

He put the report aside and smiled. "What have you got?"

"Test results on the bones," Melody replied, "confirming Dr. Lawrence's assessment. The victim suffered from rickets. That strengthens the possibility she was Latin American."

"That's good to know. Are you heading out?"

"You bet." Campbell Lawrence was waiting for Melody. He'd proved to be a very horny man, and she was enjoying every minute of it.

"So am I," Kerney said, standing up. "Do you have time to join me for a drink?"

"That's a lovely idea, but I'm afraid I can't tonight. Rain check?"

"Let me know when you're free."

"Sure thing."

Melody smiled, thinking that when it came to men in her life it was either feast or famine. Still, she felt pleased with the notion that she'd finally turned Kerney's head.

Melody left and Kerney tried without success to concentrate on work. He finally gave up and put the document away. He'd felt both annoyed and relieved when Melody turned down his invitation. He tried to think it through, but nothing came except a vague, dissatisfied feeling.

He stepped to the office door and hit the light switch. He had to get back into sync. Somehow, he didn't think that would be easy to do.

8

Sara woke to the aroma of coffee and found herself on Susie's couch covered with a lightweight throw. She sat up and looked at the night sky through the picture window. The lights of Tucson flickered, flowed, and gathered along the major roads and highways that bisected the desert floor.

She combed her fingers through her hair and found Susie in the kitchen, stirring a pot of pasta. "What time is it?"

"Almost dinnertime," Susie answered. "Welcome back to the living."

"When did I fall asleep?"

"About three o'clock this afternoon, right in midsentence."

"Can I help?"

"Pour yourself some coffee and sit yourself down. Warning: I only brew leaded sludge."

Sara got coffee, sat at the Shaker-style table, and watched Susie spear a green bean out of the pot and taste it.

"A few more minutes," Susie said, turning to face Sara. "This is simple fare. I'm not much of a cook."

"What were we talking about before I lost it?"

"Your extraordinary discovery of an honest man." Susie brought over some flatware and place mats, and arranged them on the table. "If you decide you don't want Kerney, would you arrange an introduction for me?"

Sara laughed. "He sounds that good, does he?"

"He sounds yummy," Susie said, putting a salad bowl between the place mats. "Tonight's menu is store-bought spaghetti sauce, frozen green beans, and salad with bottled dressing. However, I did cook the pasta to perfection."

"You're quite domestic."

"That's not where my charm lies," Susie said as she strained the pasta. "Nor yours. Do you really think you can't be a career officer, mother, and a wife?"

"I could handle two out of three fairly well."

"So, which one goes by the boards?" Susie asked as she slid into a chair and handed Sara a plate of food.

"I haven't a clue."

"Why not have it all?"

"I don't think Kerney would be willing to follow me around from post to post for the next ten years. Besides, neither of us discussed getting married."

"Maybe you haven't mentioned the M word to him. But you've come close, with all that talk of a stud book and getting pregnant."

Sara poked into the pasta and twisted it around the prongs of her fork. "I guess I have."

"You amaze me."

"Why?"

"You have one of the best tactical minds of any serving officer I know, and yet you don't have the foggiest notion of how to reel Kerney in."

"I'm not sure I want to be that calculating. I don't see you baiting the hook when it comes to men."

"Oh, you're so wrong. I'm just waiting for the right one to swim by."

"Okay, how would you reel Kerney in?"

"I'd ask him flat out if he's interested in marriage."

"I don't know if I'm ready to do that," Sara replied as she stabbed a green bean.

"Why not?"

Sara placed her fork on the edge of her plate. "I'm not the wife type."

"You're sure of that?"

Sara picked up her fork and then placed it back on the plate. "I don't know if I'm sure of anything anymore."

"That's promising."

"You think so?"

"Do you care for Kerney?"

"I feel more connected to him than any man I've ever known."

Susie shook her head and her chestnut hair covered her eyes. She brushed it away and grinned. "Jesus, Sara. Listen to yourself."

"I guess I'm confused."

"Finally, we're getting somewhere," Susie said. "Eat your dinner."

• • •

Ruth Pino removed her reading glasses, rubbed the bridge of her nose with a thumb, closed her notebook, and glanced at her wristwatch. Dinnertime had come and gone, and by now her ever tolerant husband had their two boys bathed and ready for bed.

The morning's chance encounter with Nestor Barela had turned out to be serendipitous. He had guided Ruth and her team to another site in the narrow valley away from the alluvial fan, where a large, undisturbed colony of Knowlton's cactus thrived. The sight of it nearly made Ruth shiver with delight.

She had no classes to teach tomorrow and would be back in the valley at first light with her graduate students. There was an incredible amount of mapping and census taking yet to be done.

To protect the plants adequately a good square mile of land, perhaps more, would be needed for a preserve. Although he had no legal responsibility to do so, Mr. Barela had volunteered to supply all the fencing material to temporarily protect the two separate sites.

She would tell Kevin Kerney about Barela's generosity the next time they spoke.

Ruth reached for her address book, and dialed Reese Carson's home telephone in Santa Fe. Reese handled all land protection programs for the New Mexico Nature Conservancy.

"Reese, Ruth Pino. I thought you might like to come up to Las Vegas tomorrow for the day."

Reese groaned. "Is this another last-minute plea to get me to lecture to your undergraduates?"

"No, I've found something I think you might like to see."

"Don't keep me hanging, Ruth. Tell me what you've got that would be worth my time."

"Knowlton's cactus," Ruth said with a smile as she settled back in her chair.

"You're joking."

"Outside San Geronimo."

"You're serious."

"Completely."

"Jesus, you know what you've got?"

"You bet I do."

Gabe turned off the shower, dried himself quickly, pulled on a pair of jeans and a lightweight sweatshirt, and slipped his feet into a pair of shower clogs.

A full day of fieldwork hadn't gotten him anywhere. He had half a mind to confront Joaquin Santistevan directly and put the squeeze on him about Rudy Espinoza. What held Gabe back was the nagging idea that Boaz hadn't been killed simply to cover up the wood theft. There had to be more to it than that. For now, he would keep digging and let Santistevan think he had nothing to worry about.

As Gabe walked downstairs he decided to follow up on Angie Romero's interesting tidbit about Joaquin's involvement with another woman during his separation from his wife. He found Orlando at the kitchen table looking through his open briefcase.

"What are you doing?" Gabe snapped.

Orlando closed the briefcase and turned to face his father. "Nothing."

"You know better than to mess with my stuff."

"Sorry. I was just . . ."

"Just what?"

"Interested, that's all."

Gabe pulled the briefcase off the table and studied his son. Orlando kept his eyes glued on the tabletop.

"You shot Rudy Espinoza," Orlando said.

"Don't you dare tell anyone about that," Gabe replied as he sat.

"People are already saying you did it. Are you going to lose your job?"

"No."

Orlando shifted nervously in his chair. "You could retire."

"Not while you're in school."

"I've been thinking about transferring to another school for my senior year."

"Why? You've got just a little more than a year until you graduate."

"I'm bored. The classes are too easy. There's no challenge."

"For chrissake, you're on the dean's list. Where would you go?"

"Albuquerque."

"And live with your mother?"

"Maybe."

"Have you talked to her about it?"

"Not yet."

"Will all your credits transfer?"

"I don't know. I just know I'm bored with school here and sick of living in Las Vegas."

Gabe let out a sigh. "You're over twenty-one and I can't make you stay, but I think it's a dumb move at this stage."

"I'm not asking for your advice or help. I plan to do it on my own."

Gabe shook his head, mostly as a reminder to himself to stop arguing with his son. "Do what you think is best. But let's talk about this again later, okay?"

"You wouldn't be pissed at me?"

"No."

"You sure?"

Gabe reached over and rumpled his son's hair. "I'm sure. But I'll miss you if you leave."

"Me, too."

"Do you still have that baseball card collection?"

"Yeah, it's in my closet. What made you think about that?"

"It flashed through my mind a couple of days ago, and I remembered all the time we spent looking for those hard-to-find cards you just had to have. You were nuts about those cards."

"Yeah." Orlando forced a smile and glanced at the briefcase. "Are you still mad at me for looking through your stuff?"

"No. Just keep what you read to yourself, and don't be sneaky, okay? I'd rather have you ask."

Orlando stood up. "Okay. I work from six to midnight."

Gabe checked the wall clock. "Well, you better go flip those burgers."

"The job sucks."

"Which makes finishing college all the more important."

"I'm going to finish, Dad. Just not here."

"It sure sounds that way."

"Later."

"Yeah."

Orlando left and Gabe stared at the wall while reality bit him in the ass. He knew Orlando's leaving was inevitable, but he'd never imagined it would happen before he finished college. He pushed himself out of the chair, made a sandwich, ate it quickly, went to his bedroom, and put on his shoes and socks. Coming downstairs he could hear his footsteps echo through the house. Maybe he should sell the goddamn place like Orlando suggested, or at least rent it out and move into something smaller.

He grabbed a jacket from the hall closet. Tonight he would hit the bars and work the Santistevan girlfriend angle.

Bernardo opened the car door, climbed into the passenger seat, and gave Orlando a broad smile. "What's up?"

Noise from cars crossing the highway bridge over the train tracks vibrated through the open windows.

"My dad is just working on the Rudy Espinoza shooting, nothing else."

"He blew Rudy away, didn't he?"

"I don't know about that."

Bernardo laughed. "Bullshit."

"Fuck you."

"Is that all you know?"

"Luiza's bones haven't been identified, and the two officers who were working on the case have been reassigned."

"Does that mean they're giving up?"

"I don't know what it means."

"It sounds like it to me."

"Every case stays open until it's solved. I know that much," Orlando said.

"They're never going to solve it," Bernardo said, putting his hand on the door latch. "Stay in touch."

"I don't think so."

"Play it that way, if you want."

Orlando shot Bernardo a hard look. "What we did doesn't bother you, does it?"

"Worrying about it won't change anything."

"That's cold."

Bernardo got out and ducked his head inside the open window. "You sure you don't want to keep your eyes and ears open, just in case?"

Orlando shook his head. "I'm out of it."

"Suit yourself."

"Just split, Bernardo. I'm already late for work."

Except for a dispatcher and one officer who was finishing her end-of-shift paperwork, the district office was empty. Gabe exchanged a few words with the woman, told the dispatcher he'd stopped by to pick up some personal items, and moved on to the shift commander's cubicle he shared with two other sergeants.

He booted up the computer, accessed Motor Vehicle records, typed in Joaquin Santistevan's name, scrolled through the file to the photograph, and printed a copy. The photo came out grainy but usable. He stuck it in his pocket and glanced across the corridor at the vacant assistant commander's office. He wondered if he would ever get to pin lieutenant bars on his collar and move in. Two days ago, his chances for the promotion looked good. Now, maybe they weren't so hot, unless he could tie Rudy Espinoza to the Carl Boaz murder. With Orlando planning to leave home, he wasn't so sure he cared.

He left the office and drove down the main strip, stopping at each bar along the way, showing Santistevan's photo and asking bartenders and customers if they knew Joaquin. None of them did.

He tried the college hangouts near the university with the same results, and decided on one more stop at the Plaza Hotel bar before calling it quits for the night. Inside, two couples—obviously out-of-town hotel guests—were sitting together at a window table that looked out at the plaza, and three men were at the bar watching a basketball game on the wall-mounted television.

He approached the bartender and showed her his shield and Joaquin's picture.

"I know him by sight, not by name," the woman said. "But he doesn't drink here. I haven't seen him for a while."

"Where did you see him?"

"At the monthly singles party. The local paper sponsors it. They use one of the banquet rooms in the hotel. I work them for the extra money."

"When was that?"

"Last year. Maybe April or May, I don't remember exactly. He came three or four times in a row."

"Did you see him connect with anybody?"

The woman laughed as she nodded at a customer holding up an empty beer glass and moved away to refill it.

"Are you kidding?" she said when she came back. "Those singles events are nothing but a feeding frenzy for hustlers of both sexes."

"Do you remember anything about Santistevan?"

"He liked to hit on young, pretty girls."

"How young?"

"Young enough to card if they wanted alcohol."

"Do you know who runs the singles party for the newspaper?"

"Viola Fisher. She coordinates it. Orders the finger food, pays for the banquet room, signs people in when they arrive—that sort of stuff."

"She keeps a roster?"

"Oh, yeah. You can't come to the party unless you take out an ad in the personals. It's in the paper every week. Haven't you seen it?"

"I usually skip over it."

The woman glanced down at Gabe's left hand. There was no wedding ring. "Maybe you should pay more attention. There are a lot of women your age who'd love a shot at you."

"That's good to know."

Kerney's apartment felt cold and looked dingy. He roamed around restlessly, tidying things up, trying not to think about Sara. But that was impossible. He stood in the middle of the small living room disgusted with the way he lived. Seeing Sara had made him want more than a crummy place and an empty bed to sleep in. Sara lit him up inside, and he didn't want to loose her or that feeling.

He was half-asleep on the couch when the telephone rang. He grabbed for it, hoping it was Sara.

"Are you awake?" Dale asked.

"More or less."

"I've been thinking about the partnership idea," Dale said. "I'd really like to do it."

"I don't see how it can happen."

"Why not?"

"I'd have to pay six million dollars in taxes to keep all ten sections. Erma's lawyer figures the payments to the IRS would be over four hundred thousand a year."

"What in the hell have you got on that mesa, a gold mine?"

"It's more like suburban sprawl pushing up land values. Everybody wants five or ten acres of paradise. The real estate developers and some area ranchers are eager to oblige."

"What are you going to do?"

"I haven't decided."

"Sell it," Dale said, "and look for something closer to my spread. Maybe around Carrizozo, or over in the Black Hills. I know a couple of ranchers who might consider a fair offer. I could put you in touch with them."

"That's a thought."

"You don't sound very enthusiastic about the idea."

"I've been distracted lately."

"The murder case?"

"That, and Sara. She showed up at my door Sunday night."

Dale let out a hoot. "No wonder you're distracted. Is she there? Let me talk to her."

"She's come and gone."

"What happened?"

"Damn if I know. I thought everything was going great, then she just up and left."

"Did you two argue?"

"No, she just took off to visit a girlfriend in Tucson. Said she had some thinking to do."

"About what?"

"I don't have a clue."

"You sound pretty low."

"I guess I am. I miss her, Dale. No woman has ever meant as much to me."

"I've been waiting a long time to hear you say that. You need a woman in you life, Kerney, and Sara's the cream of the crop."

"What should I do?"

"Ride it out. She probably just needs some breathing room. Women are like that."

"I hope so."

"I'm telling you the gospel truth."

"I don't want to think about it anymore."

"So let's change the subject," Dale said. "I still think we can put a partnership together."

"We'll talk about it later."

"Jesus, cheer up. She'll be back."

"Yeah." Kerney hung up and headed for the bedroom, hoping he could push Sara out of his mind and get a few hours sleep.

Kerney arrived at Horse Canyon Ranch as the morning sun washed the deep purple off the mountains. He eyed the headquarters as he drove down the paved ranch road, thinking that sooner or later one of those trendy, glossy magazines would undoubtedly feature Alicia Bingham and her marvelous hacienda in an issue on living the good life in northern New Mexico.

It would be a gross distortion of how the local people in the valley lived in their mobile homes, ramshackle farms, and subdivision-type stick houses plunked down in the middle of five-and ten-acre tracts. But it would sell copies, and have people from coast to coast dreaming of piñon logs crackling in a kiva fireplace, sweeping vistas of mountain ranges, and private trophy homes nestled near the wilderness.

His quick and dirty background check on Alicia Bingham had revealed that the woman was an English citizen, part of the Hollywood film scene, divorced, wealthy, and a member of several international horse breeder and riding competition organizations.

He rang the doorbell at the hacienda and waited,

wondering what, other than a love of horses, had drawn Alicia Bingham to New Mexico.

Alicia Bingham opened the door and studied the man standing under the portal at her front door. Tall, with wide, square shoulders, brown hair touched with gray at the sideburns, and keen, deep blue eyes, he was quite good looking.

She took the business card from his hand and glanced at the policeman's badge held up for her inspection.

"Griffin said you might be stopping by for a chat," Alicia said. "Do come in, Chief Kerney."

Kerney stepped inside the vestibule. Along one wall stood a large flowered vase used for umbrella storage. A pair of Wellingtons sat under a coat rack that held an assortment of rain gear, jackets, and barn coats. A three-legged occasional table opposite the coat rack contained fresh-cut flowers in a blue-and-white milk pitcher, a ceramic table lamp, and an assortment of family photographs in gold frames.

He followed Alicia Bingham into the living room. Oriental rugs were scattered around the floor, family portraits and photographs filled the walls, and chintz curtains in a spring flower print draped the long windows. Deep sofas and chairs, separated by an oversize ottoman used to hold an array of books and magazines, occupied the space in front of a large fireplace. Somehow, the very English decor blended nicely with the clean lines of the double adobe house.

"Join me in the conservatory," Alicia said as she led the way through the room.

Never having seen a conservatory before, Kerney followed along curiously. It turned out to be a sun room used for dining that took full advantage of the morning light. The round gate leg table centered in the middle of the room was antique oak with matching high ladder back chairs. On an exposed adobe wall hung a nineteenth-century sampler made by Marjorie Higgins, age ten. Below an elaborate alphabet and numbers, young Marjorie had embroidered a three-story Georgian mansion surrounded by lush grounds.

"Would you care for some coffee or tea?" Alicia asked as she sat.

"No thank you," Kerney replied, joining her at the table. He made Bingham to be somewhere in her early forties. Dressed in a gray-striped cashmere sweater and designer blue jeans, she had perfect teeth, wide set brown eyes, and short, light brown hair that covered her ears.

"I shouldn't like to rush you, but please ask your questions straight away. I have a very busy morning ahead of me."

"Emmet Griffin said you might know why Luiza left her position."

Alicia Bingham smiled. "I'm afraid during Luiza's time with us I was frantically engaged in so many different projects, I didn't give her very much attention."

"She gave you no reason for leaving?"

"Homesickness certainly was an issue for her. I don't believe she realized that she would be viewed by the local Hispanics more as an Indian than a Latina."

"She felt shunned?"

"I would say so. The locals pride themselves on their Spanish heritage. Many view Mexicans with disdain."

"She made these feelings clear to you?"

"Yes. Luiza spoke passable English. She attended a Baptist missionary school in Chiapas for several years. I was sorry to lose her. She was a very capable housekeeper."

"Did she complain of any inappropriate attention from your male employees?"

"The men flitted around her for a time until I put a stop to it. She was quite an exotic-looking creature."

"She made no complaints about anyone specifically?"

Alicia shook her head. "She simply asked me to keep the men from interrupting her at work."

"Was she more agreeable to their attentions on her free time?"

"Insofar as I could tell, no. She rarely left the ranch when I was here."

"You don't live here full-time?"

"Heavens, no. My ex-husband and I own and operate a special effects studio in Los Angeles. I divide my time between here and California."

"So, you can't say for certain what Luiza did during your absences."

"Griffin would have advised me of any concerns or issues. There were none as far as I know."

"Did Luiza leave suddenly?"

"Yes, but that's not uncommon with immigrant workers. They tend to come and go without much warning."

"Did she have a green card?"

"Yes. I follow the immigration rules carefully, Chief Kerney. As an Englishwoman, I certainly do not wish to violate any American laws that would jeopardize my permanent resident status."

"You have documentation?"

"In my files."

"Did Luiza leave any personal belongings behind?"

"As a matter of fact, she did. A box of clothing, most of which I had passed along to her. We were almost the same size. I still have them stored in the garage. I expected that she would write to have the box sent along by post, but I never heard from her."

"I'd like to see it."

"Of course."

"And the immigration forms for Luiza, if it's no bother."

"I'll get them for you." Alicia rose, left the room, and returned with a slim folder.

Kerney read through it quickly. It looked to be in order. "May I borrow this for a day or two?"

"Yes."

"If you don't think it too personal, may I ask what brought you to New Mexico?"

Alicia smiled. "When I was a young girl, I had a darling great-uncle who was in his nineties. He was my absolute favorite member of the family. He was the youngest son of a minor peer who struck out for America early in the century. Quite a few of the lads without hopes of inheriting did so during the waning years of the empire. He came to New Mexico and worked on a cattle ranch before World War I. He told such glorious stories of his adventures, I just knew someday I would have to live here."

"And now here you are," Kerney noted.

"Exactly. And loving it. Now, Chief Kerney, you must tell me something. What is this interest you have in Luiza?"

"She may have been raped and murdered."

"May have been?"

"Yes. We're still trying to identify a victim."

Alicia nodded. "Is this about the skeleton that was found last weekend?"

"Yes."

Alicia's expression turned serious. "I do hope your assumption about Luiza is wrong. It's chilling just to think about it."

"Do you have a photograph of Luiza?"

"No, I don't think so." Alicia held up a finger. "On second thought, perhaps I do. Not a photograph, actually. Come along with me."

She led Kerney out of the conservatory, through the living room, and into a media room equipped with comfortable chairs for a dozen people, a large-screen television, and expensive video camera equipment.

"We videotape our horses as part of the training program," she said, opening a cabinet. Inside were dozens of cassettes neatly stacked on shelves. "Sometimes Luiza would watch. I believe there are one or two tapes that show her clearly."

She searched through the cassettes, pulled one out, put it in a playback machine, and turned on the TV.

"Yes, this is the one," Alicia said, as she fast-forwarded

through a dressage exercise with a gray gelding. "That's Highland Boy. He'll compete in the next summer Olympics."

She pressed the remote control and the motion returned to normal speed. Luiza quickly came into view as the rider finished up with Highland Boy and turned him toward the paddock gate.

Alicia froze the frame. "Quite a lovely face."

Kerney nodded in agreement. Luiza had long jet-black hair, thick eyelashes, and delicate, almost Eurasian features. From the neck down her figure was full, with a tiny waist and wide, inviting hips. "May I borrow the tape?"

"Surely." She popped it out of the machine and handed it to Kerney. "Griffin told me that you asked him about the Barela grazing rights to the Fergurson property."

"I did."

"Are you both a policeman and a rancher?"

"In a small way. I understand you may be interested in buying the property."

"I would love to protect this side of the valley from the encroachment of subdivisions and summer homes. I'm sure Great-Uncle Howard would approve."

"I'm sure he would," Kerney said as he stood.

"Let me show you where Luiza's possessions are stored," Alicia said as she checked her wristwatch. "And then I must fly away."

She escorted Kerney to the garage, pointed out the box, and left him to search though its contents. He took it off the shelf, placed it on the hood of a green Jaguar sedan, and cut the packing tape with his pocketknife.

Inside there was nothing but clothes. He checked all the pockets and found only a hairpin and a crumpled chewing gum wrapper.

Disappointed, he closed the box, put it away, and looked around the three bay garage. It was finished, insulated, heated, and at least twice the size of his apartment. Along with the Jaguar, Bingham owned a top of the line Range Rover and a four-wheel-drive pickup truck, all in cherry condition.

He walked to his vehicle and saw Alicia Bingham leading a fine-looking saddled mare into a training paddock.

She waved to him cheerily, closed the gate, mounted the mare, and guided the horse over a series of fences and a water jump. She rode beautifully.

Emmet Griffin wandered out of the horse barn, threw a foot up on the fence, and watched his boss put the mare through her paces. Kerney joined him.

"Are you making any progress?" Griffin asked. He opened a tin of chewing tobacco and put a pinch in his mouth.

"It's hard to say. Did Luiza give notice before she quit?"

"Nope. She just left."

"How did she leave?"

"She walked away."

"Didn't you think that was unusual?"

"Not at the time. She didn't know how to drive, and most evenings, if the weather was nice, she'd go for a walk. She liked to walk."

"Was she carrying anything when she left?"

"Not that I noticed."

"Where would she walk to?"

"Mostly down to Ojitos Frios."

"Was she visiting somebody in the village?"

"I don't know."

"How was she dressed that evening?"

Griffin shrugged. "Jeans, some sort of top, I think. That's usually what she wore."

"Did she ever hitch rides?"

"Only with people she knew from the ranch."

"You're sure of that?"

"Yeah. Couple of times I'd be on the road and see some guy in front of me trying to pick her up. She'd wave him off."

"What exactly did she say to you before she left?"

"That she was going home. At the time I didn't think she meant right that minute."

"Who was here that day?"

"Me, my crew, and Richard, the boss's son. The boss was in Los Angeles that week. Richard brought a friend from college with him for the weekend, a girl."

"Tell me about Richard."

"He goes to college down in Santa Fe. He comes up on weekends, when school is out, and during summer vacations. He's twenty. A good kid."

"Did Richard ever come on to Luiza?"

"Richard doesn't like girls that way, if you get my drift."

"When did Richard and his friend leave?"

"Soon after Luiza did."

"What was his friend's name?"

"Nancy something."

"Does Richard live on campus?"

"No, Alicia bought him a condo in Santa Fe."

"Do you have the address?"

"Yeah, but I'd rather you got that information from the boss. I'm sure she won't mind telling you."

Gabe arrived at the newspaper office promptly at eight in the morning and waited for Viola Fisher to show up for work. A big-boned woman with a round, cheerful face, Fisher entered her office at eight-fifteen.

"The receptionist said you were a policeman."

Gabe had his badge case ready. Fisher took it and studied the credentials before giving it back.

"How can I help you?"

"I'd like information on Joaquin Santistevan. He attended some of your singles parties last year."

"The name rings a bell." Fisher turned to the file cabinet behind the desk, pulled out a stack of papers, and ran a finger down the pages. "Yes, here he is. He came to our Valentine's Day event a year ago in February. That's our most popular gathering."

"Was that his first time?" Gabe asked.

"Yes." Viola flipped through more papers. "Then he attended in March and April. After that, he stopped coming."

"Do you know if he met somebody?"

"I really couldn't say," Viola replied. "We use a voice mailbox system. A customer places an ad, a voice mailbox number is assigned through our special telephone line, and each person records a brief message. If a caller likes what they hear, they leave a message in return."

"Do you have records of those mailbox assignments?"

"Not unless they are still active. Once a party drops out or makes a connection, the mailbox is reassigned."

"What kind of information do you collect from your customers?"

"Age, address, and phone number. Whatever else a person is looking for romantically is usually spelled out in their recorded message and weekly personal ad."

"I'd like the telephone numbers and names of the women who attended the events from February through April of last year."

"That information is strictly confidential."

"One of those women may be able to help me solve a murder."

"Our policy is very clear. We do not release that information."

"What you're telling me is that some guy can sign up for this dating service you run, rape and murder one of your female customers, and you can't help me because a policy forbids it." Gabe got to his feet and played a bluff card. "Tell your boss I'll get a court order."

Viola looked startled. "Who was murdered?"

"I can't release that information."

Voila raised herself from her chair. "Let me speak to the city editor."

"I'll be happy to wait," Gabe replied.

In five minutes, Viola Fisher returned looking a bit chagrined. "We'll be glad to assist you, Sergeant Gonzales. All we need is your assurance that the information will be used with discretion. We don't want to create any unnecessary anxiety among our customers."

"I'll handle the matter delicately."

"Good," Viola said as she started pulling files.

Gabe left the newspaper building with the names and phone numbers of sixty-eight women. At home, he called the phone company, read off the names and numbers, and asked to have them cross-checked with Santistevan's home phone, the business phone at Buena Vista Lumber and Supply, and the telephone number of Joaquin's uncle, Isaac Medina.

"Is that all?" the phone company supervisor asked sarcastically.

"If you get any hits, I'd like a record of the calls placed by the women, starting in February of last year."

"This is going to take a while, Gabe," the supervisor said.

"Mid-afternoon?" Gabe asked hopefully.

"I'll see what I can do."

Richard Bingham weighed in at no more than 150 pounds on a six-two frame. He had long, curly hair that fell over his forehead, and he was trying hard to grow a mustache. He sat on a chair with a day pack positioned between his knees, busily filling it with textbooks and papers.

He laughed when Kerney questioned him about Luiza.

"Didn't Emmet tell you I'm gay?" he said as he zipped the pack shut.

Kerney didn't respond.

"It's no secret," Richard said. He walked to the Murphy bed, folded it against the wall, and closed the doors that hid it from view.

Bingham lived in a studio condominium of no more than 800 square feet, yet given its location in downtown Santa Fe, Kerney figured it was worth a pretty penny.

"I gotta go," Richard said. "I've got a class."

"Give me a few more minutes," Kerney replied, gesturing at the chair Richard had vacated.

Reluctantly, the boy sat.

"Did anything happen to upset Luiza the day she disappeared?"

"Well, Nancy kind of freaked her out."

"How so?"

"She wanted to get it on with Luiza."

"Nancy's gay?"

"Yeah, and she can be very butch at times."

"What happened?"

"She kept grabbing at Luiza and talking sexy to her."

"Anything else?"

"Luiza slapped her in the kitchen after Nancy grabbed her ass. That chilled Nancy out. Then Luiza split and went to her room."

"When did this happen?"

"About three o'clock in the afternoon."

"Did you see Luiza after the incident in the kitchen?"

"Not until we left the ranch. She was walking down the side of the road, about halfway between the ranch and Romeroville, when we passed her."

"Going in which direction?"

"Toward the interstate."

"Did you stop?"

"No. After what happened we didn't think Luiza wanted to talk to either of us."

"What time was that?"

"It was getting on toward dusk."

"Emmet Griffin said that Luiza never hitched rides with strangers. Did you see anyone on the road who might have given her a lift?"

"No." Richard paused for a moment. "Well, not right away."

"What about later?"

"You know where the pavement ends as you make the turn out of Romeroville heading toward Ojitos Frios?"

"I do."

"Bernardo Barela passed me in his grandfather's pickup."

"Would that be Nestor Barela's grandson?"

"Yeah. He had another guy with him. I didn't know him."

"Did Bernardo recognize you?"

"No. We were in Nancy's new Pathfinder. Her father had just bought it for her."

"Did Luiza know Bernardo?"

"Sure."

"Would she have accepted a ride from Bernardo?"

"If she wanted to get back to the ranch before dark, she might have. I don't know."

"How well do you know Bernardo?"

"Not well. He stops by at the ranch every now and then."

"Did he ever say anything to you about Luiza?"

Richard laughed. "Straight Hispanic dudes don't tend to talk about women with gay men."

"He knows you're gay?"

"Everybody knows." Richard stood up. "It's who I am. I have to go now."

Reese Carson rewound his last roll of film and returned his camera to its case. The day had turned windy and a strong gust coursed down the west slope of the mountains, picked up loose top soil from the clear-cut area, and spun a dust devil up the side of the mesa. As he turned away, his wispy, baby-fine brown hair fluttered in the wind and his red-rimmed gray eyes watered.

"Allergies," Reese said ruefully to Ruth Pino as he sniffled. "What a find you have here. It's absolutely amazing. This is the last place I'd look for Knowlton's cactus."

"I agree," Ruth said. She wiped some dust from her own eyes and watched as her graduate students moved slowly across the clear-cut area. The Knowlton's cactus census was complete—over eight thousand plants had been counted at the two separate sites—and now other indigenous plants were being studied and recorded. "But if you compare soil samples, plant life, and elevation to the San Juan County preserve, it's almost a perfect ecosystem match."

"You mean it *was* a match," Reese replied. The devastation of the woodlands turned his stomach. "This site is a disaster waiting to happen. And you could lose the second site when the erosion spreads down the valley."

"We have to move fast," Ruth said. "Spring runoff in

the canyon is going to wash away more of the alluvial fan." She pointed to the mesa. "And summer storms will cut more erosion furrows down from the ridgeline. It will be a double whammy."

Reese nodded glumly in agreement.

"Protecting the site is essential," Ruth added. "We need to restore the riparian vegetation along the streambed, reforest the woodlands, and stop the accelerated runoff."

"And fence it," Reese said.

"That's a given. Actually, we need a series of fences. One for each site and then a perimeter fence."

"How much of a perimeter?"

"If I could, I'd do the whole ten sections," Ruth answered. "The ranches east of the county road are being subdivided and sold off. Eventually, development could spread right to the national forest boundary."

"Is the leaseholder willing to keep his livestock out of the area?"

"He is, and he's willing to supply the materials so we can do some immediate fencing."

"That will help," Reese said.

"What about money to buy the property?"

"Slow down, Ruth. That isn't going to happen overnight."

"Like hell, slow down."

"We don't even know what the new owner is willing to consider."

"What can we offer him as an incentive?"

"For now, our assistance. If you're willing to complete the floral and plant community survey, I'll get a hydrologist out here to map out an emergency erosion control plan."

"When?" Ruth asked.

"This week. And I think the state forestry division would be willing to donate seedlings. I can get a volunteer crew to do the planting."

"How fast can you move?"

"I'll get on it right away. Since the land adjoins the national forest, the feds might be willing to help out."

"Putting a Band-Aid on this isn't going to solve the problem."

"I know it. I'll call my chapter board members when I get back to the office, explain the situation, and ask for authorization to begin negotiations with the owner. It shouldn't be a problem. I'll need to borrow your field notes and plant and analysis charts."

"They're in rough draft form and incomplete."

"It doesn't matter. After I get the board's permission to move, I'll need to sit down with the owner and find out if he's willing to work with us."

"He will be." Ruth reached into her back pocket and handed Reese a folded piece of paper.

"What's this?"

"A check for a thousand dollars. I took the money out of my oldest son's college fund. It's for this project only."

"You don't have to do this."

"I want those volunteers here next week and the seedlings on hand for planting." Ruth waved in response to a call from one of her students and started to walk away.

"Anything else, Dr. Pino?" Reese called after her.

Ruth turned and smiled. "We're going to have a post-setting, wire-stringing party this weekend. Bring the family, your camping gear, and enough food for two days."

"You are something," Reese said.

"Is that an RSVP?"

"I'll be here."

9

Although Carl Boaz's cabin had been thoroughly tossed during the original search, Gabe felt he'd missed something. If Boaz's journal truly reflected the amount Rudy Espinoza had agreed to pay for access to the woodcutting area, Boaz had settled for chump change.

It was hard to believe Boaz had been that stupid. Boaz had a doctorate, and had put together a sophisticated marijuana production scheme that might have gone undetected if Rudy hadn't blown him away.

Beyond that, Gabe still couldn't figure out why Rudy had iced Boaz. Why would Rudy want to kill a conspirator in what amounted to nothing more than a low-grade felony? Assuming Rudy knew about the marijuana cultivation, wouldn't he think Boaz had every reason to keep his mouth shut about the wood poaching?

He checked the time. He had hours before the phone company records on the women who attended the singles parties would be ready. He searched every

nook and cranny of the cabin, the greenhouse, and
Boaz's truck, looking for hiding places that might have
been missed. He tore out sections of the cabin walls,
shoveled topsoil out of the greenhouse nursery tables,
and stripped the interior of the truck down to the
metal. He found nothing.

Frustrated, Gabe leaned against the front fender of
the truck, and scanned the meadow and the buildings
waiting for inspiration. What was he missing? He was
about to give up when his gaze settled on the gas-powered electric generator installed on a concrete pad
halfway between the cabin and the greenhouse.

He walked to it and took a closer look. The generator, expensive and fairly new, sat on two long metal run-
ners that were bolted to the pad. He found the manufacturer's plate and a metal tag from an electrical supply
company in Lubbock, Texas.

Why would Boaz buy a generator from a company
hundreds of miles away when he could get the same
item locally? He wrote down the information, went to
the greenhouse, and climbed on the roof to inspect the
bank of south-facing solar panels. All of them were
tagged by the same Lubbock company.

At the water well, he disconnected the power supply,
removed the housing cover, pulled up the submersible
pump, and found another tag from the Lubbock supply
house.

In the cabin, Gabe sat at the table and went through
Boaz's cancelled checks, cash purchase receipts, and lists
of expenditures for construction costs he'd checked out
of the district office evidence room. Boaz had kept

detailed records of his costs to get the operation up and running. None of the items from Lubbock showed up as purchases.

Gabe looked around the cabin. The propane refrigerator and the propane stove looked new. He ran through Boaz's records again and found no documentation for the purchase of either item.

Where did Boaz get all this stuff?

He pulled the stove and refrigerator away from the wall, wrote down the make, model, and serial numbers, and used his cellular phone to call Russell Thorpe.

"Where are you?" Gabe said, when Thorpe answered.

"Lunch break at the Roadrunner."

"I need you to run some information through NCIC. Have you got a pen and paper?"

"Roger that."

Gabe read off the make, model, and serial number for each item and had Thorpe repeat the information back to him.

"How soon do you want this, Sarge?"

"ASAP."

"I'll call you right back."

Gabe used the time waiting for Thorpe to call going over Boaz's journal line by line, looking for anything that might give him an insight into the murder.

The phone rang and Gabe answered. "What have you got?"

"Three hits, Sarge. The gas-powered generator, solar panels, and the pump were stolen from a Lubbock electrical supply company. The propane refrigerator was boosted from a freight car on a railroad siding in Amarillo, and the propane cooking stove was taken from an appliance store in Midland, Texas. All within the last year. All major heists."

"Good deal," Gabe said.

"Where did you find this stuff?" Thorpe asked.

"I'll tell you later."

"You got something else you need me to do?"

"I'll call you back," Gabe said as he hurried out the cabin door to his vehicle. Angie Romero had a large-screen television in her living room that he wanted to check out.

Angie opened the front door a crack and gave Gabe a sour look. "What is it?"

"Can I come in?" Gabe asked

"What for?"

"We need to talk about your car."

"When do I get it back?" Angie asked, swinging the door wide.

"Tomorrow," Gabe said, stepping inside.

Angie's smell almost made him retreat to the front porch. She wore a frayed bathrobe, dingy gray pajamas, and a pair of tattered slippers. She ran a shaky hand through her tangled hair and looked at Gabe with blood-shot eyes.

"Mind if I look at your television?" Gabe asked as he walked to the set that stood against a wall.

"Why?"

"Did Rudy buy it?" Gabe pulled the set away from the wall.

"He gave it to me as a present."

"When?" Gabe found the manufacturer's information and wrote it down.

"You can't do that," Angie said as she crossed the room.

Gabe pushed the set back to its original position. "When did Rudy bring home the TV, Angie?"

"Maybe six months ago. You can't come in here and paw through my property."

"Where did Rudy buy it?"

"I don't know. He just brought it home one day."

Angie's closeness made her smell almost unbearable. Gabe moved quickly toward the open door. "Sorry to bother you."

Angie followed at his heels. "I want my car back."

"Tomorrow, Angie." Gabe stepped off the porch.

"It damn well better be here."

"It will be," Gabe said with a smile.

He called Thorpe with the information on the television as soon as he was out of Angie's driveway.

Thorpe called back just as Gabe pulled onto the interstate.

"The TV was stolen from the same store in Midland where the stove was boosted," he reported.

"Ten-four. Get me complete reports from the Texas authorities on all three heists."

"What have you got, Sarge?"

"I'll let you know as soon as I figure it out. Do one more thing for me."

"What's that?"

"Have Angie's Mustang towed back to her house tomorrow morning."

"That car can't be driven until it's fixed. The front end is totalled."

"I know it."

Before leaving for his class, Richard Bingham provided Kerney with his friend Nancy's full name and address. The girl lived in a dormitory on the college campus.

A private institution with a small enrollment, the school was situated in the Santa Fe foothills. The nearby mountains, million-dollar homes, and an adjacent private prep school insulated the campus and its carefully tended grounds.

Kerney found Nancy Rubin in her dorm room, introduced himself, and asked a few questions. No more than nineteen years old, Nancy had a slim, lanky body, short curly blonde hair, and a heavy New York accent. She wore three diamond studs in her right earlobe.

The girl confirmed Richard's version of the events at the ranch involving Luiza, and Kerney left feeling fairly certain that he'd gotten candid answers.

In Las Vegas, Kerney stopped at the county sheriff's office and got directions to the Box Z Ranch, where Luiza San Miguel had once been employed. The route took him along a state highway that cut through high, rolling plains and onto a narrow two-lane road that provided a panoramic view of the mountains. Where the dun-colored plains ended, massive, dark opal peaks swept beyond the limits of perception and faded into a rippling, miragelike vagueness.

The road curved away from the view and Kerney

saw the first sign of a deep trough that pierced the hilly grasslands. Soon he was hugging the lip of a canyon that cut a thousand feet below the plains and opened out in a widening valley flanked by red-rimmed table-top mesas.

The pavement turned to dirt, and the road crossed and recrossed a rocky, shallow river, and then rose to expose an expanse of rangeland that seemed to push back the mesas. After navigating a boulder-strewn bypass bulldozed around the remnants of a washed-out wooden bridge, Kerney topped out at a small rise, and stopped to take a look around.

Ten miles south, a lone butte towered where the canyon lands ended. Stands of piñon and juniper trees peppered lush pastures filled with bluestem and Indian rice grass. Patches of spring wildflowers threw color against the foot of the mesas.

Kerney drove toward the butte, taking it all in. Here the land dominated, making the small herds of cattle moving across the valley look like dots; turning the ranch road into a vague incision that faded away to nothing in the distance; putting fences, windmills, feed troughs, and stock tanks into a perspective that made man's efforts seem inconsequential.

Sheltered at the foot of the butte, the Box Z head-quarters was surrounded by groves of cottonwood trees. The houses, barns, sheds, outbuildings, and cor-rals were made of rock and in perfect condition. Behind the barn stood a pitched-roof garage with a red 1930s gasoline pump off to one side. The main ranch house was a two-story Queen Anne Victorian. The roofline was broken by two shingled dormers, and round columns supported the deep front porch.

The man who opened the front door wore a straw cowboy hat pushed back to reveal a high forehead and eyeglasses with plastic frames. Somewhere in his sixties, he had straight lips beneath a pudgy nose and deep creases in his cheeks that ran down to his chin.

"I'm looking for the owner," Kerney said.

"You found him," the man replied, glancing at Kerney's open badge case. "I'm Arlin Fullerton. What brings you out this way, Officer?"

"I have a few questions to ask you about Luiza San Miguel."

"Is something wrong?"

"I just need to find her," Kerney replied.

"She took a job last year at Horse Canyon. My wife sure hated to lose that girl," Arlin said. "If she's not there, I don't know where she's working now. We haven't kept track of her. Have you checked at Horse Canyon?"

"Yes. What was her reason for leaving the Box Z?"

"She just decided to move on, I guess."

"Did you hear from her after she left?"

"We got a card from her sometime back."

"What did it say?"

"Just that she liked her new job."

"How did you come to hire her?"

"I pay a fair wage, but not too many locals—especially the younger ones—want to work six days a week on a remote ranch. So most of my employees are Mexican. They've got their own grapevine when it comes to finding work. My wife was looking for a housekeeper when Luiza showed up."

"How did she learn about the job?"

"Word of mouth would be my guess."

"Not one of your employees?"

"She didn't know a soul when she started here."

"Did Luiza talk about herself or her family in Mexico?"

Fullerton shook his head. "Not much. She's a shy girl. Quiet. Keeps to herself."

"Did she have any clashes with other employees? Any friction, disagreements, dissension?"

"Not that I know about. She was pretty even tempered. Got along with everybody."

"Everybody?"

"Except when she got pestered."

"Who pestered her?"

"Well, it wasn't pestering to start; it was more like skirt chasing. One of the neighboring ranch boys took a shine to her. Luiza didn't like him at all. But the kid wouldn't take no for an answer. It really got Luiza's back up."

"What's the kid's name?"

"Bernardo Barela. He works on the next spread over with his uncle."

"Nestor Barela's grandson?"

"That's him."

"How do I get to their place?"

"Take the left fork out of my gate and follow the road ten miles due west. They use an old homestead as their line camp. You can't miss it. They come down from Las

Vegas most days. You should find them there. They borrowed my bulldozer this morning to do some road work."

"Thanks."

"Mind telling me what this is all about?"

"You've got a nice place here, Mr. Fullerton," Kerney said as he turned and stepped away. "Thanks, again."

At home, Gabe waited restlessly for Russell Thorpe to deliver the burglary reports that the Texas law enforcement agencies had faxed to the district office. Now that Orlando had announced his intentions to move away, the house seemed too big, and Gabe felt vaguely uncomfortable in it.

Thorpe arrived and hung around with an eager look on his face, hoping to learn what was up. Gabe thumbed through the papers, verified that the stolen items matched the information out of Texas, and looked at Thorpe.

"Go recover the stolen property at Boaz's cabin, and see what else you can find," he said.

Thorpe could barely contain a grin. "How do I keep you out of it?"

"If anyone asks, say you got an anonymous tip. Also, write up a search warrant for Angie Romero's house, get it signed, and toss the place. Take somebody with you. Who is the shift commander on duty?"

"Art Garcia is filling in for you."

"Tell him—and only him—what's up, and ask him to go with you."

"What's my probable cause for the warrant?"

"You have reason to believe that items taken in a Texas burglary are in Angie's house. Cite the Midland Police Department report. Art can help you fill in the blanks."

Gabe waved the Midland Police Department report at Thorpe. "Did you make copies for yourself?"

Thorpe nodded. "You bet."

"Good. Now go do your job."

Thorpe strode through the front door and almost bounced his way down the front porch to his unit. Gabe smiled at Thorpe's rookie enthusiasm, knowing that soon it would get washed away by harsh reality.

He read the reports again. All three Texas burglaries were professional scores, and the MO on each case was nearly identical. He wondered if the cops in West Texas even knew they had a crime ring operating in their backyards. Maybe, maybe not.

The thought slipped away as he reached for the ringing telephone.

Several miles west of the Box Z headquarters the ranch road was freshly graded and crowned. Not yet packed down and compressed, the loose dirt was soft under Kerney's tires, and his vehicle drifted into the old ruts hidden under the fresh topping spread by the bulldozer.

The road took him away from the open rangeland toward a somber line of steep-walled, forested mesas tinged purple and red. In places the mesa cliffs had been scoured bare by rock slides of massive proportions, and large boulders littered the canyon floor.

Halfway to the line camp he passed an unattended bulldozer, and the road became a worn indentation of tracks in ground-up sandstone and powder-dry clay. The road veered toward a blocky rimrock mesa, and the clay and sand gave way to shale and cobbles.

The line camp consisted of a battered mobile home on concrete blocks and a pump shed behind a falling-down single-story house with a spindlework porch. All the windows and doors were missing and part of the brick chimney had crashed through the roof. Across a bare patch of ground, next to a weathered corral containing two saddled mounts, was a horse trailer.

Kerney recognized the truck in front of the mobile home as one of the vehicles he'd seen at Nestor Barela's family compound. The sound of his arrival brought two men out on the three-step, rough-cut stairs to the trailer. The men studied Kerney as he approached the trailer.

The older man stepped down to meet him. Kerney ignored the kid, who had to be Bernardo, and kept his attention fixed on Roque.

Built along the same lines as his father, Roque sported a well-fed belly tightly cinched by a belt. A large silver buckle dug into his midsection.

"You must be really lost," Roque said with a shake of his head.

"I'm Kevin Kerney."

The amused expression vanished from Roque's face. "You're the cop who lied to my father."

"That's one way to look at it."

"What do you want?"

"I'm investigating the disappearance of Luiza San Miguel." Over Roque's shoulder Kerney saw Bernardo stiffen.

"I know the girl," Roque said. "Haven't seen her around. I heard she went back to Mexico."

"You knew her, too, didn't you?" Kerney called out to Bernardo.

"Yeah, I did." A frown line crossed Bernardo's forehead and the corners of his eyes tightened.

Kerney stepped around Roque toward Bernardo. "I understand you were interested in Luiza."

"Me? No way."

"Really?"

Bernardo shrugged. "Yeah, well maybe for a little while. But she wasn't interested in me."

Roque snorted. "That's no lie."

Bernardo shot his uncle a dirty look as he walked down the steps. "So I liked her and she didn't like me. Big deal."

"Was it a big deal?" Kerney asked.

"I don't have to waste my time with babes that don't like me."

"So, it wasn't a big deal."

"That's what I said."

"Did you see her after she went to work at the Horse Canyon Ranch?"

"Yeah, once or twice. But not to talk to."

"How about last April, outside Ojitos Frios, on the road to Romeroville? Did you see her walking?"

Bernardo shook his head.

"Is that a no?"

"No, okay?"

"You were seen on that road in your grandfather's truck with a passenger the day Luiza disappeared."

"Maybe I was, but I don't remember seeing her."

"Who was with you?"

"I don't know, man, that was a year ago. It could have been a lot of people—one of my bros, one of the family, anybody."

"Think back, Bernardo. It was a weekend evening last April. A Saturday." Kerney gave him the exact date. "Do you have any idea what you might have been doing in the area?"

"Going to work, throwing a cruise, giving somebody a ride home. What's the big deal?"

"What would take you to the mesa in the evening?" Kerney closed in on Bernardo. The boy flinched but held his ground.

"Maybe I left the gate unlocked. I could have been going to check it. Maybe we had some cattle on the road. That happens a lot."

"That all makes sense." Kerney moved even closer to break into Bernardo's personal space. He used his height advantage to force Bernardo to raise his head and look him in the eye. "But you didn't see Luiza?"

"I already said that," Bernardo replied, stepping off to one side.

"You'd remember if you did?"

"Sure."

"Look," Roque said, "if Bernardo was driving my father's truck, he was working. That's the only time he gets to use it."

"But it wasn't you in Nestor's truck with Bernardo?" Kerney asked Roque.

"Not likely," Roque said. "I always drive my own truck."

"So, who was riding with you?" Kerney asked Bernardo.

"Like I said, maybe one of my bros," Bernardo said, jamming his hands into the pocket of his jeans. "Maybe I gave somebody a ride. Who said they saw me?"

"Do you remember if you gave somebody a ride that day?"

"This is bullshit," Bernardo said. "Why the fuck are you asking me these questions again? I already answered you."

"I'm just trying to find somebody who may have seen Luiza."

"I didn't see her."

Roque jabbed his finger hard against Kerney's shoulder before he could ask another question. "Don't jack my nephew around because my father won't turn over his lease to you."

"I'm sorry if you have that impression," Kerney said.

"That's the way it sounds to me," Roque said. "You go to my father's house, lie to him about who you are, and now you show up here playing some sort of hard-ass cop game. Just leave."

"Whatever you say," Kerney said as he locked on to Bernardo again. "Did Luiza leave her Box Z job because of you?"

"Because of me? That's crazy."

"We'll talk again," Kerney said, to raise Bernardo's tension. "I'll listen to anything you have to tell me."

Bernardo turned his head, cleared his throat, spit on the ground, and said nothing.

Kerney waited a few beats, nodded good-bye to Roque, gave Bernardo a quick, even stare, and left.

The grandeur of the valley and canyonlands didn't hold Kerney's attention on the drive back. His mind stayed focused on Bernardo. Perhaps the kid had simply made some Don Juan moves on Luiza, got rejected, and—like a lot of young studs—moved on to greener pastures. But too many issues led Kerney away from such a generous conclusion. Bernardo knew the victim, had shown an interest in her, and could be placed near where Luiza had last been seen, on the same day, and at approximately the same time as her disappearance.

More damaging was the fact that some of Luiza's bones had been found on land Bernardo's family controlled. That, coupled with Bernardo's uneasiness under questioning—his body language, his defensiveness, his vague answers—raised Kerney's suspicions. He stopped at the Las Vegas district office and called Emmet Griffin.

"You said you saw Luiza occasionally refuse rides from strangers when she went out walking."

"That's what I said," Griffin replied.

"Did you ever see her refuse a ride from someone she knew?"

"I can't say that for sure."

"Meaning?"

"Once I saw Nestor Barela's grandson driving real slow on the wrong side of the road, talking to her while she was walking. It went on for maybe a minute or two. He spun his wheels and threw up a lot of dust when he left. You know, show-off kid stuff."

"You mean Bernardo?"

"That's the only grandson I know."

"Did you ask Luiza about the incident?"

"No, I didn't think anything of it at the time. She waved and smiled when I drove by. I figured she was just out on one of her evening walks."

Kerney thanked Griffin and hung up. What had Bernardo said at the line camp? He took out the pocket-size microcassette recorder he'd used to surreptitiously tape the conversation with Bernardo and Roque and played it back. On the tape Bernardo said he hadn't talked to Luiza after she started work at Horse Canyon.

According to Emmet Griffin's recollection, that was a lie.

In Anton Chico, Gabe took a look around to familiarize himself with the terrain. The phone company's records showed a customer named Bernadette Lucero had made a number of calls to Buena Vista Lumber and Supply. Bernadette had been a participant in the singles events sponsored by the Las Vegas newspaper.

A cross-check revealed frequent calls from Joaquin Santistevan to Bernadette during the workday from his office phone and late at night from his home. The pattern of calls suggested that Joaquin's reconciliation with his wife hadn't kept him from keeping company with Bernadette.

Anton Chico was Spanish for Little Anthony. Some held that the village was named after one of the original Hispanic settlers, others that it was a corruption of ancón chico, which meant "little bend."

Gabe cast his vote for the little bend theory. The village sat on a gentle rise above the Pecos River where it curved out of a progression of low-lying barrancas and flowed toward the eastern plains. Old cottonwoods graced the wide fields and pastures along the river, and the houses and farms perched above the flood plain were almost all nineteenth-century stone and adobe structures, with a few modern additions tacked on here and there.

Anton Chico and the neighboring settlements were part of a Mexican land grant still controlled by the descendants of the original colonists. Halfway between Las Vegas and Santa Rosa—a city that thrived on the tourist traffic along Interstate 40—the village was off the beaten path, and provided no amenities for travelers.

Aside from a modern public school and a post office housed in a mobile home on a large dirt lot, the village center consisted of old territorial buildings. A mercantile store, a church, a rectory, some traditional long adobe houses with narrow portals, and old stone cottages with tin roofs faced two parallel lanes.

There were no gas stations, motels, restaurants, or markets. Where the lanes converged at the outskirts of the village, the pavement ended, and dirt roads wandered to nearby farmhouses and ranches.

Gabe stopped at the post office and approached the clerk after waiting for several locals to pick up their mail and leave. A round-faced woman with silver hair, she reached for reading glasses that hung from a cord around her neck and studied Gabe's credentials.

"Do you know Bernadette Lucero?" he asked.

"Why do you want to know?"

"She applied for a job as a police dispatcher. We do a background investigation on every job applicant. It's required."

"You must mean Gloria's daughter," the woman said. She removed her glasses and let them dangle against her chest.

"Is there more than one Bernadette Lucero living in Anton Chico?"

"Not as far as I know."

"What can you tell me about her?"

"She's turned into a real good mother since she had the baby."

"How old is her child?"

"About two months. She had a boy."

"Do you know the baby's father?"

The woman shook her head. "Berna isn't married."

"How can I find her?"

"She lives next door to Gloria and Lenny."

"Can you give me a last name?"

"Alarid. Gloria is Berna's mother. She married Lenny after divorcing her first husband."

"What else can you tell me about Berna?"

"She's never been in trouble, as far as I know. She went to college up in Las Vegas for a couple of years, driving back and forth to her classes. She dropped out when she got pregnant."

"How do I get to Berna's house?"

With directions in hand, Gabe sat in his car and thumbed through the quick field notes he'd made after his last visit to Buena Vista Lumber and Supply. Twenty years as a cop had taught him to write everything down, no matter how inconsequential it seemed at the time. Lenny Alarid's name popped up, followed by the notation that he hauled piñon chips to Texas under contract to Buena Vista.

He had no idea how everything would shake out when the dust settled. But he found the developing connections intriguing.

Bernadette Lucero and the Alarids lived behind the church and rectory. A fenced lot enclosed two houses and a free-standing carport large enough for a semitractor. Surrounding the carport was an assortment of large truck trailers, a stack of spare tires, and accumulated junk. A full-size domestic sedan and a pickup truck were parked in front of a pitched roof adobe house. A smaller double-wide manufactured home, with full skirting and an add-on deck, stood nearby. At the front of the deck steps was a late model sport utility vehicle.

Behind the carport, among some cedar trees at the backside of the lot, was an old garage with an attached shed. Next to the shed was a major piñon and juniper woodpile.

Gabe drove past the open gate, turned around, parked between the two homes, and knocked first at the adobe dwelling. After a few minutes and no answer, he tried the manufactured home.

The young woman who greeted him cradled a baby in one arm. She was bright-eyed, wore her long brown hair in soft curls, and was dressed in a dark blue sweatsuit.

"Bernadette Lucero?" Gabe gave her a reassuring smile and flipped his badge case open.

"Yes."

"Do you have time for a few questions?"

"I guess so. About what?"

"May I come in?"

"Sure."

Gabe followed Bernadette inside and waited until she settled on the couch with the baby before sitting across from her.

"What a beautiful baby," he said.

Bernadette's face lit up. "Everybody says that." Holding the infant under his arms, she placed him on her knee facing Gabe.

"You must be very happy."

"I am. He's my little *jito.*" She kissed the baby on the top of his head.

"Does he look like you or like his father?"

"Oh, his father, of course."

"Joaquin must be very proud."

Bernadette's smile vanished. "You know about Joaquin?"

"Don't worry, I won't tell anyone."

"Only my mother and Lenny are supposed to know."

"Debbie doesn't know?"

"Why should she? Besides, Joaquin is leaving her soon."

"Is he going to marry you?"

"In the summer," Bernadette said, her smile returning. She bounced the baby happily on her knee and it gurgled in response.

"I really stopped by to see Lenny."

"Lenny and my mother are out of town. She goes with him sometimes on his short runs."

"I'm sorry I missed him. Maybe you can help me. Did you know Rudy Espinoza?"

"I knew Rudy. He used to cut wood for Lenny."

"Lenny sells wood?"

"He takes truckloads to Texas every fall and sells them there."

"And Rudy supplies the wood?"

"He did last year."

"What kind of truck did Rudy drive?"

"It's in the garage behind the carport. Rudy always left it here. He didn't like to drive it every day because it used too much gas. He just used it mostly when he went woodcutting."

Gabe suppressed a smile. "I hope Joaquin is taking good care of you and the baby."

"He bought me my house, my car, the furniture, and he pays all the bills. He's a good man."

"I bet he is. Joaquin and Lenny must do a lot of business together."

Bernadette nodded in agreement. "He keeps Lenny working a lot."

"A lot?"

"Well, for Lenny it's one of his biggest contracts."

"When will Lenny and Gloria get home?"

"Not until tomorrow sometime."

"Mind if I take a look at Rudy's truck in the garage?"

"Go ahead."

Gabe walked into the garage and let the grin he'd been holding back break across his face as soon as he saw the vehicle. He put on a pair of plastic gloves, opened the truck door and popped the glove box. It contained a handgun. Gabe didn't touch it. He looked closely at the exterior of the doors. On the driver's side was a random pattern of minute brown specks, quite probably Boaz's blood. He checked the tires; the tread pattern matched with those found at Boaz's cabin.

Outside, he called Thorpe on his cell phone.

"We've got a bunch of stolen stuff out of Angie's house," Russell said, before Gabe could start talking.

"Good deal. Is Art Garcia with you?"

"Roger that."

"I want you both down in Anton Chico, pronto, with a crime scene unit. I've found Rudy's truck and the handgun."

"Ten-four." Russell's voice rose in excitement. "Give me your twenty, Sarge."

Gabe gave Thorpe the directions he'd asked for, disconnected, and slipped the phone into his jacket pocket.

It was time to talk to Bernadette again. Since she had been willing to let him in the garage, she just might give him permission to take a look inside Lenny's house.

Gabe figured Bernadette was an innocent, gullible kid with nothing to hide, other than her relationship with Joaquin. He decided the best approach would be to convince Bernadette that Rudy Espinoza was the sole object of his investigation.

A brief conversation with Bernadette yielded a signed form giving Gabe permission to search, and a key to Lenny's front door.

After his phone conversation with Emmet Griffin, Kerney felt he finally had a suspect. He stopped off at a Las

Vegas hardware store, bought a lock and chain for the gate to his property, several tools, and a pair of work gloves. Then he drove out to Erma's old cabin.

All the crime scene activity had occurred on the mesa, and no one had yet searched the cabin for evidence. Dale's discovery of Erma's love letter should have triggered Kerney's interest. He wondered if anything else—like the missing skeletal remains—might be hidden under the rotting hay. It was worth checking.

He got to the cabin and started bailing out the deep, wet layer of hay with a long-handled pitchfork. Two feet down, the prongs struck a solid surface. Kerney scraped a section clean and exposed a partially rotted plank floor.

He kept bailing, throwing the hay out the open door, until the pitchfork prongs twanged against rock. He brushed away the last bit of black decomposed hay, and found the edge of the old fireplace hearthstone. The planking that butted against the stone was warped and saturated with moisture. He dug his fingers under the board and pulled it free. Wood joists for the floor rested on the original hard-packed dirt surface.

He cleaned out the rest of the hay, stood in the center of the cabin, and looked around. All he'd uncovered were the nests of pocket mice and pack rats—no bones.

Except for one small section at the side of the hearthstone, the floor squeaked and sagged under his feet. He took a closer look. The nails holding down four boards were not the same as the others.

He pulled the boards free one at a time and found another rat's nest next to a partially chewed-up, disintegrating cardboard box filled with water-stained faded stationery. Carefully, he peeled away one pulpy sheet, held it up to the sunlight that poured through a hole in the roof, and read the salutation.

Kerney scanned the contents and didn't bother to look for the signature; he recognized the handwriting. He gently removed the cardboard box, carried it to his car, popped the trunk, wrapped the box in a blanket, and put it inside.

He closed the cabin door, drove through the gate, locked it, and headed for Las Vegas. He'd promised Nestor Barela a key to the new gate lock, and it was time to deliver it.

Nestor Barela's living room was a combination of old and new. Two hand-carved, antique pine blanket chests served as side tables for an overstuffed couch and an imitation leather reclining chair that faced a television set. On one wall was a handmade shelf containing an array of framed family photographs, the largest of which, draped in black bunting, Kerney took to be of Nestor's wife. Beneath the shelf was a low wooden stool on which Nestor parked his work boots.

On the wall behind the television were two paintings. One was a portrait of a much younger Nestor Barela, and the other was a landscape of the cabin at the foot of the mesa. Both were clearly Erma's work.

Nestor sat on the edge of his reclining chair, holding the forgotten key in his hand, staring at the cardboard box on the coffee table in front of him.

Kerney said nothing and waited.

Finally Nestor looked warily at Kerney. "What happened between Erma and me occurred many years ago. I would rather my children not be told."

"From what I could tell, Erma stopped writing to you thirty years ago."

"You read them?"

"Not really."

"Our affair ended after three summers. Erma was not comfortable with it. After she stopped coming to the mesa, I hid her letters in the cabin. I couldn't bring myself to destroy them."

"I understand."

"I loved my wife, Mr. Kerney."

"You don't have to explain anything to me, Mr. Barela."

"I remained Erma's friend until she died."

"You could do no better than to have Erma as a friend."

"She used to speak to me of a young man who went to the university. The son of her college roommate."

"That was my mother."

"Erma had great affection for you."

"We were both lucky to have her friendship. Did you go to the cabin yesterday to remove Erma's letters?"

Nestor rose from his chair. "Yes. I feared the cabin might be searched because of what happened on the mesa. I didn't want the letters to be found. Will you keep my secret?"

Kerney got to his feet. "Your secret is safe with me. I do have one question for you, on a different subject. Does Bernardo frequently use your truck?"

"No. Why do you ask?"

"I'm looking for a witness who may have seen a young woman on the day she disappeared. A vehicle much like yours was reported in the area on that same day."

"Bernardo can only borrow my truck for work. That is my rule."

"Is it a hard and fast rule?"

"On occasion, when his car has not been running, I have let him use the truck."

"Do you remember when that was?"

"The last time was just after Thanksgiving. He needed to get a new water pump for his car."

"And before that?"

"It was last spring, in April, I believe. Bernardo's car would not start, and he had a friend to meet."

"Do you remember who he was meeting?"

"No."

"Do you remember the day?"

"It was on a weekend."

"I doubt it's important," Kerney said with a shrug as he held out a business card. "But I do need to talk to Bernardo. Would you ask him to call me when he has a chance?"

"I will see that he does."

"Thank you."

Kerney left the Barela compound thinking that digging up Nestor Barela's long-buried secret had unearthed another reason to suspect Bernardo. His next step was to identify the passenger in Nestor's truck, find the kid, and take a statement.

The evening wind blew hard out of the mountains. It

swirled last fall's leaves into the air, whipped through tree boughs dense with buds, and shouldered the car toward the center of the roadway.

Kerney headed for the district office. He would check in with Santa Fe, deal by phone with whatever required his immediate attention, and stay the night in Las Vegas. In the morning, he'd start looking for Bernardo's bros.

10

Minutes after checking into a Las Vegas motel, Kerney got a phone call that took him to Anton Chico. He arrived to find a group of locals lined up along the fence of the Alarid property, watching crime scene technicians gathering evidence from a pickup truck inside a garage. Several uniforms were searching large trailers parked on the lot. On the wooden deck of a modular home, a young woman barely out of her teens watched the activity with wide eyes. She wore a warm coat and held a baby bundled in a blanket against her hip.

Kerney spotted Captain Garduno in front of a single-story adobe house. Garduno, red-faced and angry, had Gabe Gonzales, Russell Thorpe, and another uniformed officer braced. Kerney stayed back and listened while Garduno butt-chewed Gabe for pursuing an investigation while on administrative leave. When Garduno finished ragging at the other two men for helping Gonzales, he saw Kerney, and walked to him.

"You heard that?" Garduno asked.

"I did. You need to know that I authorized Sergeant Gonzales to continue his investigation."

Garduno's face turned red. "We got a chain of command here, Chief. You should have informed me."

"You're right, I should have."

Garduno pulled his chin back and scanned Kerney's face. "If you want to take over my job and run the district, at least tell me to my face."

"That was not my intention, Captain."

Garduno squared his shoulders. "This is a policy violation. I have to document it for the record."

"Write it up, Captain, and make it clear in your report that I assume full responsibility for the infraction."

"Are you serious?"

"You bet I am. Send your report directly to Chief Baca."

"You mean that?"

"Consider it an order, Captain." Kerney took a step away from Garduno and stopped. "It looks like Gabe has made some progress in the case, doesn't it?" he added.

Garduno opened his mouth to speak, thought better of it, and clamped his lips together.

Gabe, Russell Thorpe, and the patrol officer—a man Kerney didn't know—nodded when he drew near. The officer wore corporal chevrons and hash marks on his uniform shirt denoting a senior patrolman with ten years of service. His name tag read Art Garcia.

"Is everything squared away?" Gabe asked.

"I think so."

Gabe introduced Kerney to Art Garcia. After shaking Garcia's hand, Kerney asked for a status report.

"We've recovered a handgun, a chain saw, and a pair of wire cutters from the truck," Gabe replied. "The gun is the same caliber used in the Boaz shooting. There's blood splatter on the driver's door, and the tires match the tread impressions we took at Boaz's cabin."

"Do you have any idea why Rudy killed Boaz?"

"According to Boaz's journal, he was squeezing Rudy for more money. I figure he knew that Rudy was pulling jobs in the San Geronimo area, and fencing hot merchandise out of Texas. My guess is Rudy wanted to make sure Boaz didn't talk."

"That's a damn good motive for murder. Have you tied Rudy into any of the San Geronimo burglaries?"

Gabe shook his head. "Not yet. But I think Lenny Alarid and Joaquin Santistevan were in on them with Rudy. I doubt Rudy was the brains behind the operation."

"Run it down for me."

"Rudy was part of an interstate burglary and fencing scheme operating between here and West Texas. We've recovered a number of items from the Boaz cabin and Angie Romero's house that were taken in major West Texas heists. I believe Rudy kept some of the stolen merchandise for himself and gave some to Boaz as partial payment for access to the woodcutting site."

"What else have you got?"

Gabe nodded at the girl on the deck. "Joaquin is supporting a wife at home, as well as Berna over there with her new baby. He bought Berna a house, a car, and furniture, which I don't think he paid for out of the salary his daddy gives him.

"Berna is Lenny's step-daughter. He makes frequent runs to West Texas, hauling firewood and wood chips for Santistevan. I don't think that's all he's been freighting."

"Do you have any hard evidence?" Kerney asked.

"No, but Berna said Lenny keeps a semitrailer on the property that he uses for special runs. She doesn't know what kind. He moved it off the property yesterday."

"You think he transferred the stolen goods?"

"That's what I would have done," Gabe replied. "I'd like to send Thorpe and Officer Garcia down to Santa Rosa to poke around. If Alarid did move the stolen merchandise, Santa Rosa would be a good spot to store it."

"Do it."

Gabe turned to Thorpe and Garcia. "Take off, guys. I want every warehouse, storage unit, or possible hiding place in Santa Rosa covered by morning. Call me at home if you find anything."

Thorpe grinned and Garcia nodded.

Kerney waited to speak until the two men were on the way to their units. "What can you tell me about Bernardo Barela that isn't in the background information Captain Garduno prepared for me?"

"Not much. He had some juvenile arrests when he was in his early teens. Mostly for getting into fights and underage drinking. Nothing serious enough to get him locked up. He was released to the custody of his parents."

"No juvenile probation?"

"Not that I know of. I think maybe he got some informal counseling."

"What kind of fights did he have?"

"Pushing and shoving matches. The usual teenage stuff."

"And the drinking?"

"Open six-packs found in a friend's car. Stopped and questioned at rowdy parties. Nothing more than that."

"Anything since then?"

"No. He seems to have straightened himself out."

"So, he's a good kid?"

"Maybe."

"You don't sound convinced."

Gabe considered his answer. "There's an edge to Bernardo. He's respectful with me, but I get the feeling it's just surface bullshit. You know how some kids cover up their insolence by acting super polite?"

"Yeah, I do."

"That's Bernardo. Underneath, he thinks he's a tough guy."

"Does he have any gang connections?"

"I don't think so."

"Do you know who he hangs with?"

"My son, Orlando, might. He's known Bernardo since high school. They played varsity baseball together."

"How can I contact Orlando?"

"He's at work." Gabe gave Kerney the name of the fast-food burger joint. "Can I ask what you've got going, Chief?"

"I've got a possible ID on the dead woman, and information that Bernardo may have had more than a passing interest in her."

"That's it?"

"He was seen in the company of an unknown companion on the road to Ojitos Frios the day the dead woman disappeared."

"That's worth checking out. Is the victim on our missing persons list?"

"She was never reported as missing."

Gabe waited for more but Kerney remained silent. "Orlando may be able to help you. He doesn't pal around with Bernardo all that much, but he probably knows who does."

"I'll stop by and talk to him."

"Captain Garduno is going to ding me for working this case, Chief. I'm getting a letter of reprimand for my personnel jacket."

"No, you're not. Garduno is going to write me up."

"You're kidding, right?"

"I'm serious. In fact, I made it an order."

Speechless, Gabe watched Kerney leave. Never in his career had Gabe ever known of a commander or supervisor ordering a subordinate to write him up. Kerney's action took Gabe off the hook, big time. The chief knew how to keep his word.

He thought about calling Orlando at work to let him know Kerney would be coming around to ask questions, and decided against it. Orlando could handle the situation without any fatherly advice.

He walked toward Berna's house. It was time to sit down with the girl and take a written statement.

Although the day had not been overly hot, the cool of the evening brought many Tucson residents out on the streets. Most stores and small businesses stayed open late to accommodate shoppers, and the wide boulevards buzzed with traffic.

Susie had made dinner reservations at a restaurant located in one of Tucson's original shopping malls. Sara expected to be dining in an enclosed, air-conditioned space filled with franchised businesses and chain department stores. Instead she found herself seated on the open patio of a bistro in a single-story, block-long building that had a mission-style feel to it.

After the meal and a lot of small talk, they wandered in and out of the bookstores, art galleries, boutiques, and antique shops that opened onto interior patios nicely landscaped with mesquites, paloverde trees, and creosote bushes.

On their way to Susie's car, Sara paused at the window of an art gallery and studied a large oil of cottonwood trees in full fall color.

She looked for the artist's signature and found it. "That's Erma Fergurson's work."

"The woman who left Kerney the land?"

"Yes."

"It's a wonderful painting."

Sara stepped toward the gallery door.

"Are you sure you want to go in?"

"Why not?"

"You've avoided any mention of Kerney for the last six hours," Susie said. "I'd hate to see you break your code of silence."

"Don't be so sarcastic."

"I bet you haven't stopped thinking about him since

you left Santa Fe," Susie said as she opened the gallery door.

Sara paused. "Would you like to see more of Erma's work or not?"

Susie smiled sweetly. "Of course I would."

The gallery had a large number of Erma's paintings. The owner, an older man, explained that he had exclusively represented Erma in Tucson for a number of years.

Sara lost herself in Erma's landscapes. There were pine forests climbing sheer mountain walls, barrel cactus ablaze in color on rolling desert sand dunes, piñon woodlands stretching across tabletop mesas, and fields of hot yellow wildflowers coursing through a valley. Erma's works celebrated the light, sky, and vastness of the land. The smallest image was priced above $10,000, and most commanded three times that amount.

The gallery owner heard Sara sigh as she finished a second, thorough inspection of Erma's paintings.

"Her works are heavily collected," he said. "I have clients who have built additions on their homes to accommodate her larger works."

"I can see why."

"These are the last, except for what is held by her estate. The prices can only go up. Are you a collector?"

"Only in my dreams."

"I have some of Erma's pencil drawings hanging in my office. Mostly studies for her earlier egg temperas and watercolors. They're quite reasonably priced. Would you like to see them?"

"I would love to," Sara said.

An hour later, Sara left the gallery with a signed, framed pencil sketch of Hermit's Peak in hand. The reasonable price had gouged a hole in her vacation funds, but Sara didn't care.

"When are you going to give it to him?" Susie asked as they walked to the car. Her eyes were smiling.

"When I get back to Santa Fe," Sara answered.

"When are you leaving?"

"Tonight."

Susie unlocked the car and got behind the wheel. "I thought so. Do me a favor before you see him."

"What's that?"

"Don't try to have everything figured out. Let Kerney tell you what he wants."

"He may not want anything."

"Do I detect a note of insecurity?"

"Maybe. Until I met Kerney, I've always encouraged the men I've known to move on."

Susie cranked the engine and pulled out of the lot. "And now?"

"I can't seem to stay that tough-minded about him."

"Tell him that."

"Those aren't words I'm comfortable saying."

"Practice. You've got all night."

"Love is scary."

"Yes!" Susie said, holding up her hand for a high five. Sara slapped Susie's open palm. "What?"

"You used the L word."

"I did, didn't I?"

"First time, about a man?"

"First time ever, about a man."

"Use it with Kerney."

"You think?"

"You'd better. Otherwise, he's fair game for the likes of me."

"No cuts. Get at the back of the line."

"Thatta girl."

Kerney studied Orlando Gonzales while he waited for the young man to finish his stint at the drive-up window of the burger joint. Orlando had his fast-food drill down to a well-oiled routine. He began filling orders as they came in over the drive-up speaker, moving quickly between drink dispenser, french fry cooker, and burger-warming trays.

Kerney saw a hint of Gabe in the boy's features, particularly the shape of his head and his chin. But his face was thinner and his eyes a bit less deeply set than his father's.

When the drive-up traffic slowed, the night manager relieved Orlando at the window and pointed in Kerney's direction.

Orlando pulled off his red company logo cap as he hurried around the counter. "Is my dad all right?"

"He's fine, although you may not see much of him until tomorrow. He's fairly busy right now."

Orlando's shoulders relaxed as he sat down. "Man, you scared me for a minute. All my boss said was that a cop wanted to see me."

"Not to worry. Gabe hasn't been hurt."

"So, who are you?"

"Kevin Kerney." Kerney displayed his shield.

Orlando read the engraved rank on the badge. "Is my dad in trouble?"

Kerney smiled reassuringly. "Not at all. He suggested that I talk to you."

Orlando shook his head in confusion. "About what?"

"Bernardo Barela."

Orlando half-closed his eyes. "He's in trouble?"

"Not necessarily," Kerney replied. "You've known Bernardo for a long time."

"Yeah, but we don't hang together very much anymore."

"When was the last time you saw him?"

"We had a couple of beers a few nights ago. Before that, it's been maybe a year since we've seen each other."

"Did he ever mention a girl by the name of Luiza San Miguel?"

Orlando's voice changed to a thin treble. "Who?"

"Luiza San Miguel."

"I don't know that name. I don't know who he's dating."

"You're not tight with Bernardo anymore?"

Orlando forced a smile. "Nah. We sort of went different ways. He's really into the ranching thing and I'm pretty much preoccupied with school."

"That's understandable. Is he popular with the girls?"

"He gets his share of attention."

"Does he brag about it?"

"Not to me."

"Has he dated anyone you know?"

Orlando mentioned some names, which Kerney wrote down.

"What about his pals?"

He gave Kerney a few more names.

After finding out how to locate Bernardo's friends, Kerney closed his notebook and put it away.

"Is Bernardo in bad trouble?" Orlando asked.

"You're worried about him."

"Well, sure. I mean, he's still a friend, sort of."

"When was your last contact with him?"

"Before this week?"

"Yes."

Orlando closed his eyes. "It was at a party. Yeah, a party." His eyes fluttered open. "I saw him there and we shot the shit for a while."

"When was that?"

"Last spring. April, maybe May."

"Did he seem upset? Agitated? In any way different?"

"No."

"Who had the party?"

"It was at some girl's apartment. I didn't know her. A bunch of us got invited on the spur of the moment."

"Was Bernardo with anyone at the party?"

"I don't think so."

"Did you do any cruising with Bernardo early last year, around Ojitos Frios?"

"I haven't cruised with Bernardo since we were in high school."

"Has Bernardo ever done anything strange or weird?"

"You mean like crazy shit? Not that I know about."

"Thanks, Orlando."

Orlando opened his mouth, closed it, and swallowed hard.

"Did you want to say something?"

"I gotta get back to work."

"Thanks, again."

Numbly, Orlando watched Kerney leave before he pulled himself out of the chair and walked woodenly to the counter. The assistant manager stepped away from the drive-up station and said something.

"What?"

"You've got three specials with cheese coming up, and three large fries. The super drinks are ready to go."

"Okay."

He stuck the drinks on the foam tray, packed the fries and ketchup packets in a bag, wrapped the burgers as they came up, bagged them, and turned toward the pass-through window. The reflection of his pale face and pinched lips in the glass startled him.

Officers Garcia and Thorpe arrived in Santa Rosa and quickly discovered that there were no warehouses or storage units in the town. But they did find a number of boarded-up, vacant filling stations, motels, and other structures on the main drag that had closed down as new commercial development spread along the frontage road by the interstate on the east side of the city.

Garcia decided to check out the vacant buildings on the off chance that Alarid was using one for storage. He assigned Thorpe to one side of the strip and took the other. After two hours of close patrols, he contacted Thorpe by radio, called off the building checks, and met with him outside the Santa Rosa State Police substation.

"I'm shutting it down," Garcia said. "Go home."

"I still think Sarge is right," Thorpe said. "Alarid has got to be warehousing the stolen merchandise somewhere."

"Not in this town."

"Maybe he's storing it in the countryside somewhere, where he won't draw attention to himself."

"Possibly. But that covers a lot of territory."

"I'd like to come back tomorrow morning and take another look around."

"We're out of our district. Let the Santa Rosa substation handle it."

"Then they'd get the bust."

"If they find anything."

"Just give me the morning."

"Don't be so gung-ho, Thorpe."

"Come on, Art."

Garcia decided there was no reason to squash Thorpe's enthusiasm. "Okay. But I want you to work with Abe Melendez. He's the sergeant in charge of the Santa Rosa substation. If you strike out, I want you back in Las Vegas by thirteen hundred. Now, go home."

Garcia watched Thorpe turn his unit around and drive down the empty street. He flicked on the dome light, made an entry in his daily log, and informed dispatch he was off duty and proceeding home.

Her name was Jessica Varela, and over the past six months Bernardo had learned a lot about her. She was thirty, divorced, had no children, and lived alone on the second floor of an old house that had been converted into two apartments. She worked as a cashier at a hardware store and took night courses at the university.

When Bernardo first saw her at the hardware store he got really turned on. She hid her face behind long blonde hair, kept her head lowered when she spoke, and only looked up to give quick, shy glances. She had a smile that seemed like she was keeping secrets, a small, skinny body, slightly rounded shoulders, and a nice set of tits.

He went into the store a lot to get stuff for the ranch, and he used each visit to talk to her at the register, asking one or two calculated questions. He'd been surprised to learn how old she was; he'd figured her to be a lot younger. He found out she was a gringa who'd kept her married name, that she'd grown up in the Midwest, and had moved to Las Vegas from Albuquerque after getting divorced.

Bernardo sat in his car across from the hardware store and watched the lights inside the building go out. The store stayed open late three nights a week, and Jessica worked on those nights when she didn't have an evening class.

He watched the employees leave and waited until Jessica reached the traffic light at the corner before pulling onto the street to follow.

She always took the same route home, so Bernardo didn't have to worry about losing her. He passed by as she pulled into her driveway, made a U-turn at the end of the block, turned off his headlights, and coasted to a stop in time to see her unlock the front door and step inside. He waited until the upstairs lights came on before getting out of his car.

Usually he just drove away after she got home, but

tonight something about the house was different; the downstairs apartment was dark. Always before the lights had been on at night.

Bernardo walked down the opposite side of the street before crossing, then strolled past Jessica's house. There was a FOR RENT sign in the downstairs window. That made him smile. The house only had one front and back entrance, and the rear door opened directly to the first floor apartment. He'd been looking for a way to get inside without being seen or heard. Trying to break in on a morning when she went to work late had always been a risky idea because of the downstairs tenants. Now that problem was solved.

He wondered what the inside of her apartment looked like. He couldn't wait to see it.

Bernardo got back in his car and drove away, thinking he'd have to move fast before the landlord found new renters. He arrived home to find his grandfather leaving his parents' house.

"*Jito*," Nestor said. "I've been looking for you."

"What is it?"

Nestor held out a business card. "That policeman, Kerney, wants to speak to you."

"Me?" Bernardo took the card.

"Yes, you. Your uncle Roque said that you've already spoken to him once, about some girl. What is this all about?"

"I don't know, *Abuelo*. What did he ask you about me?"

"Nothing really. He wanted to know if I let you use my truck."

"I already talked to him about that," Bernardo said. "I have nothing more to tell him."

"Be polite and respectful, Bernardo. Speak with Señor Kerney, answer his questions, and be done with it."

Bernardo nodded abruptly, got back in his car, and slammed the door.

"Where are you going?" Nestor asked. "It is late and you have work to do in the morning."

"I forgot something."

Bernardo peeled rubber out of the driveway, tailpipes rumbling as he shifted into a higher gear. He cruised past the burger joint, saw Orlando's car, and made a quick decision not to bother him at work. In the morning, he would call and find out if Orlando had talked to the gringo cop Kerney and what, if anything, Orlando had said.

His plans for Jessica would have to wait for a day or two.

Orlando woke up from a dream where he was lost in some strange city that was impossible to leave. No matter which way he went, every route took him back to a block of windowless, silent buildings on an empty street with no cars or people.

He got out of bed thinking that if he waited until the end of the semester to move to Albuquerque, it might be too late.

He showered, shaved, returned to his room, sat at his desk, and figured out how much money he could pull together if he split. If he used his car insurance payment, the two hundred bucks he had in savings, and his last paycheck, he could come up with about seven hundred dollars.

His stomach sank as the realization hit him that running away wouldn't change anything. His life would still be fucked. He threw the scrap of paper in the wastebasket, got to his feet, and slung his daypack over his shoulder. If he left now, maybe Dad would still be in the shower when he hit the front door. The phone rang as he reached for his jacket.

"Did a state cop named Kerney talk to you?" Bernardo asked when Orlando answered.

"Yeah, last night"

"What about?"

"You."

"What did you say?"

"Nothing."

"We need to meet."

"Why?"

"To get our stories straight, before the cop gets all suspicious."

"How did he get on to you?"

"The bitch used to work at a place out near my *abuelo*'s ranch. He's just talking to people who might have known her."

"I thought you didn't know her."

"I already told you I didn't."

"So why is the cop interested in you?"

"He's interested in both of us, bro. He asked me about driving around Ojitos Frios in my grandfather's truck with somebody last April. Does he know that was you?"

"We're screwed," Orlando said.

"Does he know that was you?" Bernardo demanded.

"No. What are we going to do?"

"Come up with something simple about where we were and what we did. Get our stories straight. Back each other up. He already talked to my grandfather. He wants to talk to me again."

"Shit!"

"We gotta meet."

"Okay."

"Some place where no one will see us. How about down by the Gallinas River where we used to party in high school?"

"That's miles from here."

"It's halfway to town from my grandfather's ranch."

"When?"

"Can you make it by ten?"

"Yeah."

"Just don't say anything to your old man."

"I'm not stupid, Bernardo," Orlando said as he hung up the phone.

He hurried down the stairs, saw his father sitting at the kitchen table, and stopped in the doorway.

"Hey, champ, who was on the phone?" Gabe asked.

"A guy from school. He wants to borrow my class notes. Gotta go."

"Give me a minute before you take off."

Orlando stepped into the kitchen. "Sure."

"My deputy chief wants to talk to you about Bernardo."

"He already did, last night."

"What did he want to know?"

"Just who Bernardo's friends were."

"What else did he ask?"

"He asked me if Bernardo was popular with the girls, and if I ever went cruising with him."

"That's it?"

"Pretty much. Oh yeah, he wanted to know about somebody named Luiza."

"Luiza who?"

"San Miguel. I don't know who she is."

"That's not a common name. More Mexican than Hispanic. You gave him the straight scoop?"

Orlando shrugged. "Sure. I really don't know who Bernardo dates. Is Bernardo like a suspect or something?"

"I don't know."

"What's this guy investigating, anyway?"

"The mesa homicide. He thinks he has an ID on the victim."

"No shit?"

"It might be a good idea for you to cool it with Bernardo for a while."

"I don't see Bernardo much anyway."

"Keep it that way until things settle down."

"Is that all?"

"Are you still planning to move to Albuquerque when school gets out?"

"Yeah."

"You don't sound so sure about it today."

"I gotta go." Orlando took an awkward step backward and his daypack banged against the door frame.

"Watch it, champ," Gabe said with a grin. "Don't hurt yourself. Maybe we can talk about it some more tonight."

Orlando nodded and smiled nervously.

"Are you feeling okay?"

"I'm fine."

"Then get out of here. I'll see you later."

"Later."

Outside, Orlando threw the daypack in the backseat of his car and cranked the engine with a shaky hand, praying that there was still a way out of the shithole he was in.

Before leaving Tucson, Sara had tried to reach Kerney by phone without any luck. She left a message on his machine, letting him know she was returning to Santa Fe, packed hurriedly, gave Susie a big hug, and hit the road. The image of Susie's approving smile stayed with her until she reached the city limits.

Sara enjoyed driving late at night. She could wrap herself in a cocoon, let her mind wander, and see where her thoughts took her. Tonight she kept thinking of Kerney and how she felt about him.

The hours it took to reach Santa Fe felt like minutes as she pulled to a stop in front of Kerney's cottage. His truck was there but his unmarked state police unit wasn't. Disappointed, she looked at the dashboard clock and realized he was probably at work.

She let herself in with the key Kerney had given her, expecting Shoe to greet her at the door with his tail wagging and the sneaker firmly in his mouth. The dog was nowhere to found, and all the pet supplies were gone from the kitchen.

Shoe's absence made her worry about both Kerney and the dog. Had Shoe run off or died? Had Kerney decided not to keep Shoe in spite of his genuine affection for the animal?

The answering machine blinked and Sara played back the messages, hoping Kerney had left one for her. Aside from her message to him and a call from a woman named Ruth Pino there was nothing else on the machine.

She went into the living room, tossed her jacket on the couch, thought about calling Kerney at work, and dropped the idea. She was too tired to think straight. A hot bath and a nap were in order. She picked up her bag and walked into the bedroom.

Without Shoe, the place felt empty.

There wasn't much left to the old settlement on the Gallinas River, just some partial stone and adobe walls, rusted pieces of tin roofing, a few sagging fence posts, and occasional piles of junk, including broken beer bottles and trash left by kids who partied at the site.

The river's floodplain had created a channel no more than three feet deep and fifty feet wide. Spring runoff filled much of the eroded streambed. Cows grazed close to the water near a locked gate on the far side where the dirt road ended.

As far as Bernardo knew the place didn't have a name. It had been settled and abandoned several times since the nineteenth century and was now part of Arlin Fullerton's Box Z spread.

He leaned against the hood of Uncle Roque's truck and watched the cows slosh their way through the water toward a low soggy bottom where spring grasses had greened up. His *tío* had gone to a spring stock sale in Roswell and wouldn't be back until tomorrow. That left Bernardo with the truck and all the time he needed to meet with Orlando.

He hoped Orlando would show so he wouldn't have to go looking for him. He heard the sound of tires on gravel, turned to see Orlando's car topping the low hill, and waved as the vehicle slowed to a stop. Orlando got out and walked to him.

Bernardo gave him a friendly smile.

"Man, you'd better have a good story we can use," Orlando said.

"First, tell me what the cop asked you."

"He asked me if we went cruising together last year in Ojitos Frios. I told him no."

"What else?"

"He wanted to know if you knew Luiza. I told him I didn't know who you were dating."

"Did he say anything about her being missing?"

"No."

"Then he's just fishing."

"I think he knows who she is. My dad said Kerney has a possible ID on the victim." A thought flashed through Orlando's mind. He stared at Bernardo.

"What?" Bernardo asked.

"How did he put us in Ojitos Frios?"

"Somebody saw us in my grandfather's truck."

"Did you tell him we were there?"

"I said I didn't remember." Bernardo tore open a pack of cigarettes and quickly lit up. "He's probably questioning everybody who knew Luiza. Don't get all bent out of shape. We'll get our shit together and it will all be cool."

Something clicked in Orlando's mind. "But he's doing a background investigation on you. Asking who your friends are. Where you were last April. If you knew Luiza. That means you're a target."

Bernardo exhaled smoke and laughed. "Did you learn that cop shit from your old man?"

"You knew Luiza, didn't you?"

Bernardo shrugged. "Yeah, I knew her."

"She never wanted to party with us that night, did she?"

Bernardo smiled. "I had to convince her."

"You meant to rape her all along."

Bernardo didn't respond.

"Do the cops know that you knew her?"

"Yeah, but it doesn't mean squat."

Orlando shook his head. "You don't get it, do you? You're a fucking suspect."

"So what?" Bernardo ground out the smoke with the heel of his boot.

Orlando turned to walk back to his car.

"Where are you going?"

"I'm splitting. I can't live with this shit anymore. I'm done with it. It's over, Bernardo."

Bernardo grabbed Orlando by the arm. "Are you going to snitch me off?"

"I didn't say that. Let go of me."

"Are you?"

Orlando yanked Bernardo's hand off his arm and pushed him away. "I don't know what I'm going to do. I'll let you know when I decide."

"That's not good enough, Orlando." Bernardo put his right hand in his back pocket and grabbed the handle of his sheath knife.

"Live with it," Orlando said.

"Can't do it, bro." Bernardo pulled the knife, took two steps, drove the blade under Orlando's rib cage, and ripped up to find the heart.

Orlando grunted once, his mouth open like a feeding fish, his eyes already empty.

Bernardo pulled the knife free and watched Orlando's blood pump out of his body as he fell to the ground. He'd read somewhere that during Vietnam the Communists would castrate dead Americans, stick their dicks in their mouths, and sew their lips together, to scare the soldiers who found the bodies. He thought about doing it to Orlando but decided not to bother. No one was ever going to see him again.

He stepped over to Orlando and slit his throat. He wanted the body drained of blood before he hauled it to the truck. When the blood flow turned to a slight trickle, he dumped the body in the truck bed and covered it with hay bales he'd brought along. Using a shovel, he dug around the sticky, deep-red blood pool, turning the soil until dry earth covered the ground.

Uncle Roque had told him to finish grading the road

to the line camp, and get the dozer back to the Box Z. From today on, anybody who used that road would be driving over Orlando's bones.

Some of Orlando's blood had squirted on his hand. Bernardo sniffed it as he drove away. It smelled good.

11

At the start of his shift, Russell Thorpe checked to see if the APB on Alarid's truck was still active. Alarid hadn't been spotted, so Thorpe got on the road to Santa Rosa. If he could pick up Alarid, it would be a significant collar.

He found Sergeant Melendez at the reception counter in the Santa Rosa substation reviewing daily shift reports. Thorpe introduced himself and told Melendez what he was looking for and why.

Melendez rolled his eyes, said there were countless places to hide a tractor trailer rig where it would never be found, and finally suggested that Thorpe do a close patrol of Puerto de Luna, a settlement ten miles southeast of Santa Rosa.

The road to Puerto de Luna hugged the edge of a low butte at the far side of the river valley until it reached a sweep of pasture and farms that bordered both sides of the river. Thorpe crossed the bridge into the village and did a quick patrol. There wasn't much to the settlement:

an old church with an adjacent cemetery, a fenced-off, abandoned one-room schoolhouse, a flat-roofed modern building with a brick facade that served as a community and senior citizen center, and several occupied houses made up the heart of the community.

He stopped at a road sign that told of the village's former status as the county seat, and its most notorious visitor, Billy the Kid, before cruising south to the end of the pavement. The road turned to gravel where two converging mesas pinched the valley close to the river, the streambed hidden behind thick bosque. He spotted several old semitrailers near barns and outbuildings, but it was clear they'd been stationary for years.

He worked a series of dirt roads, visually checking each ranch and farm that came into view, until he was a good ten miles south of the village.

Melendez had warned him not to get his hopes up, and Thorpe now understood why. As he crisscrossed and skirted buttes, mesas, arroyos, and canyonlands on rutted tracks that seemed to go nowhere, he realized that he could spend days in the boonies, find nothing, and still have hundreds of places left to search.

Back in Puerto de Luna, he stopped at the community center and talked to a cook and her elderly male assistant, who were in the kitchen preparing a midday meal for senior citizens.

"Do either of you know Lenny Alarid?" Thorpe asked as he watched the stout, middle-aged woman ladle food into a white Styrofoam container and hand it to the old man.

"I don't think so," the woman said.

The old man put the container into a portable warming cart and waited to receive the next meal.

"Do you know him?" Thorpe asked him.

The old man shook his head.

"He's a truck driver," Thorpe added.

"Lots of people around here drive trucks," the cook replied, holding out another meal.

The old man closed the lid and slid it into the cart. The thick veins in his liver-spotted hands were blood red under a thin layer of translucent skin.

"A semitruck," Thorpe said. He described Alarid's tractor trailer rig.

"Never saw it," the woman said

"I have," the old man said.

"Where?" the cook asked before Thorpe could get the question out.

"At Perfecta Velarde's barn. The truck was there yesterday when I delivered her meal to her."

"Did she have any visitors?" Thorpe asked.

"Yes. Her daughter and son-in-law. The daughter's name is Gloria. I didn't meet the man."

"Do you know Gloria's married name?"

The old man shook his head. "But she lives in Anton Chico."

"Where is Perfecta's place?"

"On the highway to Santa Rosa. The truck is parked next to the barn."

"I didn't see it on the way in."

"You can't. A hill blocks it from view. You have to be driving back to Santa Rosa to see her place from the highway."

"How far?" Thorpe asked.

"Two miles. It's just before the road curves around the mesa. You'll see it."

"Thanks."

Russell keyed the radio as he left the community center and made contact with Art Garcia.

"You were supposed to be back a half hour ago," Garcia said after acknowledging Thorpe's call.

"I may have located Alarid's truck."

"When will you know for sure?" Garcia asked sarcastically.

Thorpe took the first turn after the bridge at sixty miles an hour. "About one minute."

"Standing by," Garcia said.

Thorpe floored his unit along a straightaway, braked through a gradual curve, saw Perfecta's barn and Alarid's rig, and slowed down. "Truck in sight."

"Can you positively ID the rig?"

"Give me a minute." Russell rolled to a stop, reached for his binoculars, and focused on the lettering on the driver's door. "It's Alarid's. He's got the trailer unhitched from his cab. Looks like he's planning to leave it here."

"Give me an exact location."

Thorpe snapped off directions into the microphone. "What should I do if he tries to leave?"

"Stop him when he gets on the highway. If nobody moves, stay put. Sergeant Melendez is responding. ETA ten minutes. Sergeant Gonzales is rolling now. Good work, Thorpe."

"Ten-four."

Smiling to himself, Russell parked his unit, left the engine running, and scanned the farmhouse. All looked quiet. As he lowered the binoculars, his radio crackled and Melendez's voice came over the speaker.

"ETA five minutes. Is everything cool?"

"Roger that. Nothing's moving. Do we have a search warrant?"

"Not yet. Art Garcia is en route to magistrate court."

"Ten-four."

Melendez clicked off and Russell settled back to wait.

Lenny Alarid watched the cops from the living room window. For twenty minutes, two police cars had been parked at the end of his mother-in-law's driveway. At first Lenny told himself the cops were just taking a break and shooting the shit. Now his gut ached with the feeling that he was about to be busted.

Lenny didn't think of himself as a criminal. He wasn't a wife-beater, a drunk, or a bad-ass, and he'd never been in jail. He was forty-eight years old and had spent most of his adult life on the road, hauling whatever he could on a for-hire basis. Only a fraction of his runs consisted of hauling stolen merchandise, but the work netted him the biggest portion of his income. Without it he'd be scraping along, driving a piece of shit rig, trying to live on 15,000 dollars a year.

He took his eyes off the cops for a moment and glanced at his truck. A top-of-the-line model with a sleeping compartment and all the accessories, it had set him back over 150,000 dollars. It was midnight blue with stainless steel grillwork, a chrome bumper, custom running lights at the top of the cab, primo mud flaps, and fancy cherry red pinstriping. It was his pride and joy. But with the cargo in the box, it was about to become a big time liability.

He snorted and rubbed his belly where the gas pressure had built up. He was about to get hammered by the cops because of Rudy Espinoza's stupidity. If he hadn't murdered Carl Boaz, the cops wouldn't be here.

He switched his attention back to the cop cars just as another unit drove up, and Lenny knew for sure his goose was cooked.

Gloria, his wife, stood by his side nervously biting a fingernail. She knew exactly how he made his money. He'd married Gloria eight years ago when she still had a slender figure and a young-looking face. Then she hit forty and her body got wide, her face got fat and her arms got flabby. Lenny didn't care; he was no prize himself.

"Are they coming here?" Gloria asked.

"What do you think?"

"Don't snap at me."

Lenny grunted.

"What are you going to do?"

"Nothing."

"Can't we leave?"

"They'll just stop us on the road."

"Think of something."

"Like what?"

"Maybe they're not here for us."

"Yeah, right," Lenny said. "See the cop standing behind his car. He's got binoculars trained on the house."

The senior citizen meal delivery van came down the highway with a turn signal blinking. The cop with the binoculars halted the vehicle, talked to the driver for a minute, and sent him on his way.

"We're screwed," Lenny said. "Take your mother to the kitchen."

"I don't want to go to jail, Lenny."

"You don't know anything about my business, understand? Tell them you came along for the ride to keep me company, and don't know nothing."

"What about you?"

"I'll get a lawyer."

A fourth patrol car drove up.

"Shit!" Lenny said.

"Is it time for my meal?" Perfecta asked.

Lenny grimaced in the direction of his mother-in-law, who stood in the middle of the living room, her hands clasped on the rails of a walker. A stroke had left her partially paralyzed, and her mind was mostly mush. She barely knew who she was. Except when Gloria came to visit, the old lady had a live-in assistant, who cost Lenny a pile of money to employ.

"Take her into the kitchen," Lenny repeated, just as the phone rang.

Gloria picked it up, listened for a moment, and held it out with a shaky hand.

"I hope they bring me lamb chops and peas today," Perfecta said. "And peaches."

Gloria gave Lenny a scared look, went to her mother, and walked her through the kitchen door.

"Yeah," Lenny said into the phone.

"This is Sergeant Gonzales with the New Mexico State Police, Lenny. Who is inside the house besides your wife and mother-in-law?"

"Nobody. What do you want?"

"We're here to serve a warrant. I want you to step outside the house and stand in plain view with your hands where I can see them. Are there any guns in the house?"

"No."

"Are you armed?"

"No."

"Hang up the phone and step outside. Stay calm and nobody gets hurt."

On the porch step with his hands palms out and open, Lenny watched the four police cars come up the driveway. The front unit rolled to a stop and a uniformed sergeant with a stubby chin and square face got out of his cruiser and stood behind the car door. Behind him, three officers emerged from their units with guns drawn.

"What's this all about?" Lenny asked.

Gabe studied Lenny before responding. Alarid wore a work shirt, blue jeans, and cowboy boots that added an inch to his five seven frame. A full mustache covered his upper lip, and deep worry lines creased his low forehead. His hands were shaking.

Gabe didn't see any bulges in Lenny's clothing. He made a circular motion with his finger. "Very slowly,

Lenny, I want you to make one complete turn and then stop. Keep your hands away from your body."

Lenny finished the turn to find two of the cops within striking distance. One held a gun on him while a baby-faced officer patted him down.

"He's clean," the baby-faced cop said as he tossed Lenny's truck keys to Gabe.

"Check inside," Gabe ordered.

The cops moved into the house as Gabe walked to Lenny, smiled, and handed him some papers.

Lenny couldn't focus on the document. "What's this?"

"You want me to read it to you?"

"No."

"What's inside your trailer, Lenny?"

"You tell me."

"How about a truckload of stolen goodies from Texas?" Gabe asked.

"I don't know nothing about that."

Gabe took the papers out of Lenny's hand and waved them in his face. "This is a warrant to search your truck and trailer, Lenny. Let's try again. What's in the trailer?"

Lenny's shoulders sagged. "Water heaters, washing machines, and some other stuff."

"You got a bill of lading for the cargo?"

"No."

Gabe stepped behind Lenny, pulled his hands to the small of his back, and cuffed him.

"You arresting me?" Lenny asked.

"Yeah. Let's go take a look in the box," Gabe said. "But first let me tell you about your rights."

• • •

Lenny refused to confess to anything other than transporting one load of stolen property, still in original factory crates and boxes, boosted from a regional warehouse distribution center in El Paso.

Gabe took Alarid into the kitchen, closed the door, sat him down at the table, and had him write a voluntary confession. The kitchen was right out of the late 1940s. It had a cast-iron enamel sink positioned under a window, a run of metal kitchen cabinets painted white with a battleship gray linoleum countertop, and a badly worn tile floor. The oval kitchen table had chrome legs and a yellow top, and the matching chairs were padded with cracked vinyl cushions. On one wall hung a framed photograph of John Fitzgerald Kennedy.

While Art Garcia and Abe Melendez inventoried the stolen merchandise, Russell Thorpe stood watch over Gloria, who was in the living room feeding Perfecta her meal. Gabe had let the senior citizen van driver deliver it on his way back to the village. Through the closed door, Gabe could hear the elderly woman complaining that she wanted lamb and peas, not fish.

Gabe watched Lenny sign his name at the bottom of the paper. "Date it," he said.

Lenny scribbled the date and held out the confession.

Gabe read it and shook his head. "This isn't going to work, Lenny."

"Why not? I confessed, didn't I?"

"I forgot to explain a few things to you."

"Like what?"

"I'm going to have to book you on a murder charge."

Lenny's armpits got sweaty. "I didn't kill anybody."

"I know that. But we found Rudy's truck and the murder weapon hidden on your property. That makes you an accessory after the fact to murder."

"I didn't know he'd killed Boaz."

"The law is funny about being an accessory. If you helped Rudy in any way, you can be charged with murder. Probably second degree."

"That's crazy."

"Then there's the conspiracy charge."

"What conspiracy?"

"You paid Rudy for all that wood he poached. Don't tell me you didn't know where he got it."

Lenny rubbed his nose with a thumb. "He never told me."

"You'll have to convince a jury of that. You're looking at a shitload of felonies." Gabe ticked them off on his fingers. "Murder, conspiracy, and multiple counts of receiving and transporting stolen property. Each item in the trailer can be a separate charge against you. Have you ever been in prison?"

Lenny shook his head.

"You could get over a hundred years. What about Gloria? Has she done time before?"

"She can't testify against me."

"She might want to, if it means staying out of the slammer. After all, she's got a mother who needs looking after, and a brand-new baby grandson. You know how women get when it comes to families. I'll talk to her."

Lenny held up a hand to stop Gabe. "What do you want?"

Gabe tore off Lenny's handwritten page from the tablet and slid the pad across the table. "All of it. Your Texas contacts, who you deliver to, what Rudy boosted that you trucked out of state, where you took it, and what arrangements you had with Joaquin Santistevan."

"What do I get?"

"Probably a break from the district attorney, if you cooperate."

"What kind of break?"

"Tell you what: I'll ask the DA to drop the murder and conspiracy charges. He might even be willing to cut back on the number of receiving stolen property indictments. After all, you'll be going into court as a first-time offender."

"I'll do time?"

"Maybe, maybe not."

Lenny reached for the pad and pencil.

"Answer one question for me before you start writing," Gabe said. "How did Joaquin tip off Rudy that I was nosing around? He didn't use the office telephone."

"He used my cell phone."

"You were at the woodlot?"

"I was on the office crapper when you came into the trailer. I just stayed out of sight until you split."

• • •

By noontime, Kerney was down to the last person on the list of names Orlando Gonzales had given him. So far, none of Bernardo's friends and former high school classmates had provided any relevant information.

His last potential informant, Melissa Pena, now married and known as Melissa Valencia, worked as a secretary for an independent insurance agent. Kerney arrived at the agency and found the young woman standing behind a reception desk in a small, two-office suite, filing paperwork in a four-drawer metal cabinet.

She had long dark hair that fell below her waist and wore a jumper over a short-sleeve turtleneck top that didn't hide her pregnant belly. Kerney guessed she was in her last trimester. He identified himself and asked about Bernardo.

"I really can't tell you very much about him," Melissa said as she eased herself into her secretarial chair.

"I was told you were once good friends."

"Not me. He was my best friend's boyfriend. I kinda put up with him because of her, but I never really liked him."

"Who would that be?"

"Patricia Gomez. She went with him for three years, during high school and her first year in college."

"Didn't she have Bernardo's baby?"

"Yeah."

"Why didn't she marry him?"

"They were going to get married."

"What happened?"

"After high school, Patricia enrolled at the university and I started working here. We got an apartment together. She kept dating Bernardo. It was more than dating, if you know what I mean. Anyway, she soon got pregnant."

"How did Bernardo handle it?"

"He seemed real happy. They both did."

"And then what?"

"Patricia had a lot of problems carrying the baby, especially morning sickness. One day I came home for lunch and found her crying. Bernardo had come over, wanting sex. When she said no, he beat her up."

"Was she badly beaten?"

"Mostly he slapped her and pushed her around. She had some bruises and her face was all red."

"To your knowledge, had this happened before?"

"No. Patricia was like in shock about it."

"What did she do?"

"She broke up with him right away. Patricia isn't stupid. She wasn't going to put up with an abusing asshole."

"What did Bernardo do?"

"He kept calling and stopping by, trying to apologize. But Patricia wouldn't see or talk to him."

"Did Patricia report the incident to the police?"

Melissa shook her head. "No, but she told her parents. When school got out she moved back home and lived with them until the baby was born."

"Why did Patricia go to Denver?"

"To get away from Bernardo. He was like stalking her."

"In what way?"

"Mostly just following her when she left the house. But only when she went out alone. He wrote her a few letters about how she was making a big mistake by breaking up with him, and that he'd get even with her."

"You know this for a fact?"

"Patricia showed me the letters."

"Did she get a restraining order against Bernardo?"

"No. Her parents talked to Bernardo's parents and it all just stopped."

"I understand Bernardo pays child support."

"From what Patricia told me, Bernardo's parents had to force him to do it."

"Has Patricia had any problems with Bernardo since her move to Denver?"

"Not as far as I know."

"Would Patricia tell you if Bernardo was giving her grief?"

"Sure. She's my oldest friend. We talk on the phone a couple times a month, and she comes home to visit at least twice a year. If Bernardo was acting like a jerk, I'm sure I'd know about it."

"Do you know of any other women Bernardo has bothered?"

Melissa inclined her head and thought about the question for a moment. "It may be nothing, but talk to Jimmy Wooten."

The name wasn't familiar to Kerney. "Why should I speak to him?"

"Jimmy's home on leave from the air force. He and my husband were good friends in high school. He told my husband that he ran into Bernardo at a bar recently, and that Bernardo acted like a real creep toward some cocktail waitress. I don't know anything more than that."

Kerney got an address for Jimmy Wooten and smiled at Melissa. "I appreciate your time."

"Why are you investigating Bernardo?"

"It's a small matter," Kerney said as he walked to the office door.

Jimmy Wooten, dressed in jeans and an air force sweatshirt, stood outside his parents' ranch-style subdivision house. He ran a hand through his short, light blond hair and gave Kerney a puzzled look.

"I didn't know that hustling a barmaid was against the law," he said in response to Kerney's question about Bernardo. "Did she file a complaint, or something?"

"No," Kerney replied.

"Then what's the problem?" Jimmy asked.

"There might not be one," Kerney said. "I understand you told Melissa's husband that Bernardo acted like a creep toward the barmaid. I'd like to hear what happened."

Jimmy shook his head. "Melissa has never liked Bernardo."

"Is he your friend?"

"Not really. I knew him in high school." Jimmy's eyes narrowed. "You still haven't told me what's up."

"I'm interested in Bernardo's attitude toward women."

"That's all you're going to tell me?"

Kerney nodded. "For now. Did Bernardo come on to the waitress?"

"He tried, but she just blew him off. That got him pretty angry."

"In what way?"

"He started calling her names."

"To her face?"

"Nah, behind her back."

"What did he say to you about her?"

"That she was probably nothing but a slut who put out for anybody with a six-pack of beer and a hard dick."

"Did you think that was true?"

"From what I could tell, he was way off base."

"How so?"

"When Bernardo hit on her, she handled it real well. She showed him her wedding ring and made like a joke out of it—said her husband didn't let her date other men."

"The barmaid didn't play up to Bernardo or lead him on?"

"Not at all."

"How did Bernardo handle her rejection?"

"It pissed him off. He didn't believe she was married. He wanted to bet me he could get in her pants."

"Did you take him up on the bet?"

"No way. I told him he was full of shit and to leave her alone."

"Did anything else happen between Bernardo and the barmaid?"

"Not while I was there."

"Did you leave the bar with Bernardo?"

Wooten shook his head. "Nope. Bernardo said he was going to stay until the place closed. I don't do that kind of drinking."

"Do you remember the barmaid's name?"

"Kerri something."

"What bar does she work at?"

"The Rough Rider."

"Thanks," Kerney said. "Enjoy your leave time at home."

"You still haven't told me what this is all about."

Kerney smiled. "No, I haven't."

Kerney made a quick stop at the Rough Rider Bar and spoke with the owner, who told him that Kerri Crombie had worked all her regular shifts, including last night, and was due back at six o'clock in the evening.

He found out Crombie was married, had a little girl, and lived in a subdivision near a postsecondary vocational school just outside of the city limits.

The working-class neighborhood sat on a small bluff overlooking the Gallinas River on a parcel of land that had once been part of a National Guard training encampment. Members of the 200th Coast Artillery Battalion had trained at the camp prior to the start of World War II. Many of them died during the infamous Bataan death march after the Japanese invasion of the Philippines.

The neighborhood consisted of older flat-roof frame and stucco houses on small, rectangular lots. Over the years, some of the homeowners had converted the attached single-car garages into living spaces, added carports, and enclosed the front porches to create sun-rooms. Their front yards were neat and tidy.

Other dwellings were in disrepair. Blistered paint peeled off trim work, porches sagged, and yards were littered with discarded auto parts, motor oil cans, old water heaters, and broken lawn mowers.

Two large evergreen trees towered over the Crombie house. Planting beds bordered the walkway to the house, and a carpet of Bermuda grass stretched from the porch to the sidewalk. On the porch was a child-size plastic play table, with a miniature tea service neatly arranged for two.

Kerney knocked, got no answer, and found a woman in the backyard hanging laundry. A little girl, no more than five years old, stood at her side.

The girl saw Kerney as he walked through the back-yard gate and skipped to him. She wore bib overalls, sneakers, and a ribbon in her hair. She clutched a doll in her hand.

"Who are you?" the girl asked. She had bright red hair, just like her mother's.

"I'm Kerney. What's your name?"

"Sherry."

The woman stopped what she was doing and came toward Kerney.

"Is your last name Crombie?" he asked the girl.

"Uh huh."

"Don't talk to strangers, honey," Kerri Crombie said, as she pulled the girl away by the hand. "Can I help you?"

"I hope so, Mrs. Crombie." Kerney showed his ID

and studied the woman. Of medium build and about thirty years old, Kerri Crombie had a narrow head, curly red hair, a pale complexion, and tired eyes.

"Have you had any problems with prowlers?" he asked.

"Prowlers? No. Has somebody reported prowlers?"

"Have you seen any strange vehicles in the neighborhood?"

"No."

"Have you received any hang-up phone calls recently?"

"No."

"Have any cars followed you home from work in the last week or so?"

"No. What's this all about?"

Kerney held out Bernardo Barela's driver's license photograph. "Do you know this person?"

Kerri Crombie took the photograph and looked at it. "I know who he is. He drinks at the bar where I work."

"Has he given you any trouble?"

"No more than any other drunk who thinks barmaids are easy targets."

"Do you know him by name?"

"I think it's Bernard. No, it's Bernardo. He comes into the bar a couple of times a week."

"How long has he been drinking at the Rough Rider?"

"Ever since he turned twenty-one."

"Has he shown any unusual interest in you?"

"Mister, I've been working in bars and nightclubs for seven years. To me he's just another horny drunk with a foul mouth and wandering hands."

"You haven't seen him around your house?"

Kerri Crombie pulled her head back and the expression on her face turned serious. "Do you think he might be a stalker?"

"It's possible. I understand that you're married. Is your husband usually here when you get home from work?"

"Always. He works days and I work nights."

Kerri Crombie gave the photograph back to Kerney. He knelt down and showed it to the little girl. "Have you seen this man, Sherry?"

Sherry inspected the photograph and nodded.

"Are you sure?"

"Uh huh," Sherry said.

"Take a real close look to make sure it's not just somebody who looks like this man."

Very seriously, Sherry studied the photograph. " I saw him," she finally said.

"When?" Kerney asked.

"When I was on the front porch playing with my dolls."

"Today?" Kerney asked.

"The other day before we went to the movies."

"Did he say anything to you?" Kerney asked.

"Nope. He just walked by the house."

"Just once?"

"More than that."

"Did you see him get into a car?" Kerney asked.

"Nope."

"If you see him again when you're outside the house, I want you to go and tell your mother right away," Kerney said as he stood up. "Will you do that for me?"

"Yeah."

"Is this guy a child molester?" Kerri Crombie asked as she pulled Sherry close.

"I think he could be dangerous."

"Are you going to arrest him?"

Kerney took out a business card and wrote a note on the back. "I'll let you know if and when I do. In the meantime, be careful when you're out alone at night, and keep a close eye on Sherry. I wrote the make, model, and license number of his vehicle on the back of my card. Call me, if you see him or his car anywhere outside of work. It doesn't matter where or when. When he comes into the bar, act natural and don't say anything to raise his suspicions."

Eyes wide with worry, Kerri Crombie took the offered card. "This is spooky."

"I know. But I'd rather have you spooked than hurt."

The repair work to the ranch road was finished and the washouts, cuts, and ruts had been smoothed out and packed down. At the line camp that served as the Barela ranch headquarters, the bulldozer idled near the cattle guard. Kerney rattled over the rails and coasted to a stop in front of the trailer. Bernardo came outside and met him as he crossed to the trailer.

He lit a cigarette and gave Kerney a flat look. "My grandfather said you were looking for me."

Kerney smiled pleasantly. "We haven't been able to

identify the human remains that were found on the mesa. I thought you should know."

"You mean it wasn't Luiza, like you thought?"

"I don't think I ever said that I thought it was Luiza."

"I can put two and two together."

"I'm sure you can. We have no idea who the victim was. We can't assume it was Luiza or anyone else at this point."

"That's all you wanted to tell me?"

"Pretty much," Kerney replied. "We'll keep the case open, but unless we get lucky, it will probably remain unsolved. I'm sorry to have bothered you."

"You didn't bother me."

"Well, I leaned on you a bit the other day."

Bernardo smiled. "You were just doing your job."

"Nobody likes to think they might be a suspect."

"Hey, I told you what I knew."

Kerney nodded in agreement. "And I appreciate it."

"How come you couldn't identify the victim?"

"We can't find the complete skeleton. It could have been scattered by coyotes."

Bernardo ground out his cigarette under his boot. "That's too bad."

"Personally, I think the woman was raped before she was murdered. But you never know."

"Sounds like a tough case."

"It isn't an easy one," Kerney said with a shrug as he stepped toward Bernardo and held out his hand. "No hard feelings?"

Bernardo shook Kerney's hand and smiled. "Everything's cool."

"Good enough."

Bernardo looked pleased, which was just the way Kerney wanted him to feel. He waved good-bye as he drove away and Bernardo waved back.

Kerney had no doubt Bernardo was a budding rapist and murderer. Everything he'd learned about him fit the profile. But proving it wasn't going to be easy. If his ploy with Bernardo worked, he might let his guard down and make a mistake.

What that mistake might be Kerney couldn't predict. But Kerney had a strong hunch that, with the pressure off, Bernardo might feel free to make a move on Kerri Crombie. He decided to put a surveillance team in place to watch Bernardo.

Gabe Gonzales felt damn good about the way his day had gone. Lenny Alarid's confession had generated major busts in West Texas and New Mexico. In Albuquerque, agents had raided a damaged freight appliance store, confiscated a warehouse full of stolen goodies, and arrested the owner and several employees. In Lubbock, Midland, Amarillo, and El Paso, key members of various burglary rings had been rounded up and were undergoing interrogations. Large quantities of merchandise taken in recent West Texas heists had been seized, and three fencing operations peddling items taken in New Mexico burglaries were about to be shut down.

It was, without a doubt, one of the biggest cases Gabe had cleared in his twenty year career.

He signed the last report as Captain Garduno walked in the conference room.

"The arrest warrant for Santistevan just came in," Garduno said.

"Good deal."

"And the grand jury delivered a true bill of justified homicide on the Espinoza shooting. You can go back to work now."

Gabe couldn't tell if Garduno's remark was snide or joking. He said nothing as Garduno eased into a chair and put a department memorandum on the table. He pulled the document close and read it. Art Garcia had been bumped up to sergeant and Gabe's promotion to lieutenant had come through. He was assigned as Garduno's assistant district commander.

He clamped his jaw tight to keep from smiling and looked at Garduno. "Are you okay with this, Cap?" Gabe asked.

Garduno nodded and smiled. "Hell, I wouldn't have it any other way. You've earned it."

Gabe's smile turned into a grin. "Thanks, Cap."

"When are we going to celebrate?"

Gabe knew he'd have to invite all the troops to a promotion party, and spring for the booze and eats. Maybe he and Art Garcia could go in together on a joint bash to keep the costs down. But celebrating was the last thing his mind. Joaquin Santistevan needed to have his ass busted and thrown into jail. Gabe was looking forward to the arrest.

"I'll get back to you on that," Gabe said as he headed for the door.

To keep Santistevan from bolting, Gabe had threatened Berna with arrest if she tipped off Joaquin about the investigation. To counter the possibility that Joaquin might learn of the events in Anton Chico from some other source, Gabe had put him under constant surveillance.

No vehicles were parked outside Santistevan's house when Gabe drove by. He positioned the unmarked police unit at the end of the block and waited. For a twenty-seven-year-old, Joaquin wasn't doing badly at all. His house was a sweet little Victorian cottage in tiptop condition on a block lined with big shade trees.

Twenty minutes into the stake-out, Debbie, Joaquin's wife, arrived home and parked her five-year-old subcompact hatchback in the driveway. If cars were an indication of Joaquin's affection for the women in his life, Berna won hands down with her new sport utility vehicle.

Debbie walked to the back of the car and popped the trunk. She looked decidedly pregnant. At least Joaquin wasn't playing favorites when it came to making babies. She lifted out a bag of groceries, walked slowly up the front porch, and went inside the house.

Ben Morfin, the officer tailing Joaquin, made radio contact.

Gabe acknowledged.

"Looks like he's heading to his happy home and loving wife," Ben said. "ETA five minutes."

"'Ten-four." Gabe checked his watch and settled back to wait.

According to Lenny Alarid, Santistevan's method of targeting burglary victims was quite simple. When firewood orders came in from well-heeled customers, Joaquin would make the deliveries himself and take a look around. Did the customer have dogs or a security system? What kind of cars did the customer drive? What kind of score would a burglary yield? Were the neighbors too close by to risk a break-in?

Joaquin would ask a few innocent-sounding questions, like what the customer did for a living, or something about children and spouses, to get an idea of the family's daytime schedule.

If everything looked cool, Rudy would cruise the neighborhood for a couple of days peddling pickup loads of firewood. He would go door to door, sell a few loads here and there, and scope out the target some more. A month or so later, when no one remembered the friendly wood peddler, Rudy would pull the job.

In eighteen months, Rudy had pulled more than fifty burglaries, many of them in upscale rural Santa Fe areas, a short hour's drive from Las Vegas.

Rudy's break-ins at the weekend cabins and vacation homes around San Geronimo had also been Joaquin's idea. He'd used his time living with Uncle Isaac to scope out the best places to rob. When the firewood season ended, he sent Rudy out to rip off the second homes and mountain retreats of baby boomers who'd built expensive hideaways in the cool foothills of the Sangre de Cristo Mountains.

Santistevan's truck came into view, followed shortly by Ben's unmarked unit.

"Block him when he stops in the driveway," Gabe said into his microphone as he pulled away from the curb.

"Affirmative. There's a hunting rifle in his rear window gun rack."

"You know the drill," Gabe said.

"Here we go again," Ben replied.

When Santistevan made the turn into his driveway, Gabe accelerated, veered across the street, pointed the nose of the unit at the side of the truck, and hit the brakes. He stopped six feet short of the truck. He was out of the unit with his handgun drawn and leveled just as Santistevan reacted with a look over his shoulder.

Joaquin's right hand reached back for the rifle.

"Don't do it," Gabe said.

Joaquin's hand froze in midair.

"Check your rearview mirror," Gabe said.

Joaquin turned his head and glanced in the mirror. Another cop had a shotgun pointed at him through the rear window.

"Put both your arms out the driver's window," Gabe ordered.

Santistevan did as he was told.

"Use the outside latch to open the door."

The door opened.

"Step out slowly with your hands in view."

Ben moved to the front of the truck, his shotgun leveled on Joaquin's back.

"What's this all about?" Joaquin asked as he dismounted the truck.

"On the ground, facedown, hands locked at the back of your head," Gabe said.

Santistevan assumed the position just as Debbie came rushing out of the house and down the porch steps.

"What are you doing?" she screamed. "Let him go."

"Stop her," Gabe said to Ben as he moved in on Santistevan. He ground his knee hard on Joaquin's check, holstered his weapon, cuffed him, and pulled him to his feet.

"Why are you doing this?" Debbie yelled.

Ben had Debbie firmly in hand.

Gabe used a thumb lock to hold Santistevan still while he did a weapons pat down.

"Why are you doing this?" Debbie asked again, her voice filled with rage.

Gabe couldn't resist the impulse. "Ask his girlfriend."

12

"I want a twenty-four-hour tail on Bernardo Barela, starting now," Kerney said.

Captain Garduno winced. Even with Russell Thorpe's recent assignment to the district, he was still four officers shy of a full complement. "What have you got going, Chief?"

Kerney handed Garduno a microcassette tape. "I have no proof that Barela is our murderer, but everything I've learned about him points in that direction. I think he may have targeted another victim, a woman named Kerri Crombie. She's a waitress at a bar he frequents. Crombie's five-year-old daughter made a positive ID. She saw Barela near the family's residence. As far as I can tell, he had no legitimate reason to be in the neighborhood."

"I'll have the tape transcribed and give hard copies to the team." Garduno said. "Is Crombie at risk?"

"Barela may not think she's a good target. She's married and her husband is always home when she gets off work. Bernardo may be just sniffing around, but you never know. I've warned her to be careful. Now that Bernardo no longer thinks he's under suspicion, I want to see what he does."

Garduno ran down the district duty roster assignments in his head. He had three officers scheduled for court appearances, two attending advanced training courses in Santa Fe, and one on maternity leave. "I'm strapped for manpower, Chief," he said. "Can I get some help out of headquarters?"

"Not for a couple of days," Kerney replied. "Have Ben Morfin take the lead. Aside from Gabe Gonzales, he's your most experienced investigator. Put two uniforms in plain clothes to work with him."

"I'll have to assign Thorpe to the detail. I've got nobody else."

Kerney nodded his approval. "Make sure he's brought up to speed on surveillance tactics by Morfin. Have him ride along with Ben on the first shift."

"That means they both work double shifts."

"They can handle it. Tell Ben I don't want Barela spooked. Keep it low key all the way. Have the team use their personal vehicles, handheld radios, and cell phones. All radio transmissions on secure undercover channels only. Restrict operational need to know to your senior commanders. I will personally fire any supervisor who leaks the operation to line staff."

Garduno nodded, wrote himself a note, and waited for more.

"If he goes near Crombie, I want to know about it immediately."

"If we get anything on Barela, do you want the collar?" Garduno asked.

"I want him watched, not busted. Barela is to be picked up only if he poses a clear and present danger."

"Understood."

"Is Gabe Gonzales on his way back to the district?"

"It may be a while," Garduno answered. "He's booking Santistevan into the county jail."

"Give him my compliments on a job well done, and my congratulations on his promotion."

"I'll do that." Garduno tapped his pencil on the desktop and gave Kerney a searching look.

"What's on your mind, Captain?"

Garduno smiled uneasily. "That disciplinary report you asked me to write to Chief Baca—I'd like to forget about it. I'd rather not start my new second-in-command off with a reprimand."

"I ordered you to censure me for policy violation, not Lieutenant Gonzales."

"I know, but it would still smear egg on Gabe's face."

Kerney gave Garduno a tight smile. "You can drop it. A word of advice, Captain: When you have to chew butt, do it behind closed doors. Otherwise you humiliate your people, and it makes you look petty."

Garduno swallowed hard before replying. "Thank you."

"Tell Morfin to stay in close contact with me."

Garduno watched Kerney limp out of his office. Ouch, he thought to himself.

• • •

The dispatcher tapped on the glass partition to the radio room as Kerney walked by. He stuck his head inside and the woman gave him a pile of telephone messages. He started scanning through them on his way to the outer office. About every third message was from Ruth Pino.

"You're a hard man to reach, Chief Kerney."

He looked up to find Professor Pino standing in front of him. Her tone carried a note of displeasure and her expression wasn't cheery. He waited for more.

"I've made an appointment for you to meet with Reese Carson at the Nature Conservancy tomorrow morning."

"That's not possible, Professor," Kerney said as he returned his attention to the phone messages to hide his irritation at her pushiness. "Is the Nature Conservancy interested in the land?"

"Reese has been exploring options. Several possibilities have been discussed, including an initial purchase by the conservancy for resale to the Forest Service, or a joint purchase under the Natural Lands Protection Act."

"I'm not familiar with that law."

"It's a state statute that allows a nonprofit organization to purchase land with ninety percent public money. The conservancy would pay the remaining ten percent and manage the preserve. Isn't there some way you can free up your schedule?"

"Not tomorrow."

"We must move quickly, Chief Kerney. There are many legal issues to be ironed out before probate is settled. It is to your advantage to meet with Reese."

Kerney thumbed through more of his phone messages. Nothing appeared urgent. "I should have some time this weekend."

Pino sighed in exasperation. "I suppose that will have to do. Reese will be with me and a group of volunteers on the mesa this weekend."

"What's that all about?" Kerney stared at the last message. The brief note read "Call home. Sara" It had been logged in before noon.

"We're continuing the field survey and putting up temporary fences to protect the cactus."

"What did you say?"

"The plant and habitat assessment must be completed and protective fencing needs to be done. Nestor Barela has agreed to provide materials."

Kerney nodded, his mind sixty miles away in Santa Fe. "I'll come up to the mesa this weekend."

"When, this weekend?" Pino's voice was tinged with irritation.

"Either Saturday or Sunday," Kerney said, no longer willing to hide his exasperation with the woman.

"Very well," Pino said. A frosty look matched her chilly tone.

Kerney nodded a curt good-bye to Pino and left the building. He considered calling to see if Sara was still waiting at home for him, and decided against it. If she had already come and gone, he didn't want to get slammed by that reality.

As he gunned his unit out of the parking lot, the events of the day faded. All he could think of was Sara and what she might have to say to him when he got home.

• • •

Kerney saw Sara's Jeep and all of his uncertainty about her sudden departure rushed through his mind again. He got out of the unit not knowing what to expect, and moved slowly up the walkway to his house. He was halfway there when the door opened and Sara stepped out.

Kerney froze in his tracks. "Did you stop off to say good-bye again?"

"Where's your dog, Kerney? What happen to Shoe?"

"I sent him to an eight-year-old boy in California who desperately wanted him back."

"You didn't."

"I had to. I wasn't about to lie to the kid and keep his dog."

"But Shoe was abandoned, abused."

"Lost is more like it. The boy called me at work after Shoe arrived to thank me. Shoe is safe and his owner is happy."

"Then you did the right thing."

"It wasn't easy."

"You really liked that dog."

"You can't always have what you want. What do you want to tell me, Sara?"

"We need to talk."

"About?"

"Things. Can we talk inside?"

"Okay."

Sara stood aside as Kerney approached the front door. The expression on her face looked dead serious. He ducked past her, sat on the couch, and waited for her to join him.

She sat on the floor across from him, a good six feet away, and tucked one leg under the other.

"I didn't come here to say good-bye, Kerney. If I wanted to kiss you off, there are much easier ways to do it."

"What do you want?"

"First, I want to apologize for the way I left. But I had to get my head straight. I was feeling shy, frightened, wary, and confused."

"About what?" Kerney asked.

"You."

"I thought we were getting along well." His body felt stiff. He tried to relax, but couldn't.

"We were. Look, I came here thinking it would be great to see you and that it would just be a lot of fun. Then I wound up realizing that I couldn't treat this lightly."

"This?"

"You and me. My feelings about you aren't casual." Sara's gaze drilled into Kerney. "What do you want, Kerney?"

Kerney opened his mouth, closed it, and rubbed the back of his neck. "I don't want to lose you."

A faint smile crossed Sara's lips. "My friend Susie says I should hit you with my best shot."

"Which is?"

"A straightforward question: How do you feel about marriage?"

Kerney's felt the muscles in his shoulders loosen up. "The woman would have to be very special."

"Don't be glib."

"I take it back."

"I'm not going to give up my career."

Kerney nodded glumly. "I know that. And I can't see myself following you around from post to post for the next ten or twenty years."

"I wouldn't ask you to." She threw up her hands in frustration. "See? It's too damn impossible. Only a complete fool would jump into a part-time, long-distance marriage."

"I've been called a lot worse."

"I'm not talking about you." Sara studied Kerney's face. "Why are you grinning at me?"

Kerney's got off the couch and sat next to Sara. "I don't know. Maybe I'm feeling foolish."

Sara pulled away when Kerney tried to touch her, and got to her feet. "Don't do that." She looked down at him.

Kerney froze and the tension in his shoulders returned. The frosty look in Sara's eyes kept him from speaking.

"Tell me how you really feel," Sara said.

Kerney stood, his stomach churning. "As confused as you. I don't know what I'm doing."

"That's it?"

"No. I'm scared I might lose you, and right this minute that's all that matters. What are you feeling?"

Sara sighed. "That it's so right to be with you."

"Then let's be together, as much as we can."

Sara's eyes searched Kerney's face. "Does that mean you want a relationship with me? Something more than time together every year or two, when we can fit it in?"

"I want as much of you as I can get."

"Seriously?" Sara asked quickly.

Kerney swallowed hard. "I'll do whatever it takes to keep you in my life."

Sara's hard look faded, replaced by a soft smile. She moved to him, put her arms around his neck, and rested her head on his chest. "That sounds like a plan. Take me to bed, Kerney. We can work out the details later."

Kerney grasped Sara's waist and pulled her close. He could feel a smile spread across his face. "Is that the relationship you have in mind?"

"Partially."

In the bedroom, Sara snuggled against Kerney's shoulder.

"That was lovely," she said.

"Exceptionally lovely."

"Maybe we should just stay lovers," Sara said. "We could see each other as time allows, write, vacation together."

"Sort of a nonnuptial agreement?"

"You don't like my idea."

"It doesn't feel right."

"So marry me," Sara said.

"Seriously?"

"If you're game."

"Just like that?"

"Say yes before I back out, Kerney."

"Yes."

"I want to get married at my parents' ranch," Sara said. "We've got three weeks to pull it off."

"Have you ever been to Ireland?" Kerney asked.

"You want a honeymoon trip, too?"

"Why not?"

"This is scary, Kerney."

"Let's do it anyway."

"I bought you a present."

"What is it?" Kerney asked.

Sara turned on the bedside lamp, got up, and walked to the dresser. Kerney forgot about the gift as Sara moved across the room. She was incredibly sexy.

She came back and handed him a package.

"What is it?" he asked again.

"Open it."

Kerney pulled himself into a sitting position, unwrapped the package, saw the drawing of Hermit's Peak, and knew it was Erma's work. "My God, it's beautiful. She did it from the mesa."

"You think so?"

"Absolutely. I love it."

"Isn't it exquisite? That reminds me. You owe me a camping trip to the mesa."

"This weekend?"

"That's fine by me."

He put the drawing to one side and reached for Sara.

"What are you doing?"

"Come here."

"Don't distract me, Kerney. I have to call my mother."

"That can wait."

"No it can't. Once I tell my mother we're getting married, there's no backing out."

"Call her right now."

"I'm going to keep my maiden name." Sara leaned over and kissed him. "I love you."

"And I love you."

The answering machine message light blinked at Gabe when he got home. He hit the play button and listened to three calls from Orlando's boss at the burger joint, each more agitated than the last. Orlando had not shown up to work his shift.

It wasn't like Orlando to treat his job lightly. Unless he was sick, Gabe couldn't remember a time when Orlando had missed work. Even though Orlando's car wasn't in the driveway, Gabe went to the bottom of the stairs, called out, and got no response. To be doubly sure, he checked Orlando's room and found it empty.

The messages had come in during the first hour Orlando had been scheduled to work. Maybe something had come up at school to make him run late. Gabe called the burger joint and asked for Orlando. The night shift manager, still sounding pissed, told him Orlando had been a no-show.

Gabe's thoughts turned to Captain Garduno's briefing on the special surveillance operation Chief Kerney had ordered on Bernardo.

He got out the copy of Kerney's report Garduno had given him, read through it, and stared out the kitchen window hoping Orlando hadn't kissed off work to hang out with Bernardo.

He dialed Ben Morfin's cell phone number.

"This is Morfin."

"Ben, are you and Thorpe on station?"

"You bet," Ben said.

"Is my son with the subject?"

"Negative. The subject is home. He arrived alone and there have been no visitors."

"Thanks."

"You got a problem, Lieutenant?"

"It's probably nothing."

"You want me to keep an eye out for your son?"

"It wouldn't hurt," Gabe replied.

"What does your son drive?" Ben asked.

Gabe rattled off the information, including the license plate number.

"Got it," Ben said. "He's probably out cruising. If I see him on the streets, I'll chase him home and give you a call."

"Thanks."

"Anytime, LT. Way to go on the promotion."

"Thanks, Ben." Gabe hung up and tried to remember when Orlando was planning to visit his mother in Albuquerque. He thought it was next week, but he couldn't be sure. He punched in Theresa's numbers, and her boyfriend answered.

"Is Orlando there?"

"No. You want to talk to Theresa?"

"Just ask her when Orlando is due to visit."

There was a muffled exchange and Theresa came on the line. "Is something wrong?" she asked, sounding terse.

"Not really. Orlando isn't home and I couldn't remember when he was going down to Albuquerque to see you."

"Late next week. Why are you looking for him?"

"To tell him something."

"It must be important or you wouldn't have called me. Should I know?"

Gabe hesitated.

"Should I?"

"I wanted to tell Orlando that my promotion came through." Silence greeted his announcement.

Finally, Theresa responded. "I hope it makes you happy. Personally, I could care less."

Gabe hung up without saying another word.

He spent the next several hours at the kitchen table taking the sergeant stripes off his uniform shirts and sewing cloth lieutenant bars on the collars. He'd purchased the new insignias several months ago in a moment of optimism.

Gabe had half a mind to go looking for Orlando, but held back. Orlando didn't need an overprotective cop father looking for him in the middle of the night. He was over twenty-one, technically an adult, and a hell of a good kid to boot. If he needed a night out to blow off some steam, so be it.

Gabe stripped down to his underwear, dumped his clothes on top of the dresser, and climbed into bed. He wanted to get an early start in the morning. There was still a bunch of work to do on the Alarid–Santistevan bust, and he planned to get settled into his new office before the shift began.

Gabe checked Orlando's room early in the morning. His bed hadn't been slept in. He decided to think positively about Orlando's overnight absence. The kid didn't talk about his love life, and Gabe didn't pry. Sometimes Orlando would stay out all night, come home looking pleased with himself, and shrug off any mention of where he'd been. Within a couple of days, Orlando would start getting lots of phone calls. When that happened, Gabe didn't see much of his son until Orlando's interest in the girl cooled off.

He got to work before the day shift arrived and found a hand-carved name plaque with his new rank and name on the desk in his new office. A card rested against the plaque. The gift was from Captain Garduno.

Gabe unpacked some personal gear he'd brought from home. He put a framed enlargement of Orlando's senior high school yearbook picture on the desk and hung a few of his department commendations on the wall. Then he cleared out his paperwork from the watch commanders' cubicle and dumped it on the floor next to his office desk. He put the Alarid–Santistevan case file on top of the stack and checked with dispatch to get an update on the Barela surveillance. Bernardo had stayed home all night with no visitors.

That made Gabe feel better about things. Orlando had probably spent the night with some girl. What normal kid wouldn't trade a night of flipping burgers for a hot date with a babe? If there was a new girl in Orlando's life, maybe that was part of the reason he was restless to move. Maybe the girl was graduating, going to Albuquerque, and Orlando wanted to be with her. If so, then it all made even more sense.

He left a message on the answering machine at home

for Orlando to call him at the office, and hung up as the day shift trickled in. He spent some time accepting congratulations, along with the usual kidding, teasing, and small gifts that went with them, before the troops started work.

He put the Alarid–Santistevan files for his meeting with the ADA in his briefcase and looked up to find Art Garcia standing in the doorway. New sergeant chevrons decorated his uniform shirt.

"Those stripes look good on you, Art," Gabe said. "You want to go in on a promotion party with me?"

Garcia forced a smile. "Yeah, let's do that."

"What's wrong?"

"A rancher just called in the license plate of an abandoned vehicle south of town, on the Gallinas River. Dispatch ran it through Motor Vehicles. It's your son's car."

"Orlando didn't come home last night."

"It may mean nothing, Gabe. The rancher said kids use that spot along the river all the time to party. Maybe Orlando just left his car and went off with some friends."

"Who's the rancher?"

"Arlin Fullerton."

"Did he give you directions?"

Art held out a slip of paper.

"Call Fullerton back and have him meet me there. Tell dispatch to cancel my meeting with the DA's office. I'll reschedule later."

"You want somebody to go with you?"

Gabe shook his head as he hurried out the door.

Garcia found Captain Garduno making coffee in the break room and filled him in.

Garduno put the pot down. "Is that all you have?"

"So far."

"Is Bernardo Barela still at home?"

"No. He's sitting in a truck outside a hardware store. You want him picked up?"

"Negative. Call Chief Kerney and brief him. Then put search and rescue on standby, including bloodhounds. When did Gabe leave?"

"Two minutes ago."

"I'm on my way," Garduno said.

Orlando's car was unlocked and his keys were in the ignition. A bank envelope sat on the dashboard. Gabe reached in through the open window, picked it up, and counted the bills—over seven hundred dollars. There were two withdrawal slips and a pay stub, all with yesterday's date. Orlando had cashed his check and zeroed-out his accounts.

He looked at Garduno and fanned the bills. "Orlando would never do this with his money. Never. Or leave his keys in an unlocked car."

"Take it easy, Gabe," Garduno said. "You can't always tell what kids will do. When Orlando shows up, I'm sure he can explain everything."

"Orlando didn't party here last night. Nobody did. Look around. There's no fresh litter or beer bottles anywhere."

"Maybe the party was over there." Garduno raised his chin toward the crumbling walls of two old homesteads that flanked the dirt road. "Or maybe he's camped nearby with some friends."

Gabe looked at the dense forest on the far side of the river. "Orlando doesn't like to camp. Where the fuck is that rancher?"

"Fullerton will be here," Garduno said as he went to his unit and reached for the radio handset. "Check around those stone walls, Lieutenant."

Gabe didn't move.

Garduno took his thumb off the transmit button. "Stop thinking the worst and check the ruins, Gabe. Let's go to work and find Orlando."

Garduno waited until Gabe moved off before clicking on the handset. "I want search and rescue and every available unit at my location ASAP," he said. "Contact Chief Kerney and ask him to get up here pronto."

He dropped the handset on the car seat and went to join Gabe.

The helicopter pilot cleared the ridgeline and dropped down to follow the river. Below, Kerney could see an assembly of police cars and search and rescue vehicles, some with horse trailers. A blue domestic coupe, cordoned off with crime scene tape, sat in the middle of a dirt road. On a small rise behind the car, several uniforms were searching the ruins of old settlers' cabins.

The pilot gained altitude to keep propeller wash from disturbing the activity on the ground and planted the bird on the road a hundred yards away from the blue coupe. Kerney jumped out. Garduno and Gonzales met him halfway.

Gabe's face had worry written all over it. Garduno's impassive expression looked forced.

"What have we got?" Kerney asked.

Garduno took the lead. "Gabe's son left home yesterday morning. He cut his classes at the university, didn't show up for work last night, and never went home. One of Arlin Fullerton's ranch hands noticed Orlando's car here about noon yesterday. There was nobody around. The car wasn't reported as abandoned until this morning when Fullerton and a few of his people came back to move some cattle to another part of the ranch."

Kerney looked at Gabe. "No sign of struggle?"

"No," Gabe said flatly.

"You searched the car?"

Gabe nodded. "Nothing's missing. But I found over seven hundred dollars on the dashboard. Orlando cashed his paycheck and cleaned out his savings and checking accounts right after the bank opened yesterday morning. Withdrawal slips were in the envelope with the money."

"That gives us a time frame to work with," Kerney said. "Was the vehicle locked?"

"No, and the keys were in the ignition," Gabe said. "Orlando would never do that. He worked too damn hard for the money to buy that car."

"Did the car break down?"

"It runs just fine," Gabe answered.

"Do you have any ideas why Orlando needed so much cash?"

"None," Gabe said. "But it's every dime he had."

Garduno broke in. "Arlin Fullerton said that people park here to hike and camp in the woods or party by the river. There are several trails on the other side of the river that lead to some remote, pretty canyons."

"Orlando isn't into camping," Gabe said.

"I'm still sending the search and rescue people up there," Garduno said. "For all we know Orlando may be with some of his friends, or snuggled into a sleeping bag with some pretty young thing."

They reached Garduno's unit and stopped. "Have you found anything to suggest Orlando is with friends?" Kerney asked.

"We lifted four different sets of fingerprints from the vehicle, but that could mean anything," Garduno said.

"Is there any other physical evidence?"

Garduno shook his head. "Fullerton and his people trashed the area. They loaded the cattle on stock trucks right in the road. There's nothing but hoofprints, cow shit, and heavy-duty tire tread marks."

Kerney turned to Gabe. "When did you last see Orlando?"

"Early yesterday. About an hour before he went to the bank."

"Did the two of you talk?"

"Yeah. He said you'd questioned him about Bernardo's friends. He asked me what was up. I told you you were investigating the mesa homicide."

"How did he react to that?"

"He seemed okay with it."

"Did you talk about anything else?"

"I asked him why he was leaving early. He said he had to meet some guy from school who wanted to borrow his lecture notes. He didn't say who it was."

"Is that all?"

"Pretty much. He got a phone call while I was in the shower."

"Who from?"

"Orlando said it was from the kid who wanted to borrow his notes."

"Does Orlando have a steady girlfriend?"

"No."

"Would he tell you if he was planning to cut classes and meet some girl or go camping with friends, like Captain Garduno suggested?"

"Not necessarily. He'd know I wouldn't approve."

The search and rescue team had mounted up. Four riders crossed the river, moved through the bottom land, and disappeared into the forest. "So, it's possible Orlando decided to play hooky," Kerney said.

"Don't feed me crap," Gabe said. "Something stinks here. You know it, and I know it."

"Let's assume he came here to meet someone. Seven hundred dollars could buy two ounces of very good pot."

"Orlando doesn't use drugs," Gabe said.

Gabe was reacting like a parent, not like a cop. Kerney decided not to push the point. "Who would he come here to meet?"

"I don't fucking know," Gabe said.

"Okay, we'll talk to all his friends. But first let's see if we can find out who called him." Kerney opened his pocket notebook, tore out a page, and gave it to Garduno.

"What's that?" Gabe demanded.

"The names and phone numbers of everyone I talked

to about the mesa homicide." Kerney looked at Garduno. "Call dispatch and have them request phone company records on any calls made to Gabe's phone. Start with Bernardo."

"You're fucking crazy to think Orlando had anything to do with that."

"You wanted me to cut the crap, Lieutenant. Bernardo works twenty miles from here. He's the only person I know with a legitimate reason to be anywhere near this place during the day."

"You're way off the mark."

"Let's hope so," Kerney said.

Garduno reached inside his unit to pick up the radio handset. Gabe gave Kerney an unpleasant look, walked to the river, and stood alone with his back turned and head lowered.

Garduno finished up with dispatch, glanced at Kerney, and nodded in Gabe's direction. "He knows it could be bad, Chief."

"I understand that."

A pickup truck with three dogs in the bed stopped next to Garduno's unit, and a stocky woman with short brown hair got out. "I'm Martha Owens. Where do you want my dogs?" she asked.

Before either could answer, the dogs started barking, straining against their leashes.

Owens went to the dogs and tried to calm them. The barking continued in spite of her efforts.

"They smell something," she said.

"What?" Garduno asked.

"Either a body or blood."

"We've searched," Garduno said. "Nothing's here."

"My dogs say otherwise."

"Where?" Garduno asked, spreading his arms.

"Anne will show us. She's the best of the lot." Martha unsnapped the leash of a female hound, and the dog jumped out of the truck before Owens could drop the tailgate. The hound made for a spot just off the road and started digging while her companions in the truck kept up a steady howl.

Kerney and Garduno converged on Owens and her dog. Clumps of dirt flew as the hound dug deeper.

Martha dropped to one knee, scooped up a handful of moist dirt, and sniffed it. "It smells like blood to me. Lots of it. The ground is saturated."

"What kind of blood?" Garduno asked.

"I can't tell you that," Owens answered. "But something got slaughtered here recently."

Kerney felt the presence of someone at his side and looked over.

"Sweet Jesus, Mother Mary," Gabe said, his voice cracking.

"Don't jump to conclusions, Gabe," he said.

Gabe looked at Kerney like he was a complete stranger. "I want Bernardo in custody now."

"We'll do this my way, Lieutenant."

"What way is that, Kerney?"

"Cool it, Gabe," Garduno said.

"Fuck you, Cap. I want to know what happened to my son."

Garduno's call sign came over the radio. He hurried to his unit. "Go, dispatch."

"The phone company reports a call made from the first number you gave me to the Gonzales residence at oh-six-fifty hours, last date."

"Ten-four."

"Let's go get the son of a bitch," Gabe said.

Kerney grabbed Gabe's arm to hold him back. "Not yet. We need a plan."

"You need a fucking plan. I don't."

Kerney tightened his grip. "Give me your weapon and your shield." For a moment he thought Gabe was going to swing at him.

"You'd do that?"

"Unless you work with me, I will."

Gabe glared at Kerney. "What's your plan?"

Kerney swung his attention to Garduno. "Check with Fullerton. Find out if he slaughtered an animal here this morning. He may have had to put down an injured calf or a yearling."

"Fullerton is on his way back to his ranch house."

"Contact him ASAP." Kerney turned to Gabe. "You're going back with me to the office. We're going to see what the surveillance team has on Bernardo, and get people out backtracking on Orlando. I'll ride with you."

"To watch me?"

"You bet. Send the chopper home and keep working the search, Captain."

"Will do."

"Let's go, Lieutenant."

Garduno called dispatch and snapped off an order to make contact with Fullerton. "Patch me through when you reach him. I'll stand by."

"Ten-four."

Still clutching the microphone in his hand, Garduno watched Gabe and Kerney drive away. He threw it on the front seat of his unit in disgust, put his hands to his face, and rubbed his eyes. What a shitty, shitty day it had turned out to be.

13

At the district office, Kerney kept Gabe Gonzales at his side during the time it took to implement a sweep to gather information about Orlando's whereabouts during the last twenty-four hours. Bernardo Barela would remain under full surveillance while officers backtracked at the bank, the university, and the burger joint where Orlando worked, questioning employees, classmates, professors, and anyone else who might have seen Orlando, or knew where he could be.

Kerney pulled Ben Morfin back on duty to do followups on the people who'd been interviewed in the Luiza San Miguel slaying. He couldn't discount the possibility that it might tie in to Orlando's disappearance.

Garduno called in to report that Fullerton hadn't put down any of his livestock at the river, and the look on Gabe's face told Kerney that Gonzales was about to explode.

"Tell Fullerton we're coming out to talk to him," Kerney said.

They left the district office for the Box Z Ranch in Gabe's unit, running a silent code three. Gabe kept the unit floored until the drop-off into the canyon forced him to slow down. On the ranch road, he pushed the unit to its limit, blowing out the shocks, struts, and alignment, fighting to keep control as they pitched, bounced, and veered through rough water crossings and over jagged rock outcroppings.

Kerney didn't say a word.

They found Arlin Fullerton in the equipment barn watching one of his employees weld a new lip on the bulldozer blade.

"Did you find that missing boy yet?" Fullerton asked.

"We're still looking," Kerney said. "Did you see Bernardo yesterday?"

"Yeah, when he returned the 'dozer. He was late getting it back."

"What time was that?"

"Four o'clock, or thereabouts. He came looking for me to say he'd gouged a chuck out of the blade. Said he'd hit some hard rock while he was grading the road." Fullerton shook his head. "I don't see how he did it. That's mostly shale and sandstone he was moving around."

"How did he get back to his truck?"

"I gave him a ride."

"Did he talk about anything?"

"He told me you'd paid him a visit yesterday."

"And?"

Fullerton shook his head. "That was it, except for some small talk about how many cow and calf units his uncle planned to run during the summer."

"Did you see him after that?"

"Haven't seen him since."

"Did any of your ranch hands see anyone around the abandoned car yesterday?"

"I would have heard if they did. They have standing orders to run off trespassers and report them to me. Those kids make a mess when they party at the river, and I don't pay my people to spend their time cleaning up beer bottles, garbage, and broken glass."

"I'd like to talk to the man who first spotted the car," Kerney said.

"You'll find him at the old Cañón La Liendre headquarters. His name is Marcelo. He doesn't speak much English. It's the last ranch house on the way out."

"I've seen it from the road," Kerney said.

Although he was tired, Russell Thorpe's enthusiasm for his first solo surveillance assignment hadn't diminished. He'd followed Bernardo to an early-morning stop at a hardware store, and then to a ranch and farm supply business where Bernardo loaded up an order of steel fence posts and rolls of wire.

From there, Bernardo drove out of town on the frontage road to the San Geronimo overpass and took a blacktop highway that turned to gravel a few miles outside the village. Thorpe used the dust trail kicked up by the tires to follow Barela through the settlement to Chief Kerney's property.

With binoculars he watched Bernardo unlock the gate, drive through, and park. After twenty minutes, Ruth Pino and her students arrived in a van. He saw

Bernardo and the professor exchange a few words and then drive down the ranch road in a caravan, Bernardo leading the way.

Several hours passed before Bernardo returned alone with an empty truck and headed toward town.

Russell stayed well back of the pickup to avoid being spotted. He caught sight of the truck on the ramp to the interstate and closed the gap, keeping two cars between himself and Bernardo. Back in town, Bernardo led Russell down the main drag and onto a side street adjacent to the university, cruising through a residential neighborhood of old homes that had been converted into duplex and apartment rentals for college students.

Several blocks into the neighborhood, on a tree-lined street, Bernardo pulled to the curb, parked, and walked to a waiting car. A middle-aged man got out, shook Bernardo's hand, and took him up the sidewalk to a small two-story Victorian cottage. The man unlocked the front door and gestured for Bernardo to enter first.

Russell waited for a minute, then drove by the house slowly, jotting down the phone number on a rental sign in the front window, and the license plate number of the man's car. He circled the block and parked at the end of the street. A few minutes passed before Bernardo and the man came out and stood on the sidewalk talking. Whatever the man said made Bernardo shrug his shoulders and shake his head. The man handed something that looked like a business card to Bernardo, went to his vehicle, and drove away.

Bernardo waited until the man was out of sight

before he dropped the card into the gutter and crossed to his truck.

Russell retrieved the card after Bernardo left, caught up with him at a red light, and tailed him across the main drag to a street that fronted the old railroad station and hotel. Bernardo parked and went inside the Rough Rider Bar.

Russell sat in his hot car. The day had warmed considerably and Thorpe's air conditioner didn't work. His face and hands were covered in dust from driving with the windows down on dirt roads and his mouth felt like dry cotton.

After ten minutes of waiting, Russell decided to eat lunch. He wiped his gritty hands on his pant legs and unwrapped the sandwich he'd packed. The bread was mushy and the meat was limp. He ate it anyway, and washed it down with a warm soda, thinking that sitting inside the Rough Rider Bar with a cold beer was a much more appealing idea.

He crumpled the wax paper, tossed it on the floorboard, and looked at the business card Bernardo had thrown away. It was from a local property management company. The phone number on the card matched the number on the rental sign in the window of the house. Maybe Bernardo was thinking about getting a place of his own.

Russell's shirt collar felt sticky against the back of his neck and he could feel sweat dripping down his armpits. He checked the time. In ten minutes he was due to call in on the secure channel and give an update to dispatch. Eating something hadn't been a good idea. After yesterday's double shift, and only a few hours of sack time, the food in his stomach made him drowsy.

His eyes closed and when his head dropped to his chest, he woke up. Startled, he shook off the drowsiness. Bernardo's truck was gone and the dispatcher was calling his unit number. He pushed the transmit button on the handheld and answered.

"You're five minutes late on your call-in," the dispatcher said. "Is everything ten-four?"

Russell cursed, put his car in gear, gunned it to the main drag, and checked both directions for any sign of Bernardo. Nothing. He slammed his hand against the steering wheel in frustration.

"Respond," the dispatcher said.

"Negative," Russell said. "I've lost the subject."

"Stand by."

Russell waited with a sinking feeling that he'd fucked up.

"Return to station," the dispatcher said.

Russell swallowed hard.

"Acknowledge."

"Ten-four," Russell said.

Gabe rattled his unit over a flagstone outcropping that bisected the ranch road. The vehicle bottomed out and Kerney's head hit the roof. They drove past a stock pen that looked large enough to hold five hundred head of cattle, and into the old La Liendre ranch headquarters.

At the north end of Fullerton's half-million-acre spread, the ranch compound charmed Kerney's eye. Two side-by-side houses surrounded by mature trees faced a stone barn and horse stable that was bermed into the ground and covered with a slanted tin roof.

The older clapboard house looked to be a Victorian-style craftsman model popular during the 1920s. Ordered by catalog, the complete building package was shipped by rail, hauled to the building site, and assembled following step-by-step instructions. The screened front porch sagged a bit and a fresh coat of paint was in order, but the house looked to be in fair shape.

The newer house was flat-roofed, stuccoed, and bordered by a low fence that kept a dark-haired, four-year-old boy in and a small herd of nearby goats out. A satellite television dish was anchored to the side of the dwelling.

Gabe ground to a stop in front of the gate. The boy ran inside the house as the goats scattered to the horse stable and clattered over the tin roof, raising a racket with their hoofs.

"I'll take this one," Gabe said as he got out of the unit.

Kerney followed Gabe up the walkway, stepping around the toys the boy had been playing with. A man in bare feet, with a chubby unshaven face, stepped out to meet them.

He eyed Gabe's uniform and in Spanish asked what Gabe wanted.

"Are you Marcelo?" Gabe replied in Spanish as he stepped onto the porch. Through the screen door, Gabe could see a television. It was tuned to a Spanish-language afternoon talk show.

"Yes."

"What time yesterday did you discover the abandoned car?"

"Eleven, no later."

"And you saw no one?"

"No. I was in the feed truck. I just stopped and wrote down the license number so I could give it to the boss."

"Where were you before you found the car?" Gabe asked.

"Loading the feed truck," Marcelo said. "I always put out range supplement the day before we move cattle to a new pasture. It keeps them nearby and easier to find."

"Did you see anybody while you were loading the truck?"

"The Barelas drove by."

"How could you see them from here?"

Marcelo pointed to the large three-bin feed storage unit that stood opposite the stock pens. On high stilts with chutes under each bin, the unit was designed to fill feeder trucks quickly and easily.

"I was on top of the bins, checking to see if I needed to reorder," Marcelo said. "I can see the road from there."

"You're sure you saw Bernardo and his uncle?"

"I just saw their pickup. I don't know who was in it."

"What time was that?"

"Maybe ten or a little later."

"Which way was the pickup traveling?"

"Toward their ranch. They were in a hurry. Driving fast. I think maybe Bernardo was by himself and late getting to work. His uncle doesn't let him drive that way when he's around."

"Did you see any other vehicles on the road?"

"No. This is not a place where people go driving, except for the town kids who want to drink away from their parents' eyes. But they don't come out here much until the weather gets warmer. Did you find the owner of the car?"

"Not yet."

"I hope he's not injured up in one of those canyons," Marcelo said. "We've got bear, mountain lions, and coyotes out here that will take down a sick or crippled animal very quickly. We lose stock to them every year. If he's hurt, he could be in big trouble."

Gabe turned away from Marcelo. "Thanks for talking to me."

"Sure."

Gabe walked past Kerney, his face pale, his mouth drawn in a hard line.

Kerney gave Marcelo a business card, asked him to call if he remembered anything else, and joined Gabe in his unit.

"Did you get any of that?" Gabe asked as he backed up and started down the ranch road.

"I got it all."

"Let's go get Bernardo," Gabe said.

"Not yet."

"What more do you want, for chrissake? We got Bernardo calling Orlando at home, and a witness who puts Bernardo in the immediate vicinity an hour before Orlando's car was discovered."

"I want the same thing you do, Gabe. But first we find out what everybody working the case has uncovered."

"My son could be out there hurt or dead."

"I know how you feel."

"No, you don't know. You just think you know."

Kerney's call sign came over the radio. He picked up the microphone and responded.

"Go to secure channel," the dispatcher said.

Kerney switched over.

Garduno came on the horn. "Our subject has eluded surveillance."

"When did it happen?"

"At twelve hundred hours."

"Where?"

"The Rough Rider Bar."

"Bring Thorpe in and have him stand by."

"He's standing by."

"Swarm the city with every available officer," Kerney said. "I want that subject found."

"We're already looking. Nothing so far. Stop and detain, Chief?"

"Negative. Locate and follow only. Morfin gets the call as soon as the subject has been spotted."

"Ten-four."

"Anything from search and rescue?" Kerney asked.

"No sign of any campers in the canyons. The dogs are out and the team is still looking. They'll shut it down at nightfall."

"Ten-four." Kerney's head hit the roof as Gabe gunned the unit over the flagstone outcropping. "We're on our way back."

"This is bullshit," Gabe said as he spun the wheel and made the last turn before the county road. "For chris-

sake, tell Garduno to pick Bernardo up. We've got
enough to hold him for questioning."

The unit hit a series of bowling ball-size rocks and
Gabe fought the wheel to keep control. The ruined
undercarriage jolted Kerney's head into the roof again.

"We do it my way, or you go home," Kerney said.

One block over from Jessica Varela's apartment, Bernardo waited in his truck until the lunch hour ended and
students were hurrying out of their apartments headed
to afternoon classes. He walked down the alley between
the two streets, past the detached garages at the back of
the lots. He stopped, pushed against the side door to the
garage in Jessica's backyard, and stepped inside. Except
for some old garden tools, a rusty green push lawn mower,
and several cardboard boxes, the garage was empty. A
small window facing the back porch of the house let in a
shaft of light. The garage and the window would give
Bernardo a perfect hiding place and vantage point.

He left the garage and continued down the alley,
watching and listening for dogs. On his past visits he'd
seen only one, a young puppy kept on a leash in the front
yard at a corner house. It was far enough away from Jessica's apartment for Bernardo to easily avoid it. But he
wanted to be completely sure he hadn't overlooked any
other dogs that could draw attention to him. He heard
no barking as he walked, and saw no evidence of animals kept in the yards.

The alley wasn't used much. Weeds, leaves, and small
branches from backyard trees carpeted the lane and
there was no evidence of recent tire tracks. Bernardo

figured only meter readers and utility trucks used the alley.

He didn't see anybody outside, but a few backyard windows were open and he could hear the sounds of music every now and then. Since just about everybody in the neighborhood attended the university, Bernardo guessed some students were home studying or kicking back after morning classes.

He ran over his plan as he walked to the truck. The only access to Jessica's apartment was through the front door that led to the ground floor apartment and a staircase to the second story. He would have no trouble getting into the building. During his tour of the empty apartment with the property management dude, he'd unlocked the back door and unlatched a kitchen window. Once inside, breaking into Jessica's apartment would be no sweat. Her apartment door had been hung with the hinges on the exterior side. All he had to do was pop off the hinges and he'd be in. Then he'd rehang the door and be waiting when Jessica got back from her night class.

Bernardo had given the man from the property management company a fictitious name and a story that he was moving to town from Santa Fe to attend summer school and looking for a place to rent. If the cops questioned him it would be enough to throw them off.

He lit a cigarette and drove away, wondering what he would do to Jessica after she got home. There were so many options to consider. But he had all day to decide. The thought struck him that Jessica's long blonde hair would be a trophy worth keeping.

• • •

Russell Thorpe stopped talking and sat on the edge of his chair in the conference room with his knees locked together, looking like an overgrown, burly schoolboy who'd been sent to the principal's office.

He didn't know which made him feel worse, blowing his assignment or lying about it with a lame story about how a beer delivery truck had blocked his view of the bar just long enough to allow Bernardo to leave unnoticed.

Russell kept his gaze fixed on the wall behind the four men sitting across the conference table and waited for the ax to fall.

Captain Garduno consulted the notes he'd made while Russell had been talking. "What exactly happened at the vacant apartment?"

Russell blinked and met Garduno's hard stare. "Like I said, Bernardo met this man from a property management firm. They were inside the apartment for maybe five minutes. When they came out, they talked briefly, the man gave Bernardo his card, and then left. Bernardo threw the card away. I guess he didn't like the place."

Kerney read the name on the business card. "Aside from Ruth Pino and this Chuck Beasly, did Bernardo talk to anyone else?"

"Not as far as I know, Chief. He may have when he was in the bar."

"He didn't stop to take a piss or make a phone call?" Art Garcia asked.

"No, Sergeant."

"So, Bernardo went directly from the hardware store to the ranch supply store, to the mesa, and then met with Beasly at the apartment," Gabe said.

"That's right, Lieutenant."

"Did he buy anything at the hardware store?" Gabe asked.

"I didn't see him walk out carrying anything," Russell said.

"That's strange," Kerney said. "How long was Bernardo waiting for the hardware store to open?"

"Ten, fifteen minutes."

"You don't wait for a store to open, go in, and buy nothing," Art Garcia said.

"Maybe they didn't have what he needed," Russell suggested.

"Maybe," Gabe said.

Kerney looked at Gabe. "We'll follow up with Beasly and the hardware store."

Gabe nodded.

"That's all, Thorpe," Garduno said.

Russell stood up. "Where do you want me, Captain?"

"Out looking for Bernardo."

"Don't leave until I talk to you, Thorpe," Kerney said flatly. "I'll just be a few minutes."

"Yes, sir."

Kerney waited to speak until the door closed behind Thorpe. "Do we have anything from the field?" he asked Garduno.

"With the exception of Gabe, the teller at the bank, and the burger joint manager, so far nobody has seen or talked to Orlando since yesterday morning."

"What about the student who called and asked to borrow Orlando's class notes?"

Garduno consulted his paperwork. "We've talked to every student enrolled in Orlando's classes. No one admitted to making any such call."

"So the only verified early-morning call to Orlando we've got is from Bernardo."

"That's right, Chief."

"Do we have Kerri Crombie covered?"

"We've got her buttoned down," Garduno said. "The ADA has been calling. She wants a meeting with Gabe ASAP. Otherwise she's going to release Santistevan and Alarid."

"Let them walk," Gabe said. "We can arrest them again later."

Kerney switched his attention to Art Garcia. "Can you handle the meeting with the ADA?"

"No problem, Chief."

Kerney got to his feet and looked at Gabe. "I'll meet you at your unit."

"I'll be there."

Outside the conference room, Kerney found a nervous Russell Thorpe waiting for him. He led the young man to Garduno's office, closed the door, and searched Thorpe's face.

"You fell asleep on duty, didn't you?"

Russell blushed and nodded. "I tried not to."

"It happens to every officer at least once," Kerney said. "Most are lucky and don't get caught."

"Are you going to fire me, Chief?"

"No. But if you ever lie to me or any other supervisor

again, you'll be driving that imaginary beer truck that
stopped outside the bar. Do I make myself clear?"

Russell gulped. "Yes, sir."

"Go to work."

Outside, Gabe's unit was missing from the parking
lot. Kerney checked with the dispatcher, who said Gonzales wasn't on the air, and found Garduno in his office.

"Gabe took off," he said. "I need a vehicle."

"Take my unit." Garduno tossed Kerney his keys.
"Go easy on him, Chief. He's a good man."

"I know that."

Chuck Beasly looked at the photograph. He wore a
genial smile that seemed permanently fixed on his face.
He ran his hand through his thinning hair and nodded.

"That's the kid," he said to the state police lieutenant.
"He called yesterday to set up the appointment. I
showed him the place this morning, but he didn't take it.
I don't know why, it's a nice unit. Maybe he couldn't
afford it."

"Did he tell you anything about himself?" Gabe asked.

"Just that he was moving up from Santa Fe to go to
summer school at the university."

"What name did he give you?"

Beasly flipped a page back on his desk calendar and
ran his finger down a list of names. "Salazar. Ben
Salazar."

"How many tenants are in the building?"

"Just one. It's a duplex converted from a two-story
home. A young woman has the upstairs unit. She goes
to the university part-time."

"Her name?"

"Jessica Varela."

The name didn't ring any bells for Gabe, nor did it match with any of the people Chief Kerney had interviewed. "Was she at home when you showed the apartment?"

"I don't think so."

"What did Barela do while he was inside?"

"Is that his real name? The usual. He opened doors, looked at the backyard, checked the appliances. I gave him my standard pitch about the place. Told him it would probably rent fast and if he didn't grab it, he'd lose it."

"Was he interested?"

"I thought so, at first. He wanted to know if I was showing it to anyone else anytime soon. I told him a young couple would be looking at it this evening. He even asked me what time I was showing it."

"When are you showing it?"

"Six-thirty."

"Thanks."

Beasly walked to the office door with the lieutenant. As the officer got to his car, another police vehicle drove up and a man in civilian clothes got out. The uniformed cop froze at the side of his squad car. The guy in civvies limped to the lieutenant and started talking. The lieutenant waved a finger in the man's face and poked him hard in the chest, his face red with anger.

For a minute, Beasly thought the men were going to start fighting. But when the cop in civvies pushed the finger away from his chest and said something, the lieutenant backed down.

Beasly watched the two men get into the lieutenant's vehicle and leave, wondering what the fuck that was all about.

In front of the hardware store, Gabe killed the engine and set the brake. Kerney could have pulled his shield and weapon for any number of reasons, including insubordination and conduct unbecoming an officer. Poking the chief in the chest and calling him a stupid son of a bitch outside of Beasly's office had been a dumb thing to do.

Gabe turned and looked Kerney in the eye. "Sorry, Chief. I was way out of line. I've been acting half-crazy."

Kerney studied the mounted antelope in the store window, a centerpiece display for the chain saws arranged on tree stumps and wood logs at the animal's feet.

"You have cause," Kerney said. "No apology necessary. Let it slide."

"Did you jump on Thorpe for lying about how he lost Bernardo?"

"I read him out royally. He stays on the job."

"He's a good kid." Gabe shook his head. "Jesus, cops. We're a crazy bunch, aren't we?"

"Sometimes we are."

Inside the store, rows of caps and hats were hung on lines that ran above the center aisle, and cattle brands burned into wood boards were nailed to the walls above the shelves.

"Yeah, Bernardo was in this morning checking on something at the order desk," the manager said.

In his early thirties, the man looked impatient and

not at all happy to have cops in the store distracting his customers.

"Who did he speak to?" Gabe asked.

"Jessica talked to him."

Gabe glanced at the young woman standing behind the center aisle order counter. She was blonde and very Anglo looking. "Where is Jessica now?"

"That's her at the desk."

"Is her last name Varela?"

"You got it."

"Can you relieve her for a few minutes and give us a place where we can talk?" Kerney asked.

"Sure. Use the break room in the back. I'll have Jessica meet you there."

Just off the receiving dock, the break room doubled as a storage room for excess inventory. Jessica Varela entered and pushed some strands of hair away from her face.

"What's this all about?" Her voice carried a childlike quality.

"You spoke to Bernardo Barela this morning," Kerney said.

"I don't know why he came in." Jessica kept her head slightly lowered and gave Kerney a sidelong, timid look. "He knew the fence post driver he'd ordered wouldn't get here for another ten days. I told him that earlier in the week."

"Did he talk to you about anything else?" Kerney asked.

"He always tries to talk to me. I don't mind it if I'm not busy."

"What did he talk about?" Gabe asked.

"This morning?"

"Yes."

"Silly stuff. He wanted to know if I liked to study and do homework with other students in my classes."

"He knows you go to the university?" Kerney asked.

"Sure."

"What else does he know about you?" Gabe asked.

"That I'm divorced and that I moved up here from Albuquerque. How old I am. That's about it."

"Has he tried to date you?" Kerney asked.

Jessica shook her head and her long hair covered one eye. "I think he'd like to, but he hasn't asked. I'd turn him down anyway. He's too young and I'm not interested in dating. After what I've been through, men aren't very popular with me right now."

"What, exactly, did you tell him about your study habits?"

"Just that I like to study alone, and with my job and school and all I don't have a lot of time to socialize and stuff."

"Did you mention there was an apartment for rent in your building?" Gabe asked.

"Why would I do that?"

"He didn't ask?"

"Why should he? He doesn't know where I live."

"Have you ever seen Bernardo away from the store?" Kerney asked.

"No, just here. Did Bernardo do something wrong?"

"What time do you get off work?" Gabe said.

"Today? At five. Then I go straight to the library and study before my classes."

"What time do you get home from classes?" Kerney asked.

"Nine-thirty. You're scaring me with these questions. What's going on?"

"We think Bernardo is a stalker," Kerney said.

"And he's stalking me?" Jessica's voice quivered.

"Possibly."

"What should I do?"

"Keep to your normal routine," Gabe said. "We'll be watching Bernardo."

"What about me? Who'll be protecting me?"

"There will be a plainclothes officer following you when you leave work," Kerney said. "You'll be under constant observation."

"For how long?"

"Until the situation is resolved. I'd like to take a look inside your apartment."

"What for?"

"To make sure Bernardo hasn't been there."

"Do you think he may have?"

"It's possible. I'll need your key."

"I have a spare." Jessica reached for her purse, extracted a key chain, and gave Kerney a house key with a shaky hand. "I never should have moved here," she said. "I hate this town."

Kerney sent Gabe off on a door-to-door canvas of one part of Jessica's neighborhood while he covered the other. He worked the street behind Jessica's apartment, half expecting to find Gabe gone when he returned.

The last place he stopped was a one-story adobe

with a deep portal and territorial moldings around the windows. An old hacienda that had somehow survived the neighborhood's late-nineteenth-century conversion to Victorian architecture, it had been transformed into apartments with a series of doors that opened on to the portal.

At the last apartment, a young man, no more than five four, answered Kerney's knock. Kerney showed him Bernardo's picture.

"I saw him sitting in a pickup truck," the young man said, pointing to a spot across the street.

"When was that?"

"On my way to my one o'clock."

"He was just sitting in the truck?"

"That's all I saw."

"How long was he there?"

"I don't know."

Gabe was waiting on the sidewalk in front of Jessica's apartment when Kerney turned the corner.

"Did you get anything?" Gabe asked as Kerney approached.

"Bernardo was parked a block over at about one o'clock. Did you?"

"Nothing."

With Gabe at his heels, Kerney checked the front door, found it locked, walked to the backyard, and tried the rear door to the empty apartment. The doorknob turned and he stepped inside the kitchen of the empty apartment. ———

Gabe moved to the sink. "This window is unlatched," he said.

"I think Bernardo is ready to make his move," Kerney said.

"I hope you're right, Chief," Gabe said as he stared out the window. "What's Orlando got to do with this?" he asked softly, almost to himself.

It wasn't Kerney's question to answer. By now, Gabe had to suspect Orlando and Bernardo were somehow linked together in the Luiza San Miguel slaying. Maybe Orlando had been just a witness to the rape and murder, or maybe he was an equal partner in the crime. Whatever fell out, it was impossible to dismiss Orlando's disappearance as a coincidence.

"Let's see what pans out," Kerney replied.

They took a quick tour of Jessica's apartment to check the layout.

Bernardo threw the empty beer can out the truck window and popped open another one. There were only a few old dudes fishing along the shore of the lake at the Maxwell National Wildlife Refuge. The wintering waterfowl were gone for the season and without the birds as an attraction nobody but fishermen, a few curious tourists, and occasional picnickers came to the place during the spring and summer.

Situated on the high plains a few miles outside of Las Vegas, there wasn't much to the refuge—just marshes, the lake, cornfields planted to lure and feed migrating birds, and a view of the mountains.

Bernardo swallowed some beer, thought about Jessica Varela, and got a warm feeling in his groin. Everything he knew about her told him she was going to do exactly what he wanted, the way he wanted. Which meant he'd be able to save the best for last. That made Bernardo smile. He was going to have a real good time.

He finished the beer, flipped the can out the window, and fired up the truck. Everything was set to go. The cops were off his case, Orlando was dead and buried, and Jessica would be all alone in her apartment with no downstairs tenants for him to worry about. It couldn't be better.

On the highway into town, a state police cruiser passed him going in the opposite direction. He smiled and waved, and the cop waved back. He watched in his rearview mirror. The cop kept heading south without slowing. Cops, including Orlando's old man and that gringo with the limp, were stupid fuckers.

He checked the time. He had a couple of hours of work to do at home in the horse barn. Then he'd eat supper, clean up real good, and get ready for his date with Jessica.

Beasly and his prospective renters showed up late and didn't leave until eight o'clock. Kerney and Gabe waited until they drove away before approaching the house. Ben Morfin, who'd been glued to Barela since he'd been sighted on the highway, came on Kerney's handheld as they crossed the street.

"He's moving toward town."

"Shit," Kerney said as he unlocked the front door. "ETA?"

"Traffic is light," Ben said. "Five minutes, max."

"Talk him in to me."

"Copy that," Ben said.

With Gabe behind him, Kerney hurried up the stairs. He opened the door and used his flashlight to scan the front room. It was crammed with furniture. In the middle of the room, a Victorian loveseat faced a bentwood rocker and two walls of books sat on shelves made out of bricks and boards. Under the front window, an arrangement of plants in ceramic pots filled the top of an occasional table. Magazines and newspapers littered a glass-top coffee table and spilled over onto the floor.

"ETA two minutes," Ben said. "He's coming your way."

"Check the bedroom," Kerney said to Gabe as he opened the entry closet. It was small and stuffed with coats, jackets, boots, mops, brooms, and an upright vacuum cleaner.

"Clear," Gabe said as he came out of the bedroom.

Kerney threw an armload of coats in Gabe's arms. "Put this stuff on the bed." He grabbed the vacuum cleaner, mop, broom, and a few more coats, followed Gabe into the bedroom, and dumped the load on the floor.

"He parked three blocks away," Ben said. "He's on foot and carrying a small bag."

"Roger that," Kerney said, turning to Gabe. "I'll take the bedroom. You take the closet."

"I want first crack at him, Chief," Gabe said.

"Do it by the book, Lieutenant."

Gabe didn't answer.

Kerney shined his flashlight in Gabe's face. "Did you hear me?"

"I heard you."

"Two blocks," Ben said.

Kerney clicked his send button to acknowledge Ben's transmission. "I want Barela all the way inside, understand? We don't move until we see what he does."

Gabe nodded, switched off his flashlight, and got inside the closet.

In the bedroom, Kerney fanned his flashlight quickly over the room before killing it. The beam illuminated a row of teddy bears on a dresser top, a desk that held a lamp, clock radio, and laptop computer, and a mattress and box springs that sat on the floor covered by a comforter. The apartment felt like a hideout from the world. Kerney doubted that another human being had been invited to the apartment since the day Jessica moved in.

"He's in the garage at the back of the house," Ben said.

"We're going off the air," Kerney said. "Two radio clicks mean you move, Gabe."

"Ten-four."

Kerney left the bedroom door slightly ajar so he could see into the living room. With Gabe positioned in the closet, once Bernardo gained entry, he'd be boxed in.

Kerney glanced out the bedroom window. A gusting wind buffeted branches of an elm tree against the glass. He wondered what Gabe would do once he got his hands on Bernardo. Kerney wanted answers as badly as Gabe. Should he let Gabe step over the line, or hold him back?

The sound of footsteps on the stairs made Kerney stop thinking about Gabe. He heard the rattling of tools, followed by the sound of a hammer striking metal. It made no sense until Kerney realized Bernardo was taking the door off the hinges. The first pin popped free and clanged against the wood floor of the landing.

Two more pins fell and Kerney heard the scrape of metal against metal as Bernardo pulled the locked door free. It thudded against the threshold. A brief silence was followed by the sound of the hammer striking metal again as Bernardo rehung the door. Then the door closed and the deadbolt clicked into place.

Through the crack of the door, Kerney could see the beam of Bernardo's flashlight sweep across the living room. Bernardo put the flashlight on the coffee table, dropped to his knees, took a blanket out of the bag, and spread it on the floor. He reached into the bag again, removed a long-handled butcher knife, and placed it on the blanket. He brought out two candles, placed them on the coffee table, and lit them. Then he sat on the blanket, stripped to the waist, and started sharpening the knife with a whetstone. Finished, he put the knife down, stood up, and walked to the bedroom door.

Kerney took a step back, clicked the transmit button twice to signal Gabe, and tossed the handheld on the bed. When the door opened, he stepped forward and slapped the barrel of his semiautomatic against Bernardo's mouth. Barela reeled back into Gabe's arms.

Gabe spun him quickly, slammed him against the wall, and stuck his weapon into Bernardo's bloodied mouth, breaking teeth as he did it.

Kerney hit the light switch and Bernardo blinked in the glare.

"Where's Orlando?" Gabe asked, forcing the barrel deep into Bernardo's mouth.

"He can't talk with a gun in his mouth, Gabe," Kerney said.

"He can move his fucking head," Gabe said. "Is my son alive?"

Bernardo didn't react. Gabe cocked his weapon.

Bernardo gurgled, choking on the barrel.

"Don't kill him with the gun," Kerney said. He picked up Bernardo's butcher knife and held it out. "Use the knife. Open him up from his balls to his neck."

Gabe shook his head and jammed the gun barrel to the back of Bernardo's throat. "Fuck the knife. Is Orlando dead?"

Bernardo's eyes grew wide and he nodded.

"Did you kill him?" Gabe asked.

Bernardo nodded again.

"You pissant little fucker."

"Take the gun out of his mouth, Gabe," Kerney ordered, pulling on Gabe's arm.

"Fuck you, Kerney." Gabe's eyes bored into Bernardo. "Where is he? Where's Orlando?"

Bernardo gurgled some more.

"The gun, Gabe," Kerney said, pulling hard on Gabe's arm.

Gabe yanked the barrel out, busted Bernardo across the nose, and kneed him hard in the groin.

Blood spurted down the front of Bernardo's bare chest as he sank to the floor. He sat holding himself, gasping in pain.

Gabe holstered his weapon and held out his hand. "Give me the fucking knife, Kerney."

He took it, knelt down, and pulled Bernardo's hands

away from his groin. When the point of the butcher knife pricked Bernardo's balls, he started spilling his guts.

Arlin Fullerton brought the bulldozer out to the ranch road and started stripping dirt at the spot where Kerney had told him to start digging. Four officers, including the lieutenant who had come to the ranch with Kerney earlier in the day, stood nearby. Police cars were lined up on each side of the road, all with headlights and spotlights on.

Fullerton trenched two feet down until the blade hit a buried granite boulder. That's how Bernardo gouged the dozer's lip, he thought, as he skipped over the obstruction and started scraping away broken shale and sandstone on the other side.

The twin spotlights on the cab roof lit up the excavation as he pushed the earth into a mound at the end of the trench. It would have been faster and neater to use a backhoe or a front end loader. But Fullerton knew he could do the job. He'd logged countless hours on the 'dozer and could peel an inch of dirt away with each pass and have it be almost dead level.

The men on either side of the trench stood like statues as he worked, not talking, just staring and beaming their flashlights into the ever-deepening ditch.

Fullerton didn't want to mangle the body so it took a while to get three feet down. Even then, nothing showed. He backed up, got out of the cab, and adjusted the 'dozer spotlights to shine directly into the trench. Then he climbed down, walked to the back of the machine, got two long-handled shovels off a jerry-rigged rack, and approached Kerney.

"Two more feet and I'll hit bedrock," he said. "Best to dig by hand from here."

Kerney and the lieutenant climbed into the hole and started digging. The three other officers stood at the edge of the pit and watched. When Kerney exposed the body, the lieutenant sank to his knees and started retching, his head turned away from the crushed face.

One of the officers, a sergeant, dropped into the trench, pulled the lieutenant to his feet, and hauled him out. Kerney slammed his shovel against the side of the pit and joined the men standing around the lieutenant, who quickly broke away from the group and walked into the darkness.

Kerney followed him while the other men stood fast. One by one, their flashlights went dark.

Wisely, Arlin cut off the 'dozer's spotlights and retreated into the shadows to wait.

Gabe didn't cry as he walked down the road but his breath sounded ragged. Kerney stayed a few steps behind, keeping his distance. When Gabe stopped, a long time passed before he spoke.

"I wanted a good life for him, Chief," he said dully, his face turned away. "College, a decent job, meet the right girl, start a family. Make me proud. You know what I mean?"

"I do."

"I always thought he'd be a great father. Better than me. Kids just seemed to take to him. He had a way with kids."

Kerney didn't respond.

"Jesus, his mother is going to flip out. I need to call her. What do I say?"

"Do it later."

Gabe's back stiffened. "He was a fucking rapist, Kerney."

"Maybe Bernardo made that part up."

Gabe kept his face averted and shook his head. "You know he didn't."

"There was a lot of good in Orlando," Kerney said.

"He was my only son. My only child."

"I know."

"I raised him better than this."

"I know."

"What the fuck did I do wrong?" Gabe asked.

"You can't take the blame."

"Then who does, Chief?" Finally, Gabe turned toward Kerney. "Tell me that. Who the fuck does?"

At the trench they found Orlando's body covered by a blanket. Kerney thanked Fullerton, guided Gabe to a unit, and put him inside. Garduno met Kerney at the front of the squad car.

"I'm taking him home," Kerney said.

"Is he okay?"

"How can he be? I want somebody with him all night and all day tomorrow. Maybe longer."

"Every off-duty officer in the district will volunteer."

"Have somebody standing by for us at Gabe's house."

"Consider it done," Garduno said. "Gabe doesn't deserve this."

"Let's keep a close watch on him." Kerney glanced at

Gabe. Through the windshield, Gabe stared back at Kerney with empty eyes. "A real close watch."

"We'll stay on top of it, Chief."

Kerney looked up at the night sky. Venus dazzled like a pendant next to a three-quarter moon. He stared at it dumbly, numbed by all that had happened. He could only wonder what Gabe was going through. It had to be a thousand times worse.

"I'll take care of this," Garduno said, gesturing toward the body in the trench.

Kerney nodded, got behind the steering wheel, and drove Gabe away.

14

Kerney spent the next day in Las Vegas doing paper-work, dealing with the news media, and meeting with the ADA who had been assigned to prosecute Bernardo. Because Bernardo had lost some front teeth and sustained a broken nose, the lawyer hired by the Barelas was already making accusations of police brutality.

The ADA had questioned Kerney closely about the incidents leading up to the arrest. Without hesitating, Kerney lied about the facts. He told the ADA that Bernardo had entered Jessica's apartment armed with a deadly weapon and in the scuffle to disarm him, necessary force had been used. He knew full well he would have to perjure himself at trial, otherwise Bernardo's confession could be thrown out of court and the case dismissed.

Lying wasn't something Kerney enjoyed doing, or had ever done before in a criminal matter. But truth, in this instance, wouldn't serve justice.

The ADA seemed to buy Kerney's version of the facts, at least for the present. But Kerney needed to clue Gabe in on the spin, just in case the ADA decided to call and take a preliminary statement from Gabe over the phone.

He parked his unit, stood on the sidewalk in front of Gabe's house, and looked around. It was the first time he'd seen the neighborhood in daylight. Behind him the Las Vegas Public Library, donated to the city by Andrew Carnegie, dominated a tree-lined park that covered a city block. With its center dome, cross wings, and portico entrance, it looked like a miniature Monticello.

Gabe's house, lovingly cared for, stood directly behind the library. It was a two-and-a-half-story clapboard Victorian with a sloping mansard roof, an arched tower with circular windows, a widow's walk on the top level, and lead glass windows.

Art Garcia, dressed in civvies, his eyes ringed with dark circles, came out to meet Kerney as he opened the gate to the walkway.

Art gave Kerney a tired smile. "Chief."

"How is he?" Kerney asked.

"Sleeping. The doctor gave him a sedative. Gabe's got an appointment to see a shrink in the morning. I sent all the relatives away about two hours ago."

"Did his ex-wife come up from Albuquerque?"

"That was ugly," Art said with a nod. "She made it sound like Gabe was responsible for Orlando's murder. That nearly flipped him out."

"Is the ex-wife here now?"

"No. She checked into a motel with her boyfriend. Do you need to see her?"

Kerney shook his head. "Keep her away from Gabe if she acts up again. He doesn't need a guilt trip laid on him. He's carrying enough as it is."

"I'll let the troops know. You need to speak to Gabe? I can wake him up."

"Let him sleep. Tell him it's very important not to talk to the ADA until he speak with me."

"Will do."

"Have the funeral services for Orlando been set?"

"Not yet." Art eyed Kerney warily. "Gabe told me he put a big hurt on Bernardo to get a confession."

"I didn't see it that way. I told the ADA we used reasonable force to stop the action, and Bernardo's confession was voluntary."

Art looked relieved. "I'll tell him that when he wakes up."

"Do that, and have him call me."

Bernardo looked up from his concrete bunk and stared at Kerney through the bars of his cell. His broken nose, which had been set by the jail doctor, was covered with a bandage, and two of his upper front teeth were missing.

"I'm not talking to you," Bernardo said. "My lawyer said not to."

"You don't have to talk, just listen. You're going to prison on a life sentence without parole, if they don't fry your ass. Either way, I'm going to make the time you have in the slammer very interesting."

"What's that supposed to mean?"

"The boys in the joint are going to smack their lips when they hear that you're going to join them. You'll be somebody's girlfriend within a week. Maybe everybody's."

Bernardo flinched. "You can't do that."

Kerney smiled. "Watch me. Take my advice, Bernardo. Go with the flow. You're not going to survive in prison any other way."

"I'm walking out of here. My lawyer said he's going to get my confession suppressed because you and Gonzales beat it out of me."

"I don't think so. It will be your word against ours. But if by chance you ever live to see the light of day outside of a prison cell, let me tell you a secret, Bernardo."

"What?"

Kerney gestured with his finger. "Come here."

Cautiously, Bernardo approached the cell bars.

Kerney dropped his voice to a whisper. "I'll hunt you down and kill you."

Kerney's bluff made Bernardo's face turn white.

"Have a good day," Kerney said.

Kerney called Dale Jennings at five-thirty Saturday morning just as Sara came out of the bedroom wearing nothing but panties. She kissed him on the cheek, ruffled his hair, and moved to the kitchen, drawn by the smell of fresh coffee.

Dale answered on the first ring.

"Have you had your coffee yet?" Kerney asked, knowing full well Dale had been up for at least an hour.

"Yep. I don't have a cushy eight-to-five job like you. Gotta work for a living."

"Are you sitting down?"

"Should I be?"

"Maybe. Sara and I are getting married."

Dale whooped. "Well, I'll be damned. What a lucky son of a bitch you are."

"I know it. I want you to be my best man."

"Tell me when and tell me where."

"Montana in a week, at the Brannon ranch. Can you, Barbara, and the girls make it?"

"Wouldn't miss it. Damn, Kerney, I'm happy for you. It's about time."

"I'm pretty happy myself."

Sara came back from the kitchen, sat next to Kerney on the couch, and sipped her coffee.

"You got yourself a prize, old friend."

"My prize is nibbling on my ear as we speak."

"Barbara hasn't nibbled on my ear in a week."

"I hear that happens to old married folks."

"Stop wisecracking and put the bride-to-be on the phone. Maybe I can talk her out of making a big mistake."

"Who's wisecracking now?" Kerney held the phone out to Sara. "He's all yours."

Sara put the coffee cup down, covered the receiver with her hand, and glanced at Kerney's crotch. "You look very sexy in boxer shorts. What's that thing that's poking out?"

"A surprise."

"I like surprises." She took her hand off the receiver

and sat on Kerney's lap, facing him. "Dale, can I call you right back, in about twenty minutes?"

"Sure thing," Dale said.

"Talk to you then." Sara dropped the phone on the floor.

Kerney and Sara arrived at the old stone cabin at the foot of the mesa to find the gate open and a dozen or so vehicles neatly parked in front of a cardboard sign stapled to a wooden stake that read VOLUNTEERS PARK HERE ONLY. Another similar sign at the ranch road read SHUTTLE VAN AND DELIVERY TRUCKS ONLY.

Kerney had filled Sara in on the weekend project underway at the Knowlton cactus site, and the demand Ruth Pino had made that he meet with a Nature Conservancy staffer.

"It seems she has everything well organized," she said.

"I don't think Professor Pino leaves much to chance. I'll bet she's working her volunteers like an infantry squad on bivouac."

"She's not your favorite person."

"Maybe you can relate to her."

"Are we hiking in on our own, or taking the Ruth Pino–guided nature tour?" Sara asked as she reached for her backpack and slipped her arms into the shoulder straps.

"We'll hike," Kerney said.

He slung on his backpack and made a beeline up the side of the mesa. At the top, Sara tried to slow Kerney down. She stopped to take in the view, examine wildflowers, and adjust the harness on her pack. Each time, Kerney waited impatiently, looking preoccupied and withdrawn, before striding off again.

When they reached the windmill and stock tank, Sara tugged on Kerney's shirtsleeve. "Want to talk about it?"

"About what?"

"Your silence. This forced-march pace we're on. The fact that you haven't said five words in the last hour."

"Sorry."

"What's bothering you?"

"I can't get Gabe Gonzales out of my mind."

"You're worried about him," Sara said.

"He's a damn good man, and his life has been ripped apart. He has to live with the fact that his murdered son was a rapist."

"That can't be easy," Sara said.

"It's a hundred times worse if you're a cop."

"Can Gabe cope?"

"I hope so. I don't know."

"What about you?" Sara asked.

"Me?"

"You don't seem very happy."

Kerney looked at the high flanks of the mountains that dominated the skyline and the soft green spring grass that rippled across the mesa. "I've been trying to enjoy myself," he said, "but it isn't working. I can't hold on to this land, Sara."

"Sell it."

Kerney smiled sadly. "That's what Dale said. I've got no choice in the matter, anyway."

"Do it."

"Erma wanted me to have it."

"Erma wanted you to be happy. That was her gift to you." Sara stroked Kerney's face. "Use it to make her wish come true."

"Think she would understand?"

"Of course." Sara pulled Kerney by the collar and kissed him on the lips.

"What's that for?" Kerney asked.

"Luck. Let's go hear what kind of deal the Nature Conservancy has to offer. Just don't give the place away."

"I'm not that stupid."

Sara's voice rippled with laughter. "You'd better not be."

After arriving at the Knowlton cactus site, Kerney and Sara worked through the morning with Ruth Pino and her volunteers, setting fence posts and stringing wire. At the noon lunch break, they sat down with Reese Carson and listened to his proposal. The Nature Conservancy wanted to buy all ten sections, not only to protect the rare Knowlton cactus, but to stop any further subdivision of the land.

The open range on the mesa influenced the Nature Conservancy's decision. As one of the last grassland mesas in the area, the land was prime grazing for deer and elk migrating down from the mountains.

"It would be a wonderful plant and wildlife habitat, Mr. Kerney," Carson noted. "I hope you'll consider selling it to us."

"At full value?" Kerney asked.

"No. You sell the property to us for less than the appraisal. But it reduces your state and federal taxes. While it's not an even trade-off, you get the satisfaction of not paying the full tax burden, and insuring that the land remains intact and unspoiled."

"How much of a per-acre reduction are you looking at?" Kerney asked.

"We can negotiate that," Carson said. "If you agree in principle to the idea, we'll crunch some numbers for you at different per-acre costs. I promise you'll come out of the deal well compensated."

"Give me a ballpark figure."

"We've got to do the math first, Mr. Kerney. But you'll still be a very rich man."

Kerney mulled it over. He'd always hoped to scratch together just enough cash to get a ranch started, never expecting more would ever be possible. Even if he gave up some of the proceeds, the mesa would be protected, and he would still be able to comfortably realize his dream.

"You can verify our financial analysis with your own CPA before deciding on our offer," Reese added.

Kerney looked at Sara.

She nodded her head.

"Yes?" he asked.

"I think Erma would like to see the land stay just the way it is," she said.

Kerney smiled and turned to Carson. "Go ahead and crunch the numbers. We'll take a look at your offer."

"That's great," Reese said.

"What are you going to call the preserve?" Sara asked.

"We usually retain the most commonly used place name," Reese said.

"I think it should be called the Fergurson Mesa Ranch," Sara said.

"Or the Erma Fergurson Ranch," Kerney offered.

"Or the Erma Fergurson Mesa Ranch Preserve," Sara countered.

Reese Carson smiled at Kerney and Sara. "If we strike a deal, and the two of you can agree, you can stipulate the name. I'll put it in the contract as a condition of the sale."

Two weeks after Orlando's funeral, Gabe knew that everything had changed forever. The terrible burning sensation in his stomach never stopped and at night sleep came only after he took a sedative. But the pills didn't keep away the dreams that left him dazed in the morning, wondering if he'd been sleeping or hallucinating.

One dream recurred over and over. In it, he was standing at the edge of the trench looking down at Orlando's crushed body, watching it decay to an anonymous skeleton, all traces of identity dissolved away.

Each time he would awake from the dream with throbbing temples and a racing heart.

Gabe's shrink had him keep a daily journal of his thoughts and feelings. Gabe didn't write down anything about his dream, and not much about how he felt, for that matter. He just didn't have the words for it. He doubted there were any.

In his sessions, the shrink kept pushing him to talk about his grief, anger, and pain. Although he felt empty and drained, Gabe faked it well enough to get a green light to return to duty.

He sat on the living room couch, bit into the sandwich, chewed mechanically, and stared at the television. Tomorrow he was due back to work. Yesterday, Theresa and her boyfriend had come up from Albuquerque to cart away some of Orlando's things as keepsakes. After they left, Gabe had packed up everything else—Orlando's clothes, books, old toys, the stereo, the TV, the linens and pillows from the bed, even the baseball card collection—and had taken it all to the dump. Then he'd cleaned the room from top to bottom and locked the door.

He put his half-eaten sandwich on the plate and went to the kitchen. All his thank-you notes for the sympathy cards were ready to be mailed. Chief Kerney wouldn't get his note until he got back from his honeymoon in Ireland. He gathered them up, took them to the mailbox outside the public library, and dropped them down the chute.

This was the first night that he wasn't being watched like a hawk by some cop pretending to keep him company. It felt good not to bullshit people that he was doing all right.

On his way back to the house, Gabe looked at the moon and saw two bright stars nearby. He didn't know much about stars, constellations, or astronomy. Maybe they were satellites. But satellites weren't supposed to flicker.

Orlando would have known whether they were stars or not, Gabe thought as he stood in his front yard. But Orlando would never be around to tell him such things again.

He placed the muzzle of the pistol in his ear, but couldn't pull the trigger. His hand shook so hard the weapon banged against his cheekbone. He lowered the gun and stared at the house his grandfather had built, wondering why he'd put all his time, money, and effort into restoring it. His family was shattered and his pride in what the house once represented no longer mattered.

He leveled the gun at the living room window and pulled off a round. The lead glass shattered. He kept pointing and firing at every window in the front of the house until the handgun emptied. Lights went on inside the neighboring houses. As the growing sound of a siren pierced the night, Gabe walked to the porch step, sat, and stared at the ground. Glare from a spotlight washed over him, and Art Garcia's voice came out of the darkness.

"Toss the handgun, Gabe."

The weapon felt heavy in Gabe's hand. "It's empty."

"Please, Gabe, lose the gun," Art said, almost pleading, as he came up the walkway.

Gabe flipped it onto the grass and started crying, unable to hold back the sobs.

Art sat on the porch step, put an arm around Gabe's shoulders, and waited for the crying to stop.

When Gabe opened his eyes, he saw Russell Thorpe, Ben Morfin, Captain Garduno, and several state and city patrol officers standing in the front yard.

Embarrassed, he dropped his head, took a deep breath, and let it out slowly. "What am I gonna do, Art?" he asked softly.

Art patted Gabe's shoulder. "You'll get through it."

ALSO AVAILABLE FROM

MICHAEL
McGARRITY

MEXICAN HAT

SERPENT GATE

TULAROSA

Visit
❖ **Pocket Books** ❖
online at

www.SimonSays.com

Keep up on the latest new
releases from your favorite
authors, as well as author
appearances, news, chats,
special offers and more.

SIMON & SCHUSTER
A VIACOM COMPANY
www.SimonSays.com

Pocket
Books